Count the Days

Count the Days

Lin Summerfield

Walker and Company
New York

First published in the United States of America in 1991
by Walker Publishing Company, Inc.,
720 Fifth Avenue, New York, NY 10019

Originally published in Great Britain.

Library of Congress Cataloging-in-Publication Data
Summerfield, Lin, 1952-
Count the days / Lin Summerfield.
p. cm.
"Originally published in Great Britain"
--T.P. verso
ISBN 0-8027-5796-0
I. Title
PR6069.U36C68   1991
823'.914--dc20
91-14124
CIP

Printed in the United States of America
2 4 6 8 10 9 7 5 3 1

For my mother, who – fortunately for me –
bears no resemblance to Cassie's mother
Isabel Wade.

Also in memory of my grandmother, who
was the model for Cassie's 'Gran'.

1

Margie Thoroughgood disappeared on a Monday morning.

I know it was Monday because the weekend's misadventures had caught up with me and I was in the headmaster's office when the call came through. Mr Riordan and I were gazing at each other across his desk in a kind of despair, he as unable to express his disappointment in me as I was to explain my actions. Ashamed, I lowered my gaze to the telephone, praying it would ring the way telephones do in films at the crucial moment and so save me.

I was no stranger to Mr Riordan's office, nor to the grave, sad look he wore when trying to understand a child's bad behaviour. But this time it was different; this time I knew what I had done was serious enough for police involvement.

'Why, Cassie?' Mr Riordan asked suddenly. 'Why?' And this room with its thick olive green carpet, grey filing cabinet and ancient desk seemed the only real place in the whole world.

'Don't know, sir.'

'Whose idea was it, yours or David's?'

'His, sir.' I licked my dry lips and stared through the window at the sumachs on the far side of the playground. The leaves were changing colour now and the once velvety sumach fruits, which somehow reminded me of Gran's best tablecloth, were shrivelled and dusty. I wished I was outside, hidden among those trees so I didn't have to see my headmaster's face.

'All his idea?'

'Yes, sir.' I was telling the truth. It had been David's idea to climb the fence into the school playground last Saturday, and David who broke the first milk bottle. How far away it seemed now, as distant as the summer holidays, or even last Christmas.

'Sixty milk bottles,' said Mr Riordan with awful emphasis. '*Sixty*. And then the window. Who broke the window?'

I looked down at the rectangle of pink blotting paper on the desk. How could I tell anyone how wonderful I felt while we were smashing those bottles? Or how, carried away by excitement and the illusion of power, I had picked up the stone and hurled it through the cloakroom window?

'I did, sir,' I mumbled. In breaking the window I had also broken the spell. David and I stopped suddenly, both realising with horror what we had done. The woman who lived next door to the school was just coming to investigate the sounds of breaking glass as we fled. And here I was, facing the music while David remained in semi-anonymity – I hadn't given his surname – at the Catholic school in town.

I knew Mr Riordan would ask me why again, and I was frantically working on some complicated story, strictly of the cock-and-bull order, when the phone rang. He gave me a look that said I needn't relax yet before he answered it.

'Hello? Oh, hello, Mrs Thoroughgood. What can I do for you?'

I brushed the back of my hand across my nose, trying to look unconcerned. Mrs Thoroughgood was a school governor, as well as a Parish Councillor and member of the Wickstead Library Committee, and we were all in awe of her. Was it possible she had heard of the broken window and was calling to demand police action? I rubbed my nose again, violently.

'Yes, I see. So Margie didn't come home at lunchtime? No, I don't recall actually seeing her this morning, either. Hold on a moment, Mrs Thoroughgood. I happen to have a girl from Margie's class with me right now.' He covered the mouthpiece and looked up at me. 'Cassie, is Margie Thoroughgood here today?'

'No, sir.'

'What about this morning? Wasn't she here then?'

'No, sir.'

'Have you seen her at all today?'

I shook my head. When Margie was absent you noticed it. I called her 'The Girl Who Has Everything' because, as far as I was concerned, Margie owned all the things the rest of us could only dream about. Even Dawn, my best friend, whose father was assistant manager at the plastics factory in town, didn't own a three-foot high doll with a whole suitcaseful of clothes. And Margie was beautiful. She had white-blonde hair and blue eyes, an already developing bust, and the knack of standing and sitting in such a way that showed these attributes to advantage. But more than anything I envied Margie's bike, one of the new, small-wheeled Moultons with a silver frame. Mine was about fourth-hand and painted a horrible mushroom colour.

And Margie was popular: always the centre of playground attention, always dominating the conversation and suggesting which games we played. She had a new Best Friend every week, and she would stroll about the village with her arm around the chosen one, whispering her secrets and sharing her sweets until someone new won her interest. The girls she cast off would sulk, perhaps even cry over it for a day or two, and then forgive her; there was always the hope of winning her back, after all. Besides, she never did it in a really cruel way. It was almost as if this chopping and changing were completely beyond her control: the same kind of wild energy that compelled her to do another string of cartwheels when the bell had sounded and the rest of us were lining up. Margie could get away with an awful lot, except with Miss Saunders – which was something I could never understand – and usually took full advantage of the fact.

And now, now she was missing, I couldn't help feeling a bit pleased to think that perhaps Margie Thoroughgood had taken things too far at last.

'Cassie, run and fetch Miss Saunders, will you?' said Mr Riordan. 'Oh, and don't say anything to anyone about Margie yet, there's a good girl.'

'Right, sir,' I said importantly. 'Sir – will you want to see me any more?'

'Surely you didn't think I'd finished with you yet? No, you'd better wait outside until I've dealt with this, and until I've decided what to do with you. Run and fetch Miss Saunders now.'

As I left the office, I heard him say, 'Look, let's not panic, Mrs Thoroughgood. All children get into scrapes at times – ' She must have cut him short there, and I could imagine her outraged 'Not my Margie!'

Everyone looked up when I entered the classroom. They had all seen the broken window and must have guessed I was the culprit when Mr Riordan summoned me. I enjoyed seeing the disappointment on their faces, especially the boys', because I hadn't returned in tears. I gave Miss Saunders the message in a tight, excited voice.

'Did he say what it's about, Cassie?'

'Yes, miss.' I glanced at Dawn, who sat in the front row. 'But I've not to tell.'

A look of irritation crossed my teacher's face, as if it were my fault, and she rose wearily, scraping her chair on the floor. I was aching to run to Dawn and whisper, 'Margie Thoroughgood's disappeared! Spread it!' But my sense of self-importance won. Once they all knew, it would fade my own glory; I had to hold this piece of excitement to myself a while longer. So I marched out, businesslike behind Miss Saunders, widening my eyes at Dawn to show her that something was up.

Miss Saunders was young, young enough to wear her hair in a fashionable 'beehive' and wear stiletto heels. All the other classes envied ours in having her for our teacher, and ours grieved over the fact that we'd be leaving the Primary next year and wouldn't see her again. This was where Margie and I had something in common; we were practically the only ones not to have a crush on her. In my opinion, she was too exotic-looking to be beautiful, while Margie disdained to have crushes on anyone.

I waited outside the office while decisions were being made over what to do about Margie. I was thinking how odd Mr Riordan and Miss Saunders looked together: he resembling Desmond Morris on *Zoo Time*, she the rare and dazzling creature under his scrutiny. There were rumours that Mr Riordan was getting a divorce, and there was no doubt in the minds of Class Six that he would then marry Miss Saunders. What horrid children they'd make; ugly little things with red hair and monkey eyes.

They were not in the office very long, and when they emerged, both looking anxious, they went off down the passage without a word to me. I began to feel the situation could be serious. It was just on half-past two, which meant Margie had been missing for six hours. I couldn't remember her ever playing hooky before. She'd had the odd day off for sore throats and tummy upsets like the rest of us, but she'd always brought a note from her mother. Besides, Margie liked school. My theory was that she had done it for a dare, which meant somebody else in the school knew about it. That theory was reinforced when Mr Riordan returned with Petey Scammel, the class stinkpot. But he went into the office alone, leaving Petey with me.

'Did you hear about Margie?' Petey asked, in a voice dangerously loud considering where we were.

'Of course.'

'I saw her this morning. She was getting into a car with a man.'

'What man?' I didn't believe him.

'Just a man. Mr Riordan's going to phone the police. I bet she's been kidnapped.'

I considered this for a minute. The Thoroughgoods were quite well off, I supposed, but probably not so rich that they could afford the thousands kidnappers usually demanded. When I pointed this out, Petey suggested we ask the vicar to hold a village whip-round.

'I don't think it's at all funny,' I said severely. 'If you're speaking the truth, Petey Scammel, it could be something much worse than kidnapping.'

Petey stared at me, a tuft of hair sticking up from the crown of his head like an exclamation mark. He might have smelled of the guinea pigs he kept in his back yard, but Petey was never slow on the uptake.

'What . . . done in, you mean?' He shook his head. 'No, not Margie. She's too smart for that. Bet you half a crown she's hiding somewhere, Cassie?'

'Not on.'

'Okay. But I still think it's the most exciting thing that's ever happened in Upper Grisham.'

So did I at that stage, although I wouldn't have admitted it.

In a little while, Mr Riordan called Petey into the office and sent me back to my class. He'd deal with me tomorrow, he said. I was angry at having missed the nature programme we always listened to on the school radio every Monday afternoon, and when I passed the broken cloakroom window I felt like picking up a stone and breaking another one.

Before we went home, Miss Saunders gave us a lecture on never talking to strangers, or taking sweets or accepting lifts from them. She didn't say anything about Margie, though. We could hear the infants singing 'Now the day is over' in the classroom next door, and I realised it was only a quarter past three. Every-

11

thing was odd about this afternoon, I thought; just like the time the Jehovah's Witnesses said the world was coming to an end and Gran kept me off school because she believed them. Everything *felt* odd. We were leaving early while the little ones were late, and outside in the playground mothers were grumbling and looking at their watches.

'So, what do you do if a strange man offers you sweets?' asked Miss Saunders. 'Dawn?'

'Say no and walk away,' said Dawn, parrot-fashion.

'And if he's persistent and tries to follow you? Cassie?'

'Run and tell the first lady you see.'

'That's right. Or if there's a shop nearby, you could run in there and tell the shopkeeper. Now, I want you all to go straight home this afternoon. No hanging about in the rec., and that includes you boys too.'

Dawn scowled at her fingers. Not so much because she resented being told what to do, as I did, but because scowling was her natural expression. I decided that if Dawn wanted to stick to our original plan of being first to the churchyard in order to find the best conkers, then that would be fine by me. Miss Saunders, unlike Mr Riordan, might often be defied without too serious consequences.

It was a good year for conkers. They were large and plentiful and a stiff breeze that day had brought hundreds of them down. Dawn and I scrabbled among the grassy mounds and tombstones, filling the pockets of our gaberdines, while at the same time keeping a sharp eye out for Cyril Jennings, who was responsible for maintaining the churchyard and who was not sympathetic to conker hunters. When our pockets would hold no more we went over to the war memorial and sat down to examine our haul. We played the traditional game with them, as well as a form of jacks and marbles with the smaller ones, but mostly we collected them just for the satisfaction of having them; it was a strange child indeed who could not be found with a pocketful of shiny conkers every autumn in our village.

'I don't think the others are coming,' I said after a while. 'Perhaps we ought to go home now, Dawnie.'

'Why? We're perfectly safe here.'

'I don't know. If my gran's heard about Margie she'll be worried. So will your mum and dad.'

'No, they won't. We're out early today, aren't we? They're not to know that.' She bent low over her conkers.

That was just like Dawn; complacent, moody, unhurried. I seldom knew what she was thinking, and she rarely told me. She would be silent for hours, and sometimes I wondered if she even knew I was there. Yet if I stayed away or started talking to someone else, she'd appear at my side, say, 'C'mon, Cassie,' and I'd meekly follow her wherever she led me.

Ours was a strange friendship. I don't know what the attraction was for Dawn, but for me it was her very moodiness, her long silences and her bright, blue-eyed scowls, which added up to an irresistible mystery. I felt we had some secret understanding between us, something sensed and respected by others, although as indefinable to them as it was to me. And because of this, I sometimes allowed her to lead me astray.

'You're not frightened, are you, Cassie?' Dawn asked suddenly.

'Of course not. Like you said, we're perfectly safe here.'

'I mean of your gran. It'll be bad enough when Mr Riordan tells her about the window.'

'He won't tell her,' I said confidently. 'He'll forget with all this fuss about Margie. Anyway, I don't care if he does. I can do anything I like when my dad's not here.' Which was far from the truth. Dad was the one who let me get away with murder, but as soon as he had to go abroad again Gran got out her apron strings. I think she lived in terror of me breaking my neck, getting abducted or catching head lice.

A tall, thin figure dressed in black and approaching from the oldest part of the churchyard made me jump.

'How many times do I have to tell you children not to play around the war memorial?' barked Father Steven. 'I don't mind you coming to look for conkers, but this isn't a playground, you know. And didn't Petey Scammel just tell me you were all supposed to go straight home today and no hanging about?'

We stood up awkwardly, staring at the sun reflected in his round, rimless glasses.

'Well? Isn't that what your teacher said?'

13

'Yes, Father Steven,' said Dawn. She could be really sugary when she chose.

'But we thought we would be safe enouth here,' I added.

Father Steven was not impressed by what I meant to sound like a declaration of faith.

'Never mind what you thought, Cassie Wade. It's high time you learned to do as you're told. And why weren't you at Sunday school yesterday?'

'My gran wouldn't let me. She thought I had a cold coming.' Another lie. I'd hidden behind the Boy Scout hut so I could save my collection money for sweets.

'Then I'll expect to see you in church next Sunday as usual. Now off you go home, the pair of you. And no stopping or speaking to strangers on the way. Understood?'

'Yes, Father.'

'And no more playing around the war memorial. Show some respect for the dead.'

'Yes, Father.'

We turned and hurried back along the path to the side gate, Dawn daring to stop for one last conker. If Father Steven knew about Margie, chances were the entire village did, too; even right at the top of Joshua Road, which was where I lived. Nothing stayed quiet for long in a little place like Upper Grisham.

'I bet Margie wishes she were here now,' I said, turning back to see the tops of the churchyard trees still bright with the last of the afternoon sun.

'She might be dead.'

'That's what I mean.'

'You are *silly*, Cassie.'

After I left Dawn I began to run. Fear of Gran's anger, the silence around me, the man Petey said had taken Margie in his car – all combined to make me run and not stop until I reached my own front gate.

Gran was peeking out from behind the net curtain, so I thought I'd better stop and unload the conkers from my gaberdine pocket. They rolled across the road, where they would probably be squashed by a passing car.

I didn't want them any more.

2

Our house was the last one at the top end of Joshua Road. It wasn't old, being built in the thirties, but seemed old in comparison with the new council houses which were mushrooming in the heart of Upper Grisham. Nor was it a large house, though once again comparison made it seem so. We had fireplaces in the bedrooms and our bath was downstairs in the kitchen. I remember how Margie Thoroughgood had laughed when I told her this.

'A bath in the kitchen? It's crazy!' The laugh was surprisingly good-natured, though; for Margie could often be hurtful. Yet on the one occasion she visited me at home – I think it was my birthday tea – she made me feel good about my life by describing everything she saw as 'fun'.

Our living-room was seldom bright. The sun only shone through the small window on winter mornings when it was low in the sky, our furniture was dark and cumbersome, and Gran aired her washing right in front of the fire. Consequently, I never felt cheerful or at ease in that room until the curtains were drawn and the light switched on. Then it was quite cosy, and sometimes Gran even agreed to move the clothes horse so we could toast her home-made bread and tea cakes.

It was a polished room, though you didn't fully appreciate this until the light was on. Gran polished the table, chairs and side-board three times a week, and once I even caught her buffing up the aspidistra. Cleaning was a religion to her, a lifetime habit she couldn't, or wouldn't break. From five o'clock in the morning until seven in the evening she was 'on the go', as she aptly described it. Most of the work was unnecessary as far as I could see. Baking her own bread and cakes, for example, when we had a grocer's in the village which sold bread still warm from the bakery in town. It wasn't as if Dad kept her short of money, either; that was regular and generous enough. I think Gran just liked making work for herself.

We only used the best room when Dad was home, at Christmas, or when the aunties came from London for the annual duty visit. The furniture in here was more modern and so, Gran insisted, bound to wear out quickly if we kept using it. So she turned it into a showpiece, and I was never allowed to enter, under severest penalties, except on those special occasions. What I didn't understand then was how much Gran hated this room because it reminded her of my wayward mother. Later on, when I discovered this, I began to associate it with her, too: spotless, bright, but cold and unwelcoming.

We didn't watch much television, although Dad had bought us one of the latest models with the new, larger screen. Gran was a little afraid of it, and the performance she went through to put the thing on was unbelievable. First, she would move everything else right out of the way, isolating the set in a corner of the room 'in case of fire'. Then she carefully inspected the plug before inserting it in the socket – I don't know what she was looking for and I don't suppose she did either. Finally, and having seated me at a distance to safeguard my eyes, she would make a little dart at the On-Off switch, always springing back as though it was red hot. She preferred the radio, or 'wireless' as she still called it, conveniently forgetting how our old forties set had gone up in flames and taken the curtain with it.

I liked to read in the evenings, the advantage over television being that if I liked or didn't understand a passage I could go back and read it again. We had a lot of books. The rickety (and highly polished) bookshelf made by Dad in his last year at school held dozens of them, all arranged in order of importance. The Bible, the Family Doctor, Nuttall's Standard Dictionary, and all the other dull volumes occupied the top shelf. Murder mysteries belonging to my mother – and in constant danger of being thrown out – came underneath. The bottom shelf held the most interesting selection, and I was allowed to read any of these without first taking them to Gran to be vetted. *Victoria's Golden Reign, Hans Brinker*, and the old Amy Cruse biography of Robert Louis Stevenson were my favourites. And then there was 'Gran's book', the great family joke. She had bought *The New World* from a travelling salesman, believing it to be a history of America. It was actually a sort of Jehovah's Witness handbook. Dad could never reach for something to read without spotting it and teasing her mercilessly.

Dad's job was with CSE – Combined Services Entertainments – which was then part of the British Forces Broadcasting Service, and he was abroad a lot organising shows for the troops. He took the job after my mother walked out on us, so it was like losing two parents to me. But Dad always came back, filling the house with presents, the sound of his laughter, and endless tunes on his flute. Mother never came back. I used to ask about her, why didn't she come to see me and where was she? But Gran became so cross that I soon learned to keep quiet about it. That was water under the bridge, I was told. Five years of flowing water and I couldn't remember what the boat looked like any more. The first Christmas after she left, when I was six, she sent a Christmas stocking and a card signed *Mummy and Uncle Ray* -- whoever he was. It was a pretty card, though. The three wise men outlined against a desert sky with the words 'Silent Night' written above in glitter. Gran threw it away.

The smell of boiling clothes and washing powder was still in the house when I arrived home – it being Monday and Gran a traditionalist with the housework. She hadn't heard about Margie, and was only looking out of the window because she saw Colin Woodruff going by at half-past three and wondered if her clock could be wrong.

'No, we were let out early,' I said, almost choking to give her the news. 'Gran, you'll never guess what! Margie Thorough-good's disappeared!'

'Margie who?'

'You know Mrs Thoroughgood, Gran. That blonde woman who belongs to all the clubs and the council and everything. You once said if she looks down her nose any further she'll get eyeballs in her nostrils. You know,' I prompted. 'Her daughter. The one with the silver Moulton bike.'

Gran had lost track of my point by now and was carefully rubbing Vaseline on her rough elbows. 'Yes, well. I've told you before,' she said absently, 'the bike you've got is good enough for you to tear about on. One of those new ones would be broken within the week.'

17

'Gran, you're not listening! I said Margie's *disappeared*! Petey Scammel – you know, that boy who smells like a guinea pig's hutch – he saw her get in some man's car this morning and no one's seen her since. She didn't turn up for school this morning, nor this afternoon. Mrs Thoroughgood phoned because she didn't go home for lunch. Mr Riordan's phoned the police. That's why we were sent home early. Gran, do you think it'll be on the news? Can we turn it on and see?'

Gran peered at me over her raised, greasy elbow. 'If you were sent home early, how is it you arrived here the same time as usual?'

'The vicar stopped to speak to us.' Only a half-lie.

'Did he ask why you weren't at Sunday school yesterday?' She narrowed her eyes at me. 'You were seen sitting on the step outside the Boy Scout hut. Eating sweets on a Sunday morning! I suppose that's what you do with your collection money, is it?'

I sat down at the tea table in despair; I couldn't keep anything a secret from Gran. Sometimes I wondered if she paid people to follow me and spy on me. The worst part about it was that she took a positive delight in confronting me with what she knew. I'd have to be up pretty early in the day to pull one over on her, she'd say. I supposed it was only a matter of time before she heard about the milk bottles and the cloakroom window.

'We'll pick that bone later,' said Gran, coming from the kitchen with the boiled eggs we always had as 'makeshift' on washdays. 'Now, what's all this about Margie Thoroughgood?'

I told her again, going into greater detail – and perhaps over-dramatising Mr Riordan's reactions – while cutting toast soldiers to dip in my eggs.

Gran listened patiently, her green eyes searching my face as though looking for evidence that this was just one of my stories designed to cover some misdeed of my own. And there, in the dark living-room, as I listened to the loud ticking of Gran's antique French clock, it did seem likely that the whole thing might have come from my imagination.

We put the television on at six o'clock for the regional news, but there was nothing about Margie. I wondered if we would have to go to school tomorrow if she was still missing. Or would it count like Colonel Cartwright's funeral and Princess Margaret's wedding and we'd be given the day off? Gran didn't think that was very likely.

'Anyway, I'd rather know you're safe in school than roaming the village,' she said.

'Margie's mother thought she was safe in school. Only she never got there, did she?'

Gran frowned. 'I think I'll walk you there myself tomorrow.'

'Oh, Gran! I wouldn't get into some stranger's car. I'm not that stupid!'

'All the same, better safe than sorry. I know I shouldn't have any peace of mind otherwise.'

I felt my infamous temper beginning to rise. It was no good Dad telling me to 'count to ten' as a way of governing myself, he didn't have as many trials as I did. How was I going to feel when everyone saw me being escorted to school? They'd say Cassie Wade was a baby, too afraid to walk alone. I could still remember the taunts and sniggers of a couple of years ago because Gran wouldn't let me leave off my liberty bodice. This was the last straw; even Dawn would laugh, and I couldn't bear that.

'What about me?' I yelled. 'What about my peace of mind? They'll all laugh at me if you take me to school!'

'Of course they won't. I bet they'll all have someone with them tomorrow. No, it's no good you getting in a state, Cassie. I'm not letting you go alone, and that's that. Whatever would your father say?'

'I don't care what he'd say.' I was beginning to grizzle. 'I'm nearly eleven. I'll be at the High School next year and you still treat me like a kid. At this rate I'll still be wearing ankle socks by the time I get married.'

'That's if anyone'll have you.'

I was about to give her my favourite spiteful retort – that as she didn't care about me I'd run away to find my mother – when there was a knock on the back door. I knew this must be a neighbour because only strangers came to the front, and when Gran led Colin Woodruff's mother into the room I flushed to think the woman must have heard me shouting.

'Isn't it awful about the Thoroughgood girl, Mrs Wade?' she stage-whispered. 'No one's safe these days. Honestly, you never used to hear of this sort of thing years ago. Children could play in the street in safety and you could turn your back on them for five minutes without having to worry –' She broke off, looking at me. 'Well, you know what I mean, Mrs Wade.'

'Won't you sit down?' Gran adopted her gracious hostess voice, apologising for the state of the place when she knew it was spotless. I would have been ashamed, except that half the women in the village behaved exactly like it.

'The thing is,' Mrs Woodruff said, 'I don't think it would be a good idea to let the children walk to and from school unaccompanied until this business is over. So I propose taking your Cassie in the car with my Colin and the little Jeeves boy.'

'But I always walk with Dawn!' I protestd. 'She'll be waiting for me!'

'That's all right, Cassie,' said Mrs Woodruff with a hint of impatience. 'There's room in the car for Dawn as well.'

Gran looked at her watch. 'It's getting near bath time for you, Cassie.' That was for our neighbour's benefit. Bath night was Friday; the rest of the week it was a strip wash in front of the kitchen sink.

'I must say,' Gran resumed, 'I was inclined to believe this was just one of Cassie's tales at first. Especially as there was nothing on the news about it.'

'It's too early for it to be on the news. After all, it may just be some childish prank.'

'A fine prank, worrying her poor parents half to death! There's one thing I will say about Cassie; she'll never go off without telling me where she's going and who with.' They both looked at me with something approaching approval.

'Nor my Colin,' said Mrs Woodruff. 'I've always drummed it into his head. Tell us where you're going, who with, and what time you expect to be home.'

'Of course, it's not so bad with boys,' said Gran mildly.

'Oh, I wouldn't be too sure of that. There's all manner of perverts walking the streets these days –'

'Cassie,' Gran interrupted, 'Go and have your bath now, there's a good girl.'

Life in our village had changed abruptly by morning. We saw police cars everywhere instead of old Constable Seagle on his bike. They came to question our class individually, as well as making house-to-house calls, and I saw the searches going on across the fields and meadows as Mrs Woodruff drove us to school. That evening, we saw Upper Grisham on the regional television news, and they showed the school photograph of Margie, which was taken last summer before she had her hair cut.

'Marjorie Jane Thoroughgood,' said the newscaster. I hadn't known her middle name was the same as mine.

Later in the week, we learned that an Animal Defenders Club badge had been found behind the Boy Scout hut. Margie had owned such a badge and her father insisted she was wearing it when she left the house on Monday morning, so everyone began to assume the worst. I didn't know what to do. Gran would be angry if she knew I'd been playing behind the hut, but keeping quiet would be a waste of police time and surely punishable. So I told Gran and she took me to the police station in town, where I explained how I lost the badge over two months ago and could identify it as mine by a scratch on the front. I felt important answering their questions, but it led to a strange, frightening confrontation with Margie's mother.

We were waiting for Mrs Woodruff to collect us from school on Thursday afternoon when Mrs Thoroughgood came running into the playground. I hardly recognised her at first; she was so changed from the sophisticated woman who sat on the Parish Council and who organised our school sports day. She wore no make-up, her hair hung about her face in rat's tails, and she looked old and ill. 'Cassie! Cassie!' she screamed, grabbing my shoulders and shaking me. 'Are you sure – absolutely positive – it was your badge they found?'

'Yes, Mrs Thoroughgood.'

'My Margie had one like it. Cassie, how do you know it's yours?'

'I-it's got a – a scratch on the stag's head,' I stammered. Her fingernails were digging into my shoulders and hurting me. 'And I remember where I lost it. It was rusty when they found it, Mrs Thoroughgood. That proves it's been lying there for some time.'

Still she wasn't convinced. She kept shaking me and repeating, 'Are you sure, Cassie? Are you *sure*?' until Mr Riordan came out and calmed her.

'Rust – yes, I see.' She released me and gazed around at the children who were waiting for their parents. 'So Margie may still

21

be safe!' she muttered, her eyes darting as though looking for a white-blonde head in the little crowd, a broad, confident smile among the frightened stares.

Mr Riordan had to drive her home, and he didn't look very happy about it.

'She's gone funny in the head,' said Dawn. 'Poor bitch.'

We'd hardly discussed Margie's possible fate since Monday, when it still seemed likely she was merely in a scrape. Since then, Petey's story of her getting into a car with a man had been corroborated by Mrs Rabbs, the President of Upper Grisham WI, but she was elderly, short-sighted, and often got so confused she couldn't tell you which day it was. Their statements resulted in an Identikit picture, however, which went up all over the village. Mrs Woodruff looked at one and said she'd never seen anything so like Mr Average in her life before. But there was one thing both Petey and Mrs Rabbs were sure of; the car Margie had got into was green.

We hadn't discussed it because, apart from the police questions, the attitude of the adults somehow forbade it. They were watching us carefully, supervising everything we did and listening to our conversations, which naturally became stilted and self-conscious. Perhaps they thought it unhealthy to talk about Margie, as if something bad would happen to one of us through mentioning her name, in the way you caught nits by touching the head of a nit-infested child. But Mrs Thoroughgood's sudden appearance in the playground seemed to break the spell.

'Do you think Margie's dead?' I asked Dawn.

'It's more than likely, I'd say.' She rolled her exercise book into a telescope and peered through it. 'And she must have known the man to get into the car with him.'

I wasn't too sure about that. A casual approach – 'Hello, darlin'. Need a lift to school, then?' – in the main village street and in daylight. Margie, confident she could handle anything, would have accepted eagerly.

'Poor Margie,' I said.

'It was her own fault. She always did think she knew it all.'

I could have pointed out that the same thing might be said for Dawn.

'Do you sometimes think it can't be real?'

'Cassie, why do you say such stupid things? Of course it's real.'

22

'I know it is. I meant, don't you think it can't be?'

Dawn shrugged. If I said something she didn't understand she seldom made the effort. Not that I could blame her.

On Friday, Mrs Thoroughgood made an appeal on television. If Margie was alive, she said, would whoever was holding her please let her go? Take her somewhere – some street from where she could find her way home?

Her tearful face turned to the woman reporter. 'I want to tell whoever has her what it feels like not to know. Ever since we knew she was missing, I've been counting the hours, then the days. And every day that passes, I feel there's less . . . less hope . . . ' She covered her face with her hands.

It was then only day five, and none of us could guess at that time how the days would turn to weeks, the weeks to months, before Mrs Thoroughgood finally knew what had happened to Margie.

3

It was cold by the time Dad arrived home in November and Gran, pointing to the abundance of berries in the hedgerows, predicted a hard winter. I had long taken my tent – a faded black-out curtain hung over a skipping rope – in from the back lawn and resigned myself to indoor games. No more playing safari, nomads or gypsies this year, no more such games ever, in fact. Next summer holidays we would be looking forward to starting at the High School in town, where they called playtime 'break', and nobody dreamed of rolling about on the grass like a little kid.

There was the eleven plus exam looming in the New Year and Margie's disappearance still hung over us, so the welcome home I gave my dad was a rather subdued one. Perhaps he sensed my anxieties, because for a moment he seemed to look at me with an odd, worried expression. He swept me up in his arms as usual, hoisting me way off the ground, and as usual he said, 'You're getting heavy, Cassie. Far too heavy for poor old Dad to lift you!' But his laughter was restrained, his gaiety almost forced. I snuggled up to him, squashed my face against his neck to breathe in his warm, comforting smell. Not the smooth, talc-powdery smell of Mr Riordan, or the sweatiness of Dawn's father, but exclusively that of my dad.

He broke away to hug and kiss Gran, and I glanced furtively at his cases. I didn't want him to think I only cared about what wonderful present he might have brought me, but I couldn't help looking all the same. Before he unpacked, however, there was a ritual to be endured. Dad began it with the traditional, awful words: 'Well, has my Cassie been behaving herself?'

Gran had a list of all my scrapes and misdeeds ready – a mental list, although I'm sure she did have a real, paper one hidden somewhere – and I had to watch my dad's face changing from an expression of worry to disappointment, mock horror, and back to worry again. When he shook his head at me and uttered the mournful, reproving, 'Oh, Cassie!' I knew it was time for the second part of the ritual. Gran, either softening toward me or thinking perhaps that a wholly bad report reflected on herself, began on all the gold and silver stars I had won at school.

'And Miss Saunders had to tell her off for choosing books from the library that were too simple for her. She got ten out of ten for reading and writing, didn't you Cassie?'

'I won a prize at Sunday school too, Daddy,' I said. 'I did the best "Temptation of Our Lord" and I won a book, *Children of The Bible*. Do you want to see it, Daddy?'

'Later, Cass. Show me after tea. I want to get unpacked first. Are you coming to help me?'

I looked at Gran, wondering if it had been a good idea to mention Sunday school in front of her when only last week Father Steven had been asking about my recent absences. Gran shook her head slightly and I sighed with relief; she was going to keep quiet.

I followed Dad upstairs, making myself useful by dragging the lightest of his cases behind me. What would have happened if the broken milk bottle incident had ever come to his and Gran's ears I trembled to think. No presents, no hugs, and possibly a good hiding. I hadn't gone unpunished for the episode, though. Mr Riordan had kept me in every playtime for a fortnight, setting me various and impossible tasks such as an essay on 'Ten Dangers from Broken Glass'. At last he was satisfied – and I was convinced – that I'd never deliberately smash anything again. We would put it behind us, he said, and concentrate on school work, bearing in mind that all-important exam in February. He smiled at me and I felt awful; I cried right there in front of him. Now, looking at Dad and imagining his face if he knew what I had done, I felt my eyes starting to burn again.

Dad was usually a hopeless suitcase packer, so I was amazed to see everything folded flat, even his socks, instead of being all screwed up like so much rubbish. I couldn't help remarking on it.

'You've even wrapped your shoes in tissue paper.'

'Well, your gran only has a go at me for creasing everything. I though I'd give her a shock this time.'

Was it my imagination, or did he really look embarrassed?

I sat on the edge of his bed, the double bed he'd once shared with my mother, and I watched him carefully putting his clothes away in the drawers and cupboards. Every shirt had been expertly starched and ironed, and there were several I'd never seen before. He had a new pullover too; a hand-knitted one with panels of complicated cable stitch in his favourite shade of green. So Dad had met a woman, and the relationship was advanced enough for her to be ironing his shirts and knitting for him. I was hardly surprised; Dad was still young, athletic and good-looking, so there had always been the chance he would find someone else once his divorce came through. Gran never discussed the subject with me, although I once heard her telling Mrs Woodruff that she was much in favour of his remarrying – 'Providing the right young woman came along.' I liked the idea, too. I sensed an empty space in his life that Gran and I could never fill, realised there was a special kind of love that had nothing to do with the kind a man feels for his mother and daughter. I wanted to question him, of course. Excited yet a little jealous, pleased for him yet anxious, I wanted reassurance that my world was not going to change too radically, that my life wasn't going to set me even further apart from other children than I already felt. Several times I opened my mouth and felt the word 'Dad ... ?' rising in my throat, only to fall back again. When I finally did force it out and he looked up expectantly, all I could say was, 'Give us a tune on your flute?'

It was a request he could never refuse, and when he had found his flute case among the piles of clothes I settled myself cross-legged on the bed to listen. As far back as I could remember, Dad never let a day go by without giving someone a tune on his flute. And one of the few things I could remember with any clarity about my mother was her utter contempt for that instrument, so it was natural that hearing it here in the room where she used to sleep made me think about her. As Dad played, I gazed around at the evidence of her long-ago presence.

Admittedly, she hadn't left much: one or two dresses she'd obviously considered too old-fashioned to take with her, the pretty cushion and chairback cover; and the dressing-table set – of blue glass and as dated as the dresses – was unmistakably hers. She left no jewellery, no make-up or perfume, although I seemed to recall her owning vast quantities of these things. And I recalled seeing her at that dressing-table, carefully applying lipstick in preparation for an evening out somewhere. Whether this was on one occasion or many times, transformed in my memory by the same mysterious process that rolls every childhood Christmas into one, I can't be sure. But I see her sitting there, her hair freshly curled and shining, the pink evening dress that rustled and rasped as she moved, her long fingers delicately sorting through a tangle of necklaces in her musical jewellery box. I believe I went and stood beside her, staring at her reflection and wondering why she liked going out so much when she knew Dad preferred quiet evenings at home. She turned to me, smiling slightly, giving me a look that said I shouldn't really be in her room. I watched her for some moments, baffled yet enthralled by the mystery of all those little pots and jars before her, half-awed by the skill needed to keep an adult face youthful and attractive. I think I felt glad I would have such expert guidance when I grew up.

Mother's dressing-table triggered off less pleasant memories, too. She didn't get on well with Gran, who was her mother-in-law and who disapproved of women wearing make-up at all, let alone every day. Their bones of contention were many, but it was the question of personal vanity which caused most strife, and my mother was very vain. She dreamed of a life central in local society, of being the perfect hostess to people like the Thorough-goods and Colonel Cartwright. She even contemplated buying a twenty-four volume encyclopaedia for me – at five years of age – because Colonel Cartwright force-fed his children on the *Britan-nica*. And when she learned that Mrs Thoroughgood bought her own and Margie's clothes in London we had no peace. The Wades had to do the same, or better, in everything. Consequently, the rows grew in heat and frequency. How well I remembered their raised voices, my mother's demands, her dresses and perfume, while her face was no more than a blur.

'Wake up, Cassie!' My father took his lips from the flute just long enough to rouse my thoughts, then I felt obliged to clap in time to 'Portsmouth', which was a great favourite of ours.

If only life could go on like this for ever; Dad playing his flute, impressing my schoolfriends with his talent, Gran building up the fire in the living-room, poking at the coals to encourage a good, toasting blaze. If only the eleven plus wasn't looming in February, the frightening new school where the girls wore nylon stockings and talked about boys incessantly. I thought of Dawn doing her Adam Faith impersonation:

> *'What do ya warn' if ya don't warn' muh-nee?*
> *What do ya warn' if ya don't warn' luv? . . . '*

She'd have no trouble fitting in at Wickstead High School. In fact, she was actually looking forward to it, preparing the rest of us with useful advice from her older sister, such as calling Arithmetic 'Maths' and never admitting that you read *Bunty*.

I thought of Margie Thoroughgood. She wasn't particularly interested in boys or pop music, but she had the poise and confidence to see her through the upheaval of changing schools. Besides, Margie had a good brain when she chose to use it; she would almost certainly have passed the exam and got into the top stream.

I tried to imagine the girls of Class Six together on the town-bound bus, heading for our very first day. Dawn, Sylvia, Christine, the twins. I saw them all so clearly. Everyone but Margie. However hard I tried I couldn't picture her face, excited and expectant as it would have been, among ours.

They made us pray for her at school. That is, Mr Riordan inserted a petition for her safety following the Lord's Prayer at morning assembly, to which we bellowed 'Amen' with much feeling but little faith. Already we were beginning to think of Margie as past. She had been missing now for over thirty days.

My hands, which had been clapping automatically to the music of Dad's flute, suddenly fell to my lap. Dad looked up, slowly lowered the flute, although his lips remained puckered.

'Sorry,' I said. 'I was just thinking, that's all.'

'I heard about the Thoroughgood girl. Was she a special friend of yours?'

'Not really, Daddy. Though I suppose at one time I saw a lot of her.'

'Want to talk about it, Cass?'

'There's not much to tell.' It wasn't an episode I was particularly proud of because I'd deserted Dawn for the honour of Margie's company. 'I gave her one of my fossils – the trilobite –

and she gave me a butterfly necklace on my birthday. Gran didn't want me to keep it because she thought it looked too expensive. We were only friends for a couple of weeks.'

It had all begun when I met Margie coming home from the Sunshine Corner Club one evening. The village hall had been so crowded with kids that I hadn't seen her before and was surprised; playing silly games with beanbags and I-Spy wasn't Margie's usual idea of fun.

'It's a bore, isn't it?' she said, meaning the club. 'I only go there because the old man who runs it is chairman of the PC and a great friend of Mummy's.' She began to sing the club song in a mocking voice:

> 'Sunshine Corner, oh it's mighty fine,
> It's for children under ninety-nine,
> All are welcome, seats are given free,
> Here at Sunshine Corner is the place for me.

'Yuk! Why do you go, Cassie?'

'Why? Well, it's good for a laugh, I suppose.'

We walked along the road together, taking the mickey out of poor Mr Donald, the PC chairman and rather clueless club leader. And it was *fun*. Margie had a way of making you feel good about yourself, that you were doing and saying the right things, that you *belonged*.

The next afternoon we took chocolate spread sandwiches, a bottle of Vimto and a bag of cherries and had a picnic in the cow-patted field next to the water tower. Margie sprawled in a patch of clover and began half-heartedly searching for four-leaved specimens. The strong sunlight made her hair look absolutely white, her eyes even paler blue; and I wondered how it was she tanned so well with her colouring while I, with dark hair and eyes, always spent every summer smothered in calamine lotion.

'You are lucky, Margie,' I said, really thinking aloud.

Margie didn't ask me why. She simply took it for granted I meant her looks, laughed and tossed her head. No wonder everyone wanted to be her friend.

This particular intimacy survived little more than a week, however; then Margie lost interest in me and attached herself to a new girl. I minded very much at first and tried to win her back with bribes of sweets. But Dawn was there to soften the blow, treating me rather like a wilful child who has had its own way and found no good came of it. I began to regard the whole episode as shameful, a self-inflicted wound to my pride – especially with regard to those bribes – and decided I had learned my lesson.

'She must have got at least half a crown's worth of pineapple chunks and spearmint pips out of me, Daddy,' I said, laughing because I was embarrassed and wished I hadn't told him.

'Did you really regret losing Margie's friendship so much, Cassie?' He looked sorry for me, and that hurt.

'Not really, no. Not after a while.'

'That's good, because from what you've told me Margie wasn't always a very nice little girl. So you weren't one of her regular crowd, then?'

'Not one of those who were always tagging along, like Sylvia.'

'No, I didn't think so.'

'We used to play in her garden a lot, though.' Used to. Again the past tense. 'Everyone's saying she's dead, Daddy.'

'It's a possibility you'll have to accept, Cass.' He looked at my hands, still folded in my lap, took one in his own and examined it as though searching for dirt in my nails the way Gran did. How small my hand looked cradled in his. 'Cassie, I want you to promise me you'll never speak to strangers, whatever they – '

'Daddy, we've had all this at school from Mr Riordan and Miss Saunders. And Gran's been giving me the same.'

'Well, now you're getting it from me as well.' I made an impatient movement, which he checked with his hands on my shoulders. 'No, Cassie, you're going to listen to me. A man like that would use all sorts of tricks to entice a little girl to go with him. For instance, he might say he has some puppies and would you like to go and see them? He might even say your gran is ill and she's sent him to fetch you home. But you remember, Cassie; the answer is always "No."'

I nodded slowly. 'But Daddy, suppose Gran really was ill and needed me?'

'Then she'd get Mrs Woodruff to telephone the school.'

This seemed a wholly unsatisfactory arrangement to me, but Dad needn't have worried; nothing in the world would have induced me to so much as cross the street with a stranger. He

30

insisted I make him a solemn promise, however, then he took a small package from one of his cases and handed it to me.

'This isn't a Christmas present, mind. I've already given that to your gran to hide until the day, and don't you go looking for it, either.'

It was a necklace of small shells, all painted in different colours and having a curious smell about them, like scented seaweed. Dad's presents were always special to me, but this was the first time he had brought me a necklace, or any jewellery in fact. I wondered if it was my imagination again, or if this necklace had been chosen by a woman. Somehow it didn't have Dad's touch; it was too delicately pretty, too feminine. And he was unusually anxious that I should like it.

'It's fab!' I said, using Dawn's pet word. That year, everything that wasn't 'square' was 'fab', and this was the first time I had used the word without feeling self-conscious and a fraud. Even so, Dad laughed.

'Fab, eh? That's exactly what I hoped you'd say. I'm glad you like it, Cassie.' He fastened it round my neck and I ran downstairs to show Gran.

Dad's homecomings were always a cause for celebration, and I used this particular occasion to wangle an invitation for Dawn to come to tea. It wasn't too easy as Gran didn't have a high opinion of my friend; she was sullen, Gran said, and when she did condescend to speak it might as well have been in a foreign tongue with all those silly 'fab' words. But I wheedled and nagged – 'Dad won't be home for Christmas and I want him to see Dawn' – until she relented. I would have been too embarrassed to ask Gran if she thought Dad had a new girlfriend, so I meant to ask Dawn's opinion.

We had our tea in the seldom-used front room because Dad was home and Gran, not without a little grumble, lit a fire in there for us. The fireplace was quite hideous to my eyes, surrounded by bottle green tiles with snowdrops painted on them so you thought of snow even before a roaring fire and you shivered. But Dawn, true to her contrary nature, took a fancy to it and I had a job dragging her to the table where she was supposed to concentrate on Dad and put her powers of feminine instinct to work.

'Well, how's your father, Dawn?' said Dad, winking mysteriously at Gran as if he sensed the plotting behind this afternoon.

'Very well, thank you,' said Dawn politely.

'That's good. Are you looking forward to starting at the new school next year? It must be very exciting for you.'

'Mmm.' Dawn nodded, her mouth full of cake.

'But of course, you have an older sister there already, don't you? It won't be so strange for you.'

Dawn's eyes met mine briefly. He was hinting, and none too delicately, that he hoped he could rely on her to look after me.

I think I must have pulled a face, because Dawn suddenly said, 'You look well, Mr Wade,' which brought us safely back to the task in hand. ''Course, it must be rotten for you, stuck away from home all the time.' Gran glared at her. 'And I'll bet you miss Cassie, too.'

'Yes, I miss her very much.'

The most obvious next question would be, Why don't you get a job closer to home? But Dawn was much too sophisticated and wise to ask it. Instead, she began to talk about her mother, the new pullover she was knitting for Dawn, the wonderful Sunday lunches she cooked (Gran glared again), the fact that Mrs Holgate was the indispensable family anchor. Dad listened gravely, but his eyes were twinkling, and I knew it was because of his presence that Gran suddenly melted toward Dawn. She patted her cloud of hair and made her take another slice of Battenburg.

We talked in private later, Dawn and I, and she examined the shell necklace while I described Dad's beautifully ironed shirts.

'I think you're right,' she said at last. 'Looks like you could be getting yourself a wicked stepmother, Cassie.' She bared her teeth and waved her hands, like toasting forks, in front of my face. 'Poor old Cassie!'

Of course, I knew anyone my dad liked just had to be all right. His new girlfriend would be warm and kind, and she wouldn't object to an eleven-year-old daughter. I knew that much because I knew my dad so well. But what would Gran do? I'd lived with her all my life, but if Dad remarried he might want me to go and live with him and his new wife somewhere a long way away.

Why did there have to be so many changes all at once?

The police came to our school again just before Christmas, and this time they questioned every child, not only us in Class Six. Detective Inspector Washkansky (I'd overheard Miss Saunders telling someone his name sounded like a Polish soap powder) and Sergeant Jordan were both kind and softly spoken; yet I trembled and blushed when it came my turn to go into the headmaster's office.

Miss Saunders was present too. She announced me, and though I was so nervous I felt I needed the lavatory, it also made me feel grand and important.

I looked at Washkansky. He had a fatherly sort of face and smiled reassuringly all the time; but there was a weariness about him, as if he'd lost several nights' sleep in a row, and I had an immediate sympathy for him; I knew very well by now that grown-ups had their problems, too.

He began in a conversational way.

'Hello, Cassie. That's a nice name. Is it short for Cassandra?'

Everyone asked me that. 'No, sir. I was christened Cassie. Cassie Jane Wade.'

'And you're in the same class as Margie?'

'Yes, sir. But I wasn't – I mean, I'm not a particular friend of hers.'

'Well, that doesn't matter, Cassie. I expect you see her outside of school sometimes, don't you? And that's what I'm especially interested in at the moment. Do you know if she has other friends, apart from those here at school? Older friends, perhaps? Take as much time as you like, Cassie, but please think very carefully.'

I gazed at the blotting paper on Mr Riordan's desk, trying to look deep in thought. But at first the only thing to enter my head was the fact that the mobile library would pull up in the playground at any minute, and I didn't want to miss it. The young librarian liked me and always had something new to recommend. Sometimes he even put aside a book he knew I would enjoy days before the fortnightly visit. He wouldn't have done that for Margie. Margie didn't like reading much, and whenever she took out a library book it was always a title sure to impress – but she seldom actually read it. I remembered the last time she went out to the van: she grabbed *The Girlhood of Queen Victoria*, just because she knew I wanted it. That, like her other library books, remained in her desk until it was time to return it.

I looked up at the Inspector, and he nodded, smiling. 'Take as much time as you like, dear.' But Miss Saunders frowned, and I believe if it had been up to her she would have turfed me out by the ear for wasting time. I tried really hard to think.

There was one lad Margie had been especially fond of. He was the fifteen-year-old son of our coalman, a surly boy with ginger hair, grimed-in skin and the unlikely name of Rodney. On Saturdays, he helped his father on the round, and Margie often used to wait at the bottom of our road for him. Why she liked him so much I never knew. But I didn't believe the feeling was mutual, because Rodney sometimes tried to avoid her.

Then I thought of Conny Jennings. He loved Margie, even though she was always teasing him and calling him names because he was backward. Conny's father, Cyril, was a kind of general handyman to the village, earning his beer money by trimming hedges, mending paths, keeping the churchyard and rec. in order and even sharpening knives. Sometimes he did a bit of poaching, too. It was Cyril who chased us out of the churchyard in the conker season, and we were all afraid of him – especially when he was sober and particularly foul-tempered.

Conny must have been about nineteen or twenty, and so far his education had consisted of trailing his father around Upper Grisham to help with the heavy work, or roaming off alone across the fields when the old man couldn't be bothered with him. Sometimes Conny would follow us, hoping to be asked to join in a game; but as we grew older, more sensible of the company we kept – and perhaps crueller, too – these invitations became rare. Poor Conny would watch from a distance, bouncing a football with all the skill of a two-year-old, occasionally calling in his strange, gravelly voice, 'Anyone wanna kick?' and nobody bothered to answer.

But it was Margie his eyes sought the most. If she was in a good mood she'd humour him, offer him sweets and ruffle his hair as if he were a little boy. If not, she'd call him 'Dumbo' and threaten to tell Constable Seagle he'd been pinching from Cartwright's orchard again. That used to make the rest of us laugh.

The funny thing about Conny was that although he was so backward ('Daft as a brush,' Gran said) he knew the names of every wild plant, when and where to find them, and which were poisonous. He could even tell you one or two Latin names. Father

Steven had taught him all this, but I still thought it was wonderful that someone who couldn't read, count, or even tie his own shoelaces could remember so much. Dad once said it was as though his mind, deficient in every other way, became a sponge to absorb these facts simply because Conny loved wildlife.

I told all this to Inspector Washkansky. 'But I wouldn't call Rodney or Conny a special friend of Margie's.'

'Well, that's all right, Cassie. You've been very helpful.'

Miss Saunders, looking displeased, sent me back to my class.

We still saw a lot of the police in Grisham, and whenever they spent a long time at somebody's house our suspicions automatically fell on that person. One man, a former admirer of Mrs Thoroughgood's, was actually taken to the police station in town – helping with enquiries, as Gran said ominously. But nothing came of it. The landlord of Grisham's only pub was prime suspect for a while, solely on the grounds of his having a bitter, invalid wife. I overheard Gran telling Mrs Woodruff he had 'suppressions' and was 'likely to turn' – whatever that meant. Again, nothing came of it.

Christmas, and after over seventy days, Margie's disappearance was still national news. We had become used to seeing her picture in the newspapers and on television, and somehow it made us all feel important because we knew her. But despite the publicity, and the number of police working on the case – and from the top CID men to our own Constable Seagle and Sergeant Carlo, that number must have been great – the investigation was getting nowhere.

4

Gran was right in her predictions for a hard winter. As far as I can remember, it only snowed twice in our region, but the snow lay frozen fast to the ground for over six weeks before the thaw set in. East Anglian winters are often savage, especially for those living in the more remote villages, and though we weren't cut off that year we soon tired of the endless white beyond our windows and the unbelievable hardness of the ground beneath our feet when we did venture out. The playing field, where the mud rose in peaks and swirls after the last football match, was painful to walk across, even in my thick-soled Start-Rite shoes, and a fall in the playground hurt much more than usual.

Gran had a touch of arthritis in her fingers and left knee, which always became worse in cold weather, so she seldom went out during that January and February and we bought all our groceries from Jack Knowles. Jack had a mobile shop and called at Upper Grisham three times a week, bringing all the news from neighbouring villages along with the groceries. I didn't like Jack much, and I hated having to go out to the van to help carry the shopping. He had a disconcerting way of looking at me; his head on one side, top incisors protruding from wet lips, eyes sparkling as though he found me amusing. But what I disliked about him most was his habit of always saying the same things, asking me the same questions.

'They haven't found the girl that went missing, then?' he'd say, and Gran would shake her head gravely. 'Terrible, isn't it? You knew her, didn't you, Cassie?' I would nod. 'I'll never understand what sort of bloke could go around hurting kiddies.' And so on, three times a week.

Now, as we entered February, he had a new theme.

'I hope you're well prepared for that eleven plus, young Cassie. It's not far off now, after all. Know the twelve times table? What's the capital of Denmark, then? Can you divide seventy-three into two thousand and eight?'

As if I wasn't feeling bad enough about it.

My weak subject was Arithmetic. I could barely multiply, and long division was as much a mystery to me as it would have been to one of the infant class. So Gran – and no doubt prompted by my mumbled answers to Jack's questions – made me revise Arithmetic every evening of the week before the exam. It didn't help much. Between us we conquered the division, but Gran had never learned fractions, and she had the vague idea that the decimal point was some cliff on the Cornish coast. The end of my pencil became very chewed and every night I went to bed with splinters in my teeth. I hoped my English and General Knowledge would be enough to pull me through.

The morning of the great day was dark and bitterly cold. I sat shivering at the breakfast table while Gran bustled about making tea and scrambled eggs, and grabbing the poker to prod the slow fire every time she passed. All the while, she was giving me instructions: how I was to answer when spoken to, what frame of mind I ought to put myself in.

'I dreamt about it last night,' I said. 'I dreamt they'd invented some new subject, something far more important than Arithmetic or English, and we hadn't been taught it.'

'Just a silly dream, Cassie. I know you'll do very well.'

'Suppose I don't pass, Gran?'

'You'll pass all right. So you haven't quite got the hang of those fractions yet; what does that matter? Fractions are only one little thing. They set more store by your reading and writing because that opens the way to other subjects. They don't fail people just for not knowing fractions, Cassie.'

I wasn't convinced, and I had to force down the scrambled eggs and a cup of tea. Before I picked up my satchel and put on my gloves, Gran gave me a kiss for good luck.

'Just do your best, Cass. That's all anyone can do. And remember, passing the eleven plus is a good start in life, but failing it isn't the end of everything.'

She'll never know how much those words cheered me, or how I began then to realise what a sensible woman she was. Gran might not have learned fractions or passed exams, but she had more sense than any professor.

We were expected to make our own way to town, although children from villages further out were being taken by a special bus. Dawn and I went in Mrs Woodruff's car with Colin, who looked in danger of being sick at any moment. I repeated Gran's words of wisdom confidently, only to see his mother's eyes glaring at me in the rear view mirror.

'It might not be the end of everything for you, Cassie Wade,' she snapped, 'but we expect Colin to enter a profession, and passing this exam is vital to him.'

I shrugged, turned to the window and said no more.

Wickstead High School, where the girls were to take the exam, stood on a hill on the far side of town, and I had only seen it once before. That was a long time ago, during one of the rambling Sunday walks Dad and I used to take when my mother was still at home, and, naturally I suppose, the impression I had carried in my mind all that time was a false one. I saw now that the building was almost certainly post-war, light and airy, rather than the workhouse-type monstrosity I'd pictured. Mrs Woodruff followed the signs which indicated eleven-plus candidates were to be met in the first quad, and drove us slowly past a science lab, where I could see a row of bunsen burners on a bench near the window. Would we study real science in our first year? And would we do the sort of experiments with chemicals that Dad remembered from his school-days? Perhaps here I would finally decide what sort of career I wanted for myself. I'd listened to the ambitions of other girls – air hostess, nurse, hairdresser – and I'd shuddered. I wanted to do something interesting, and different; something that would make Dad proud of me and Gran say, 'I always knew she'd do well.' Today would be the very first step.

Whatever the results of this exam all of the girls would attend Wickstead High, but in different streams – A to E – according to individual ability. I had hopes of reaching the B-stream, as did most of the Grisham girls; we knew our primary school had a good record for passes, and many ex-pupils then went on to collect a healthy bunch of O and A levels.

The boys would either go to Wickstead Grammar or the Secondary Modern, and they were to sit their exam today at the former. So when Mrs Woodruff had deposited us in the quad she drove away eagerly. It was a well-known fact that she had already bought part of the Grammar School uniform for Colin. The last I saw of him was his pale face, staring desperately out of the rear view mirror and mouthing something that looked a plea for mercy. But I was too anxious for myself to spare him much sympathy.

We hung our coats on pegs in the corridor, bright-coloured coats which betrayed their owners as strangers among all the grey gaberdines. Just then, two girls in the grey blazers and skirts of the school uniform came by. They gave us a contemptuous look, and one of them groaned, 'More eleven-plussers, I suppose.'

I turned to Dawn anxiously. We had been told to put our coats here, but could it be possible we'd misheard and pinched someone else's pegs? Dawn had her blue-eyed glare fixed on the girls, and before I could stop her, she snapped, 'And you must be last year's rejects.'

One of the girls, greasy-haired and spotty, with a thin, chapped mouth, approached us as if she couldn't believe what she had just heard. I backed away slightly, but Dawn didn't move; she was going to get us into trouble before we'd even started at this school.

'I'll remember your face, kid,' said the girl. Then, turning to me, 'Yours, too. And you'd better remember my name. I'm Myrtle Baines, and I'm a prefect; so you'll have to watch it.'

Dawn placed her hands on her hips and tossed her head arrogantly. 'You're no prefect. You're in my sister's class. My sister's Julie Holgate, so you're the one who'd better watch it. C'mon, Cassie.' She took my arm and dragged me off to the gym, where we were to assemble before going to the exam rooms.

'Dawn, I wish you hadn't answered her back,' I said. My voice sounded very like a whine. 'Suppose she really is a prefect?'

'She isn't, I tell you. She's just the school bully.'

'And we're on the wrong side of her already.'

'Oh, for God's sake, Cassie! You've got to stand up for yourself here; no running to teachers in this place. Number One Rule – if you can't look after yourself, don't go telling tales.'

She went on ahead of me into the gym, where I spotted one or two others from our class amongst a crowd of strangers. I told myself Dawn was just showing off. She wanted me to see the advantage she had by knowing so much about the school through her sister. All the same, I wished I hadn't been with her when she crossed that awful, spotty Myrtle.

We were taken to the exam rooms upstairs in alphabetical order, which meant Dawn and I were separated. I sat next to a coloured girl who put a set of jacks on her desk for good luck, then asked me what I thought I was staring at. The only one I could see from Upper Grisham in our room was Sylvia Tanner. It was then that I noticed an empty desk a few places behind Sylvia. We were still in alphabetical order, and I knew the vacant place must be Margie's. Poor Margie. A few days had passed since I last gave her a thought, and that made me feel guilty. Several times that morning, in between wrestling with long division and decimal points, I looked up at that empty place.

The afternoon was easier. We had to write an essay, and we could choose from a long, imaginative list of subjects. Perhaps, because she had been on my mind so much that morning, any subject I picked would have provided scope for the inclusion of Margie. As it was, 'Summer Days' was a natural setting for the missing girl.

I wrote about our wild-flower collection, begun so eagerly in the short period when Margie was my Best Friend and never completed. One day, we had gone on a wild-flower hunt. Armed with large bags in which to put our specimens and Margie's *Observer's* book, we scoured the fields and hedgerows around the village. We had just finished a picnic lunch of peanut butter sandwiches when Margie spotted something yellow on the edge of the field. She ran to investigate, and returned with a flower neither of us had ever seen before.

'I bet it's a wild orchid,' she said confidently. 'It's so beautiful.'

But the *Observer's* book had some pages missing – Margie was so careless with her belongings – and we couldn't identify it.

'Let's ask Conny,' I suggested, aware that his awkward figure had been crouched in the long grass behind us for some time.

He came, half running, half skipping, when we called, pleased as could be that someone wanted him. And his face lit with pride when he understood it was his expert knowledge we sought.

'Here,' said Margie, 'you know all about plants and things. What's this called?'

Conny cradled the flower in his great hands as gently as if it had been one of his pet mice. 'Toadflax,' he growled, almost incoherently. 'Thass toadflax. Pretty, unnit?'

Poor Conny. Just as he was offering the flower back, his eyes unable to conceal the admiration he felt for Margie, she snatched it from him, crushed it and threw it to the ground.

'Toadflax? It's called *toadflax*? I thought it was an orchid!'

It was difficult to say which angered her most: the flower for having such an ugly name, or Conny for telling her.

She ran off, leaving me to gather up the picnic things. Conny helped me.

'Her don't mean it,' he muttered. 'Her don't mean it.'

On another occasion, when half a dozen of us were idling around the rec. one evening, Margie really got Conny into trouble. It was about eight o'clock, the sun had already set and it was that time of day when the light is beginning to fade and you know you ought to be going home, but the scent of garden bonfires and new evening coolness persuades you to stay just a while longer.

Margie suggested we play Mr Castle, a sort of cross between Hide and Seek, It, and Statues, with a few complicated rules that no one could ever remember thrown in for good measure. Margie volunteered to be It and named the cricket pavilion as Home. While she counted to a hundred, in fives, the rest of us hid among the bushes bordering two sides of the rec. I headed for the corner because there was a low wooden fence there, and you could hop over it until the catcher was safely past and then sneak to Home.

Conny was already there, squatting behind a prickly bush and sucking his dirty fingers. I wasn't alarmed, or even the least surprised; Conny turned up all over the place, especially when Margie was around. I pulled his hand away from his mouth.

'You'll get worms,' I said.

Conny frowned at his nails, then held his head back and grinned, as though he thought having worms a very desirable thing.

'You've got to keep very quiet, Conny,' I told him. 'We're playing Mr Castle, and Margie is It.'

'All right, Cassie. Can I play?'

'Only if you keep quiet.'

But Conny couldn't keep quiet. He giggled, cupping a grubby

hand over his mouth like a small child laughing when he shouldn't. More than once, he whispered, 'She won't find us here, will she, Cassie? Margie won't find us here.'

Exasperated, I got up to chance a bolt for Home, but Margie saw me, and then Conny shouted, 'Run, Cassie!'

I ran and ran, not even daring to look over my shoulder until my hands slapped the pavilion wall and I screamed, *'Home for Cassie!'*

But where was Margie? She was easily the fastest runner in the school, which was why she never minded being It, and she should have caught me with little trouble. I turned around. There was no sign of anyone, and until Sylvia Tanner appeared from behind the pavilion I had an uneasy idea I was being made a fool of.

'Where's Margie?' Sylvia asked, pulling a twig from her hair.

One by one, the others crept out, looked around them, then sauntered toward us.

'Margie's playing silly buggers with us,' said Dawn. 'C'mon, Cassie. Let's go home. It's getting dark now, anyway.'

Just then, Cyril Jennings, Conny's father, came striding across the rec. He was an ugly, bullet-headed man, with skin that always looked sunburned, even in winter, and eyes like organ stops. He carried the bright red plastic shopping bag that usually contained the results of his poaching. Probably he was on his way to sell his latest haul in the pub.

He saw us and stopped, his face in the sneer that told me he was stone-cold sober. Gran used to say drink could turn a man nasty – only with Cyril it was the other way around. Beer made him affable, almost gentlemanly; the lack of it turned him into a foul-tempered, loud-mouthed brute whom everyone avoided.

Cyril turned to me first. 'You seen that son o' mine, Cassie Wade?'

'No.' I refused to be polite.

'What about you, Dawn Holgate?'

'No. And if I had I wouldn't tell you.'

Cyril made a threatening gesture with his fist and Dawn flinched slightly, though she still managed to keep her defiant look.

But Conny, peering out of the bushes and unable to bear the tension, decided to give himself up. Perhaps it wouldn't have been so bad if Margie hadn't stepped out behind him, but she had to show us all that Margie Thoroughgood wasn't afraid of anyone, and somehow her smirking and preening made it look as if they'd been up to something in the bushes; at least, that was what Cyril must have thought. He strode over to his son and began hitting him around the head.

'How many times do I have to tell you? How – many – *times*? If you don't stay away from these girls you'll end up in a home!'

Conny made not the slightest effort to defend himself, although he was quite big and strong enough to floor his father if he chose. Instead, he hunched his shoulders and whimpered.

'I ain't done nuthin', Dad! I ain't done nuthin'!'

'I'll give you "ain't done nuthin!" I'll give *you*!' The last word was accompanied by a punch between the shoulders. 'Now you get on home and don't you dare come out no more tonight. You hear?'

When they had gone, Cyril still making a racket that could probably be heard all over Grisham, I looked at Margie and saw she was laughing. It was at that moment that I lost all traces of the admiration I once felt for her and decided I didn't really like her much at all.

I stopped writing five minutes before the allotted time was up to read back over my essay. I found I had not stuck as strictly to the theme as I'd intended, so I hastily scribbled a few more sentences, which threw the entire piece out of balance in my opinion. It was ruined; foolishly ruined because of my day-dreaming. I felt angry with Margie.

'You should worry,' said Dawn in the car on the way home. 'My mind was a complete blank for twenty minutes. I didn't even finish my essay.'

'But at least what you did write must have made sense. I'm not at all sure mine did.'

'Cassie, every time you say you've written a bad essay you get top marks. How did you get on, Col?'

My eyes met Mrs Woodruff's in the rear view mirror. She looked smug, confident of Colin's success. Which was more than Colin did.

'Not too bad,' he muttered.

Further discussion revealed we'd all had the same problems in the Arithmetic test, all found the same sticking points, and I began to feel easier about my own effort. Dawn was right about my essays, too. I was a poor judge of my compositions, and the very ones I thought I had mucked up usually got the best marks. My spirits started to rise, so that by the time we reached Upper Grisham I could even dismiss the thought of Myrtle Baines from my mind. Everything was going to be all right, and I could hardly wait to get home and tell Gran.

I had been promised a special tea today, and I ran indoors expectantly, sniffing the air for smells of cake-baking. But although the table was laid ready, all I could see were muffins piled on to a plate ready for toasting, and we had muffins nearly every day. Gran was folding washing in the kitchen, and the look she gave me sent me into a panic. All I could think of was that she must have heard about the broken milk bottles. But that had been months ago, and I had led a near-blameless life since. Hadn't I?

'Gran, what's the matter?'

'Nothing, Cassie. Take your things off and have a warm by the fire. Then you can tell me how you got on and all about it.'

That hardly sounded like a prelude to bone-picking. I unbuttoned my coat slowly, watching Gran and wondering why she hadn't baked a cake.

'Aren't you well, Gran?' I asked.

'I'm all right. Shouldn't I be, then?'

'Well, I kind of thought – I mean, I thought we were going to have something special tonight?'

She turned her back to me, busily folding a blouse. 'I know, Cass. I meant to bake a chocolate sponge, but I just didn't have the time.'

'Didn't have time?' I yelled, almost crying with disappointment. 'Why didn't you have time? You promised, Gran!'

'I know I did. But I had a visitor, and that took up most of the afternoon. I'm sorry, Cassie. I know you were looking forward to it, but I'll make it up to you, I promise. Don't get in a paddy, now. I've got too much to think about.'

I sat down by the fire, glaring into the flames. All the day's news was spoiled now, and I had a mind to refuse to eat the muffins. Gran had never broken her promise before. No matter how busy she was, whoever came to distract her, if she had made

44

a promise she would keep it. It was then that I noticed a faint perfume in the air. Not the kind that cost twelve-and-six from Boots, either, but the really expensive perfume people like Mrs Thoroughgood wore. While Gran was still busy in the kitchen, I went and peered into the front room. The scent was more powerful in there, and tea things – the best china, too – were set out on the table. I tiptoed in and touched the teapot. It was cold, so the visitor had left some time ago, but she had left evidence of her identity: a certain shade of lipstick on her cup, a certain brand of cigarette, only half-smoked, in the ashtray. The scent was the final proof.

'Gran!' I called. 'I remember this perfume. It's the one Mother used to wear, isn't it?' She didn't answer, and I turned around. 'Gran, she's been here, hasn't she? My mother's been here?'

Gran stood in the doorway, still holding the folded blouse, looking at me with the same odd expression I'd seen when I first came in.

'Yes, she was here.'

'Well? What did she want?' My lips were dry and my knees began to tremble, but not through excitement.

'Come and sit down, Cassie. Over here, by the fire.'

I did as she asked, watching her all the time, although she wasn't looking at me any more.

'What does she want?' I repeated.

'She wants to see you, Cassie.'

'She's out of luck, then. 'Cos I don't want to see her.'

'Just listen, Cass, will you? Since she left your father she's done pretty well for herself. Got a shop in Ipswich; a fashion shop as far as I can make out. She's bought a house there, too.'

'Why did she bother coming here then? Come to visit the poor relations, I suppose? Well, I hope she's brought me an expensive present.'

'Now, Cassie! I won't have you speak in that way. She *is* your mother, after all, and she deserves some respect. She just wants to see you, have you over to stay with her for a week or so.'

'No, Gran! No! I don't want to! She's sent me one Christmas card since she left. One! Oh, and I forgot; one Christmas stocking that took her five minutes to buy in Woolies and cost her all of half a crown.' I flung myself back in my chair, feeling defiant, pleased with myself for the sarcasm I considered very adult and worldly wise. Gran soon set me straight on that.

'You're eleven, Cassie,' she said. 'A child still. I don't pretend to know anything about the law or how this business of reasonable access works. As for her coming to see you, I don't think I can do anything to prevent her. But remember, your father is abroad for so much of the time and I'm getting on in years. It may be that, should your mother want you to go and live with her, a judge could well decide that's the best thing for you.'

I went upstairs to change out of my best winter dress, which Gran had insisted I wear that day. Live with my mother? I didn't even know my mother any more. Any judge who decided I would be better off with a stranger than with my gran would have to be extremely hard-hearted, and if it came to it I should tell him so. I banged my fist on the window-sill and it made a hollow, rather weak thump. Yes, I should tell him so.

I looked over the fields behind our house, an unrelenting sea of white, then at the trees in the dell that had once belonged to Colonel Cartwright. Sometimes I could see pictures in the bare branches, and then it was difficult to imagine summer-time, when we played beneath them and looked up to a sky of green leaves that shuddered and chattered with invisible birds.

It would be like that with my mother. I'd be miserable there, and as the months went by it would be difficult to remember the times when I had lived with Gran and been happy. Why did she have to come back now, after all these years?

I sat on my bed and cried.

5

And that was when my troubles really began – with my mother's reappearance that afternoon in February. These days, I suppose it would be called a Tug-of-Love, but as far as I could see love had little enough to do with it. And I was being pulled in three directions instead of two. Every time somebody knocked on our door I flew into a panic, thinking it was her come to take me away, and I would dart upstairs to hide in the linen cupboard. But it was Easter before she finally did turn up. Typical of her, I thought. She acted on the spur of the moment, when the mood took her, or when she didn't have anything better to do with her time.

I was arranging a vase of daffodils in the living-room when I heard the click of the latch on our back gate. Gran had gone to the village grocery store for some spice; she always baked her own hot cross buns, which we ate buttered and still warm from the oven for Good Friday tea. She had promised to let me help make them this year and I was eager to begin. So when I heard the latch I ran to the door expectantly and flung it open.

My mother had changed very much, unless my memory was at fault, and I had to look hard before I was sure this woman was really her. She was still slim, but not so tall as I'd always thought, and her hair had changed from ash-blonde curls, which she used to pile high on the top of her head, to a rich brown, like mine but cropped short and close. She wore a smart suit of silvery grey with a white frilly blouse and black court shoes, and she carried a practical-looking shoulder bag instead of the high fashion clasp handbags I remembered. She recognised me immediately – though why I should have been surprised at this I don't know – and opened her mouth to speak. It was too much for me. I slammed the door and ran upstairs to hide in the linen cupboard.

In a little while she gave up knocking and calling to me and I hoped she had gone away. I crawled out of the cupboard and sat on the top stair, praying that Gran would soon be home to tell me everything was all right and we could get on with preparing the hot cross buns. But Gran was likely to stop for a gossip with the shopkeeper, and if she met one of our Joshua Road neighbours it would take her half an hour to get home. I went into the front bedroom, Dad's room, from where I could see a long way down the road. Her small figure with its crown of short, thick grey hair would have been unmistakable even without that awful yellow coat. Gran looked older than her sixty years, and suddenly lonely, too, as she plodded along with the familiar wicker shopping basket. A widow for so many years, only one grandchild, and she not always as grateful as she ought to be. I wished I had gone to the shop with her instead of loafing in front of the fire with last week's *Bunty*. And if my mother was still outside Gran would come home to find her there, haughty and irritable on her doorstep.

I went back downstairs reluctantly and opened the door. My mother was pacing about in the garden, casting quick, nervous glances at the neighbouring houses as if she were ashamed to be seen.

'You'd better come in then,' I said. My voice startled her and – or perhaps it was only my imagination – her face paled.

'Cassie, *darling*!' she gushed once she had regained her poise. 'Didn't you recognise Mother?' But I detected an edge of annoyance and stood well back to let her in.

'Why don't you sit down? Gran's just gone to the shop. I'm expecting her back any minute.' I pushed the door shut behind me, enclosing us in the small dark living-room where her expensive perfume made the air sweet and sickly.

'Is that all you have to say to me after all this time, Cassie?' She pounced on me without warning, both arms trapping me against her, the brooch she wore scratching my nose. 'My poor Cassie! Did you really think Mother had left you for good? Poor, poor child!'

'You're hurting me!' I squealed as she manoeuvred me to a more comfortable position, the brooch narrowly missing my eye. 'You're hurting me!'

She released me then, her hands gesturing indifference. 'Well, I could hardly expect you to be overjoyed, I suppose, but I did anticipate a little more warmth, Cassie. Stand back, darling, and let Mother have a look at you.'

I obeyed, watching her eyes travel critically from my head to my feet and back again. When she ordered me to turn around, I obliged meekly.

'You're not very big for eleven, are you? Still, that's no real disadvantage. Generally, I believe men are apt to feel intimidated by tall women.'

'I thought you ran a shop, not a white slave market.'

'Cassie! Whatever has your grandmother been teaching you? I've never heard such an expression from a little girl! And for your information, I don't run a shop – I own it. No, Cassie, I was simply thinking of your future. Of course, you may well choose a career and a late marriage, and I hope for your sake that you do. A woman should never settle for being a wife and mother if she has the ability to make more of herself. But whatever she does, a young woman owes it to herself to be well groomed and as attractive as possible. Does your grandmother take you to the hairdresser regularly?'

Why didn't Gran hurry up? I needed her support badly.

'No, I've never been to the hairdresser. Gran cuts my hair herself.'

'I thought as much. You should always have your hair cut by a professional, Cassie. I'll arrange for you to – '

Just then, Gran walked in. She glanced at me briefly, then eyed my mother.

'Well, Isabel,' she said. 'I thought that was your car parked down the road.'

A car? My mother could drive a car? There were few women drivers in our area at the time, and only one that I knew of in Grisham. I begrudged the admiration, but that was real achievement.

'Cassie,' said Gran, 'go and make a pot of tea. I hope you don't mind tea, Isabel, but we never drink coffee.'

'Of course not.' That remark was open to interpretation. Of course she didn't mind, or of course these unsophisticated bumpkins didn't drink coffee.

I put the kettle on and laid the tea tray. Ours was a gas cooker and I found it impossible to hear their conversation above the noise of the heating kettle, so I crept closer to the door.

'I don't know what you mean by that, Lilian,' my mother was saying. 'I simply parked further down because the road up here is so narrow.'

'You weren't thinking of taking Cassie away with you while I was out, then?'

'Of course not! For one thing, I didn't know you were out. And for another, do you seriously believe the child would have come with me? She slammed the door in my face and ran upstairs at first. I spent ages banging and calling before I could persuade her to let me in. Besides, I wouldn't be so stupid as to just take her off somewhere without telling anyone, not after that terrible business last year.'

'No, Isabel. I don't think you would. I'm sorry.'

They were silent for a moment, then my mother said, 'You know, when I first heard that a child from Upper Grisham was missing, I fainted. I felt sure it must be Cassie. Then when I heard it wasn't – well, that's when I knew I had to see her again.'

'What a pity you never bothered to come before.'

'I wrote, Lilian. I wrote regularly. But she never wrote back.' Another silence. Then my mother, hesitantly: 'She did get my letters, didn't she?'

'No, Isabel. Now then, don't lose your temper with me. It wasn't my idea to keep your letters from her, it was Arthur's. He thought they would only upset her, and if you couldn't be bothered to come and see her it would be better to sever all contact completely.'

'I meant to come and see her.' My mother's voice had taken on a childish, petulant whine. 'But you know how it is when you're trying to set up in business.'

'No, I don't know,' said Gran. 'I wouldn't, would I?'

'I had to travel a lot for my employers. Then, once I had the capital to go it alone, well, I just couldn't afford to take days off here and there. All I've done since I left has been for Cassie.'

'What rot, Isabel! If you cared about her at all you would have stayed and been a real mother to her.'

'But I wanted to make something for her, for her future. I don't want Cassie to leave school and marry the first man who comes along. I don't want her to make the same mistakes as I did.'

It was just about the worst thing she could have said.

'So, you married my son and then decided you'd made a mistake, did you?' Gran snapped.

'I'm not blaming Arthur, Lilian – '

'You've changed then.'

'What I'm saying is, it was a mistake for both of us. You often used to say so yourself. Do you think it would have been good for Cassie to grow up with Arthur and me squabbling all the time?'

The kettle began its shrill singing and I made the tea in the precise way Gran had taught me: one spoonful for each person, one for the pot, take the pot to the kettle and not vice versa. Whatever shortcomings I might have in the line of personal grooming, at least I could make a good cup of tea. I inspected the contents of the biscuit tin. We had chocolate-covered wafers and home-made raisin biscuits, but I took the stale Rich Tea and put them on a plain white plate. So, my mother had written to me. But she could drive; she could have come in person. She was only here now because she'd heard about Margie and that made her feel guilty about me.

'Not those, Cassie!' Gran frowned at the Rich Tea when I took the tray in. 'For heaven's sake, child!'

'Please, don't bother on my account,' said my mother. 'I never eat biscuits or cake. Very bad for the figure and complexion, Cassie. Another thing, I hope you won't learn to smoke cigarettes at your new school.' (She had just lit a Capstan herself.) 'Smoking is very bad for young people. It causes little red veins on your cheeks and makes your breath nasty.'

I brought the teapot in and placed it on a table mat while my mother watched.

'Does she have the small bedroom window open at night?' she asked. 'I'm a great believer in fresh air at all times. And if you don't mind my saying so, Lilian, it's rather stuffy in this room.'

I could see that Gran did mind, but she answered quite evenly, 'Cassie has to be kept warm. She's prone to bronchitis.'

'She never used to be.'

'Isabel, perhaps you'd like to show Cassie the photo of your shop if you have it with you.'

At once, my mother forgot her concern for my welfare and became very lively. She was proud of herself and her achievements and seemed anxious that we should be suitably impressed.

She took a large, glossy photograph from her bag, pulling her chair closer to mine.

'This is the shop from the outside. It doesn't look big, I know, but I'm planning to expand.'

I nodded. The double-fronted shop looked big enough to me, and the name above the door – Isabel Alexander, my mother's maiden name – made it seem very grand too. I couldn't see much of the fashions on display in the windows because of sunlight reflected in the glass.

'Well, what do you think?' my mother asked eagerly.

'It's very nice,' I said.

'Very nice? Isn't that just typical of this child?' I wondered how she could presume to know what was 'typical' of me when she hadn't seen me for so many years. 'Is that really all you can say, Cassie?'

'I can't tell very much from a photo.'

'No, well, perhaps you'll come and visit me soon and then I can show you the real thing. Wouldn't that be nice?' She spoke as though offering me a week at the seaside.

But she soon tired of trying to hold a conversation with me and turned her full attention on Gran. Her talk was mostly about herself and her shop, and though Gran didn't care for her and didn't understand business she listened politely, now and then nodding her head and uttering appreciative sounds. I watched my mother carefully, taking stock of her and judging. My first impression had been that she was much altered; now I saw I had been mistaken. The hairstyle was changed and the make-up was bolder, but I realised the woman inside was still the same. Her mannerisms were the old, familiar ones, the ambitions still governed her life. Only now she seemed to have ambitions for me as well.

I tried to imagine what it would be like living with her. She would dine out most of the time, I supposed, and that would be fun. Probably she threw a party once a week, inviting all the rich, important people she knew, and there would be champagne and caviare. I decided I must ask her whether caviare came in a tin or whether you bought it by the pint like shrimps. Then there was the shop which took up so much of her time, and I imagined dozens of assistants scurrying about under her critical gaze, piles of fashionable dresses in their arms. There would be plush carpets that made it look as if you were gliding instead of walking, people talking in whispers, all the prices marked in guineas, and of course my mother's expensive perfume heavy in the air. She would send me to a private school, a small establishment set in acres of well-kept gardens, where the girls wore a pretty cream and blue uniform instead of the dull grey of the local High School. No Myrtle Baines there, and no teachers who repelled you at the slightest hint of tale-telling. Perhaps there would even be stables and a tennis court.

I looked at Gran, suddenly overwhelmed by my disloyal thoughts. What on earth would she do while I was enjoying myself eating out at smart restaurants and riding horses? I wouldn't see Dawn any more and if Margie Thoroughgood was ever found how would I know? I'd miss Father Steven and Mr Riordan. I'd even miss Jack Knowles, who pestered me with the same remarks and questions every week. Maybe Dad wouldn't want to come and see me when he knew I was with Mother, either; he'd feel I'd deserted him. But poor Gran, she'd feel it most of all. I pictured her looking out on the back garden, empty without me, the way Mrs Thoroughgood looked out at her garden now. I felt my eyes starting to burn and I fidgeted, trying to think of other things.

'Cassie seems impressed,' said my mother, looking pleased. 'Is there anything you'd like to ask me, darling?'

'How do you buy caviare?'

'What? Well, from a shop of course.'

'I mean, what in? A tin or a packet?' I think I had the vague idea that caviare was a superior type of spinach.

'In a little pot. Really, Cassie, I'm sure I don't know what makes you think of such questions. No one has mentioned the subject as far as I recall. I meant did you want to ask me anything about my shop or my new house?'

I looked at Gran. There was a limited number of questions one could ask about a new house and I couldn't think of any.

'Well, would you like to come and stay with me? Just for the weekend, say. Perhaps a week.'

'What, right now?'

My mother laughed. 'No, not right now, you silly child. I'll have to prepare a room for you first and that will take time. I was thinking of the summer holidays.'

Gran answered for me. 'I'm sure she'd enjoy it, Isabel. You'll have to keep in touch with me so we can arrange a week that suits you and doesn't clash with any plans Arthur may have.'

This satisfied my mother and she prepared to leave. She hoped we wouldn't think her rude, she said, but this room really was too stuffy for her comfort.

'Would you like to walk with me to my car, Cassie? Go and put your coat on, then.'

Gran nodded when I looked at her doubtfully, mouthing the word 'best', which meant I was to put on my Sunday coat and not the plain duffle I wore to school.

My mother did not offer to hold my hand or even bother to speak, apart from the odd comment on changes in Joshua Road, as we walked along together. I had the feeling she was critical of me – of the way I walked (I was the kind of child who tripped over every twig and stone), of the way I held my head, and even of my pretty red coat with the fur-edged collar.

Luckily for me, the sight of Cyril Jennings returning from some job in the village distracted her.

'Oh, Lord!' she whispered. 'He's not still around, is he? It's a mercy that boy of his is a mental defective. I'd hate to think of a normal lad in Cyril's care.'

I couldn't help making a small 'Huh!' at the back of my throat. Dad had once said that was the real tragedy; that if Conny had been normal he would have been more able to stand up to his father. As it was, Dad said, Conny was a great deal more sensitive than many so-called 'normal' people, and had a tremendous sense of loyalty to Cyril simply because he *was* his father.

My mother, however, seemed to take the 'Huh' as a sign of my agreement and gave me an approving look.

Cyril, evidently already well-oiled and half supported by pushing his bike, touched his cap at my mother and even nodded at me. Although I could never bring myself to be more than coldly civil toward the man, I saw no reason to put him out of his beery good humour with rudeness – he might have taken it out on Conny. So I gave him a self-conscious 'Good morning'; but my mother walked ahead as if she hadn't seen him.

When we reached her car, a blue Prefect, she fumbled in her handbag and produced two ten-shilling notes, thrusting them into my pocket as if they were a secret pay-off.

'There! Buy something pretty for your hair. And a decent pair of gloves. You must protect your hands in cold weather, Cassie. Hands age quicker than anything.'

I dare say it would have been appropriate to mumble an obedient 'Yes, Mother'. Instead, I crinkled the two notes between my fingers and thought of the big Easter egg in Jack Knowles' van. Then my mother flung her arms around me, and once again I felt my nose in collision with her brooch.

'Be a good girl for your grandmother,' she said. 'Don't wander off or speak to strangers. And whatever you do, stay away from that Jennings boy. He's not right in the head, and – well, you never know. Stay away from him, Cassie. I'll keep in touch and we'll arrange something for the summer holidays. I can see that your gran has very little dress sense – such an awful coat, Cassie! So we'll use the time to fit you out with a complete new wardrobe. You don't want to start at your new school feeling odd girl out because your clothes are old-fashioned, do you?'

'There's a uniform,' I said dully, 'so it won't matter.' But she didn't seem to hear me.

She released me, got into her car and drove away with a careless wave. That's it, I thought; we won't see her again until next Christmas, if ever.

But why didn't she take any notice when I told her about the uniform? Could it be that she hadn't been thinking about Wickstead High at all? I walked back along Joshua Road, slowly at first, then I began to hurry. Gran had said she didn't know anything about the law and custody rights, but I was sure no one could force me to leave her and go to live with my mother.

The lead story on the national television news that evening was the disappearance of a ten-year-old Welsh girl, Myfanwy Davies. She had been on her way to an aunt's house in a village near Pontardawe, mid-South Wales – and was last seen getting into a green car. Like Margie, Myfanywy was flaxen-haired with blue eyes and a confident, outgoing nature. The police were so sure of a connection that men from the South Suffolk CID were already on their way to Wales.

That was the day we all began to feel there could be no doubt any more. As I overheard Gran telling Mrs Woodruff, if the man who abducted the Welsh child was the same one who offered Margie a lift to school, both girls were almost certainly dead.

6

Once again I was in Mr Riordan's office, apprehensively facing him across the wide desk and wondering what I could possibly have done wrong this time. My headmaster had a good technique when dealing personally with wrongdoers. He would wait a good half-minute after you knocked at the door before calling, 'Come in!' with a weary, exasperated voice. Then, when you entered, he'd look up briefly, say 'Ah, Cassie,' and keep you waiting a further five minutes while he pretended to be searching for something in the filing cabinet. What I hadn't realised before today was that this was his usual way of dealing with everyone, whether they were in trouble or not.

'You can sit down, Cassie,' he said, and I did so, folding my hands in my lap and trying to look demure.

He opened one of the desk drawers and took out a small pile of exercise books, which he then sealed in a large buff envelope.

'You know where the Thoroughgoods live, don't you, Cassie?'

'Yes, sir.'

'Do you think you could deliver these to Mrs Thoroughgood for me? They're Margie's exercise books. Her mother telephoned this morning and asked if she could have them.' I must have looked doubtful because he added, 'Tomorrow's Saturday, so you can do it tomorrow afternoon.'

'All right, Mr Riordan.' I took the package but made no attempt to leave the office.

'Anything the matter, Cassie?'

'I – well, I haven't seen Mrs Thoroughgood for ages, sir. Is she – I mean, I won't know what to say to her.'

Mr Riordan screwed the top on his fountain pen. 'Would you rather I asked someone else to do this, Cassie? I'll understand if you don't feel able to face her. I simply chose you because I felt you would be wise enough not to chatter or ask questions.'

'No, it's all right, sir. I don't really mind, and I won't ask questions.' The sense of importance overrode any qualms and I clasped the package tighter. 'I shan't mention Margie unless she does.'

'That's very sensible, Cassie.' He unscrewed the pen top again, slowly, thoughtfully. 'You know, she might *want* to talk about Margie.'

'Do you think so, sir?'

'I think we must face up to the likelihood of Margie being dead. Mrs Thoroughgood has accepted it; she's gradually coming to terms with it. Bereavement is a fact of life, Cassie, and some of us have difficulty in dealing with a bereaved person. We're inclined to avoid the subject because we feel it may cause distress.' He spoke carefully, looking to see the impression he was making. 'When my father died – I was a small boy at the time – I remember my mother saying, "If only they'd talk to me about him. It's as if he never existed." That hurt my mother very badly. Do you understand my meaning, Cassie?'

'I think so, sir. You mean that if Mrs Thoroughgood wants to talk about Margie I should just let her and not try to change the subject.'

Mr Riordan nodded. 'That's right. I know it seems I'm asking a lot of you, Cassie. But I wouldn't ask if I didn't think you could handle it. As I said, Mrs Thoroughgood wants those exercise books very much. I'd take them myself if I had the time – '

'That's all right, sir,' I interrupted. The responsibility made me feel very adult and worldly wise, and I also thought that it was a noble thing for me to do. After all, when the Animal Defenders badge was found hadn't Mrs Thoroughgood practically accused me of being a liar and attention-seeker?

The Thoroughgoods lived in the part of Upper Grisham that was generally known as the Old Village. That is, they lived in one of the old roads but in a modern house. Allgoods was set further back than its neighbours and enclosed by an eight-foot-high privet hedge which looked as though it hadn't been trimmed since the previous summer. It was a white house with large windows, and to me it looked exactly like the American family houses we saw so much of in the films and on television. I imagined Elvis Presley lived in one just like it. There was a conservatory as well – Gran called it a 'glass lean-to' – where Mr Thoroughgood grew tomatoes and Margie used to keep her stick insects.

I had played in the back garden many times, had even been inside the house when Margie took several of us in for orangeade after a particularly long session on the magazines we were always writing. But entering by the front way made me feel like a trespasser. 'Still, Mr Riordan sent me,' I said to the sleek Siamese cat, Margie's pet, who followed me to the front door. 'So it must be all right.' The cat turned sapphire eyes on me, his mouth opening in a silent miaow, waiting for me to ring the door bell and gain him admittance.

Mrs Thoroughgood took her time answering, and when she saw me on the step she was clearly bewildered. Perhaps she had seen a child's shadow through the glass and for a moment believed it could only be Margie.

'Oh, hello, Cassie. I haven't seen you for a long while. What can I do for you, dear?'

'I've brought you something, Mrs Thoroughgood.' I looked down at the cat, who was rubbing against my calves, his back arched luxuriously.

'You'd better come in, then. You too, Muffin.'

'Is that his name? It's a funny name for a Siamese.' Then, before I could stop myself, 'I thought Margie said his name was Chula. Oh, I'm sorry, Mrs Thoroughgood.'

She closed the front door and with her hands on my shoulders guided me into the sitting-room. 'Margie gave him a different name every week. I always call him Muffin, but it doesn't really matter what name we use because he's stone deaf.'

'Oh, poor Muffin.'

'Sit down, Cassie. Would you like some tea? It's very near tea time.'

'Well, I – all right. Thank you.'

The Thoroughgoods' sitting-room was very light and I thought of Gran and her obsessive polishing. She'd want to polish a room like this three times a day instead of three times a week. One thing I hadn't known about Margie's parents before was that they were great readers. I looked at their overloaded bookcases and yearned to investigate more closely. I couldn't imagine what sort of book would keep Mrs Thoroughgood entertained for longer than five minutes at a stretch. At least, not the Mrs Thoroughgood I used to know. She had changed so much in the months since Margie disappeared. She still dressed like some minor British film star and was as meticulous as ever with her make-up, but she was thinner, paler, and held herself as though she felt permanently cold. And I couldn't imagine the Mrs Thoroughgood of last year inviting an eleven-year-old to take tea in her sitting-room.

She returned with the tea tray, which she placed on a low table with a smoked glass top.

'Well!' She smiled the too-bright smile that has to be forced. 'It's good to see you, Cassie. How's your gran?'

'Very well, thank you.'

'Good. I'll bet you're glad to have the eleven plus over with, aren't you?'

I nodded, looking at the plate of iced buns and wondering whether I would be offered more than one, and if so whether she'd think me a pig for accepting.

'I brought you these,' I said, handing her the package. 'Mr Riordan said you wanted them.'

'Oh, thank you. But I thought he'd be bringing them himself.'

'He says he's very busy.' I saw the look of disappointment on her face and realised what a lame excuse my headmaster had made. It would have taken five minutes of his time to deliver the books himself. Just five minutes. I understood now; what he had told me about people's attitudes to bereavement had in fact been a confession.

'He has an awful lot to do,' was my equally lame excuse for him.

'Yes, I suppose so.' She fingered the package lightly. 'Why don't you take your coat off, Cassie? You won't feel the benefit when you go out otherwise.'

I laughed. 'My gran says exactly the same thing.'

'Cassie, why did you apologise just now? When you said Margie told you the cat's name was Chula?'

'I don't know.'

'So many people do. Or they avoid me altogether. Even my

closest friends seem to make a conscious effort not to look at her picture whenever they come here.' She gazed at Margie's photograph on the sideboard, compelling me to do the same. It was the picture they had shown on the television news when Margie first disappeared.

'They tell us not to talk about her,' I said. 'The teachers and some of the parents, I mean. Or if they don't actually say not to, they give us a funny look if we do.'

Mrs Thoroughgood nodded, though she wasn't looking at me. I thought she was beautiful. So beautiful she gave me a peculiar, achey sort of feeling across my chest.

'Shall I pour the tea, Mrs Thoroughgood?'

'No, that's all right, Cassie.' Obviously mindful of her china, she took the pot before I should touch it and poured two rather strong cups of what she told me was Earl Grey. 'Do help yourself, dear,' she said, indicating the plate of iced buns with a vague wave of her hand.

'Thanks.' While I was eating, self-conscious and terrified I would drop crumbs on her carpet, she opened the package and began sorting through Margie's exercise books.

'I used to love reading through Margie's work,' she said. 'Especially her compositions. She wrote about you once, Cassie. Did you know that? It was after she'd been to your house for your birthday tea. Would you like to read it?'

I didn't want to say no. Poor Mrs Thoroughgood looked and sounded so lonely; and it seemed important to her that I read it. So I nodded and she handed me the blue English composition book.

Margie's handwriting was large and round. I had forgotten that, and how much I used to envy it in comparison with my own vile scrawl. She had written 'Margie Thoroughgood', not 'Marjorie', which I knew she hated, on the front cover. And underneath,

> *If this book should chance to roam,*
> *Box its ears and send it home,*
> *To Margie at Allgoods, Old Mill Road.*

Class Six thought that was rather clever and Margie basked in the satisfaction of having started a fashion. Later, I discovered my

61

father used to scribble the same requests in his school-books, so it wasn't exactly original.

The composition Mrs Thoroughgood wanted me to read was the first one in the book, a What-I-did-last-weekend type of essay. I read slowly, with even more concentration than was usual with me.

Last Saturday afternoon I went to Cassie Wade's birthday tea. Cassie lives with her gran at the top of Joshua Road because her daddy works abroad a lot and she hasn't got a mother. I gave her a present of a necklace, a little orange butterfly on a chain. Cassie liked it very much and I was very pleased because I picked it out myself.

Cassie's gran makes all her own cakes and I think they taste much nicer than shop ones. We had egg sandwiches and peanut butter sandwiches and a jelly shaped like a rabbit. Patty Jeeves didn't want to eat it because it was like a rabbit and we all laughed at her. There was two sorts of cake. One was a real birthday cake with icing and ten candles on it. The other was a sponge and when it was cut it had a pattern inside like squares on a draughts board. I thought that was clever.

After tea we played some games in the garden and Mary Thorby was sick down her frock. Before I went home I thanked Cassie's granny for a nice time and she said give my love to your mother.

I looked up at Mrs Thoroughgood and found her watching me closely, waiting for my reaction. I didn't know what to say, so I turned back to the essay and pretended to read it again. As I bent my head I became aware of a bright orange glint on my chest, the butterfly necklace, and quickly covered it with my hand, thinking Mrs Thoroughgood would be upset to see it.

'This is a good essay,' I said without looking up. 'I think she should have got a gold star for it. I couldn't write anything half so good.' I blushed, feeling I had said too much, or not enough, wondering if she actually expected me to say anything at all.

We drank our tea silently, Mrs Thoroughgood not taking her eyes from the exercise book, which I had on my lap. It seemed to me as though some change came over her while we sat there, sipping from the rose-patterned china cups. She glanced at me once or twice. Indeed, apart from the exercise book, I was the only thing in the room her eyes seemed capable of focusing on.

The rest of the time they were distant, large and pale blue like Margie's, but blind-looking eyes and – *wild*, I thought. I cleared my throat as a prelude to speaking and she looked up again.

'How is Mr Thoroughgood?' I asked.

'He is well.' How peculiar that sounded; precise, like a foreign student of English. He is well.

'Oh. Good. Does he still work in London?' Mr Thoroughgood did something in advertising. I wasn't sure what, but Dawn – who made it her business to know everyone else's – said it involved a lot of art work and he got paid quite a bit for it.

'Yes,' said Mrs Thoroughgood. 'Still in London.'

'Oh.' I couldn't think of anything else to say, and as she didn't seem inclined to help me out I began to pet Muffin.

Making conversation with adults wasn't usually difficult for me (with the possible exception of Father Steven and Mr Riordan). In fact, I enjoyed talking to older people; or showing off, as Gran termed it. But I was shy of Mrs Thoroughgood and it wasn't because of Margie, either. Nor, as I realised later, was it because I felt overawed by her beauty and sophistication. It was those eyes, rarely still but seldom focusing; as if she were watching a scene invisible to me in the same way a cat will often appear to be watching something that isn't there.

'Would you like to see Margie's room?' she asked suddenly.

'Oh, I – don't know, Mrs Thoroughgood. I'm not sure if – '

'It's all right, Cassie. Margie wouldn't mind.'

I *did* want to see it. Out of curiosity, perhaps, or the enjoyable idea of doing something right for all the wrong reasons. So I followed her, remembering the time Gran and I visited the house of a recently dead great aunt. I had wanted to touch everything in that house, to touch the exact spot where the old lady's hand had come to rest before she died. I was supposed to be an over-sensitive child (because of my mother, Gran maintained) and even glimpsing the funeral procession of a total stranger was apt to give me nightmares. Yet, like some other sensitive children, I sought out the very things which troubled me most, enjoying the shivers so much during daylight hours that it was almost worth the night terrors.

Margie's bedroom was like something straight out of the type of glossy magazines my mother used to read. Pastel blue cur-tains, carpet and bedspread, and white furniture. *White* – unheard of for a child's room in those days. Soft toys, including a giraffe and a zebra, occupied the window-sill and cupboard tops, and there was a very smart dressing-table set that I immediately began to covet.

'I change the bed linen every week,' said Mrs Thoroughgood. 'Even though – I still change it.'

I understood that. When our cat had been run over three years before, I had still felt compelled to put fresh milk in his dish – just in case. 'In case,' I told Gran, 'it wasn't Tigger, after all. Perhaps it was another cat Mrs Woodruff saw and our Tiggy just went off on an adventure. Perhaps Tiggy'll come back.'

I understood, and was about to tell Mrs Thoroughgood so, when she spoke again.

'Do you know how long it's been, Cassie? How long Margie has been missing?'

'Two hundred and eleven days,' I said, almost automatically.

She nodded, not at all surprised by my answer. 'Two hundred and eleven days. You've been counting too, then?'

'In my diary. Sometimes I forget for a while.' It sounded like a confession. 'Then I have to count back. I think it's right, though.'

'Yes, Cassie. It's right. And every one of those two hundred and eleven days I've come into this room, in the afternoons – at tea time. And then . . .' She picked up one of the soft toys, a tiger, and stroked its ears. 'Then I feel closer to Margie. It's almost as if I can expect her to come walking through the door at any moment. Do you like Margie's room, Cassie?'

'It's very pretty, Mrs Thoroughgood.'

'Yes. Margie chose all the furnishings herself, you know. And she insisted on having her room downstairs so that Muffin could come in and out of the window as he pleased during the night. She loved to have him sleep on her bed. This is the first time I've come in here with someone else, Cassie. Even when my husband is at home I've always come into this room alone. But maybe the next time you visit . . . You will visit me again, won't you dear?'

'Well, I suppose – '

'Please say yes, Cassie. Please, my dear?' She placed her hands on my shoulders, briefly reminding me of that afternoon in the playground.

'Of course I will, Mrs Thoroughgood.'

'Thank you, Cassie. I promise you'll always be very welcome.'

I'll never forget the smile she gave me just then; it was a smile of genuine affection and gratitude. And it was the beginning of a curious friendship – one I was sometimes to regret.

The following day, a Sunday, Myfanwy Davies was found in a Shropshire field. She had been strangled, her small body trussed up in a polythene sheet and buried in a shallow grave.

Gran cried when she heard the news, just as if it had been Margie they'd found. Later, I heard her whispering to Mrs Woodruff that the child must have been 'interfered with' because she had been half-clothed. That expression, 'interfered with', preyed on my mind. I realised, because of the awful way the words were uttered, that it was Gran's euphemism for something even more horrific than strangulation.

I began to have nightmares. My mother would force me to go and live with her; then, due to some piece of neglect on her part, I would be taken away, strangled, and – *interfered with*.

One night I dreamt I was walking through the fields when I saw Margie's hand sticking out of the earth. I dug with my hands, further and further down, expecting to see her half-naked body, her pale blue eyes wide open, staring up at the stinging nettles around her grave. But I didn't reach her. There was only her hand, the little gold signet ring on her second finger, sticking out of the crumbly, moist earth.

The police were still certain of a connection between the two girls, and they took tracker dogs into the fields around Upper Grisham. Every adult and child in the village was questioned again as they searched for a link. I guessed they were looking for a Grisham man who had recently been to Wales, or a Welshman who had been in Suffolk last October.

'Well, I think it's stupid,' Dawn pronounced. 'It could just as easily be someone from Outer Mongolia. My dad says a smart dog doesn't shit in its own kennel.'

I thought over her words again later that week when Gran said we'd had a letter from Dad. He was coming home soon, he said, and he would be bringing a friend. The mysterious girlfriend, no doubt.

Then I saw the envelope. It was postmarked from Swansea.

7

Gran and I always went shopping in Wickstead, our nearest town, on Saturdays. Usually in the morning as Gran liked to get it 'over and done with', but because Dad was going to meet us and take us to tea we caught the two-fifteen bus that particular day. I was getting to the age when conforming suddenly becomes all-important and no longer docilely submitted to Gran's ideas of what an eleven-year-old should wear. But Gran still had the final word on such matters and there I was, resplendent in my Sunday-best coat and an unbearably silly hat that looked like a ruined soufflé. I planned an appeal to Dad, who was more reasonable, and in the mean time prayed I wouldn't meet anyone I knew in town.

In any case, shopping bored me and I couldn't understand why Gran would never let me stay at home, or at least leave me in the library while she trotted round the shops. She would ask what vegetables I'd like with the Sunday lunch and I'd stand there yawning or staring without much hope toward the toy shop.

'What are you going to do when you get married?' she would ask in exasperation. 'That's if anyone'll have you.'

'I shan't get married,' I'd answer.

'You'll still have to eat. You won't always have your old Gran to look after you, you know.'

I waited outside the butcher's, pressing my forehead to the window and watching Gran interrogate the junior assistant about the quantity of fat and gristle in the mince. She was a fussy shopper, and always very particular about meat. I just wished she'd be more adventurous. We had mince every Saturday, and roast beef – which was cheaper than chicken then – every Sunday. I tried to attract her attention, hoping to interest her in the flabby, freckled Lincolnshire sausages which, although I had never tasted them before, seemed to me the most delicious meal possible in the entire world. As I waved to her frantically, drumming my fingers against the glass and pulling faces, I felt a hand on my shoulder.

'Hello, Cassie. Waiting for your gran?' Mrs Thoroughgood was bending slightly so that her face was level with mine, as if she were speaking to a much younger child.

'Yes, Mrs Thoroughgood. Then we're meeting my dad. He's taking us to Marion's tea shop.'

'Oh, that's nice. I have tea there myself sometimes.'

I wondered if she was hinting she'd like to join us and if she expected me to invite her. Luckily, Gran came out of the butcher's just then and relieved me of the difficulty.

'The price of meat these days!' she complained to Mrs Thoroughgood without any other form of salutation.

'I know, isn't it dreadful? I can see the day coming when lamb will cost five shillings a pound.'

Gran pulled a face. 'Nothing could surprise me less, I can tell you. Well, how are you keeping, Rochelle?'

'I'm fine, thank you.'

I hadn't known her Christian name before. Rochelle. I thought that was beautiful; beautiful and sad, like her. And I admired my gran for daring to address her by it. I would never be able to think of her as anything but Mrs Thoroughgood.

'I was wondering if Cassie would like to come to tea with me again one day next week,' she said, smiling at me.

Gran frowned. She didn't know anything about the first time because to tell her would have been to invite a lecture on how to behave, what to say and do.

'Can I, Gran?' I whined. Going to tea at someone's house – as opposed to going to a tea-shop – seemed a sophisticated, adult thing to do. 'Oh, go on! Can I?'

'I don't know. You mustn't be a nuisance, Cassie.'

'Oh, she isn't, Mrs Wade.' Mrs Thoroughgood patted my shoulder.

'Well, I suppose I had better say yes.' Gran could never give in graciously. 'But if she starts making a pest of herself, just you send her packing.'

Mrs Thoroughgood promised to do so, and we agreed on the

following Tuesday, straight after school. When she had gone, I had to explain to Gran all about Mr Riordan and the exercise books. She seemed satisfied from that point of view, but still slightly disgruntled about the tea.

'I can't for the life of me see why she wants you to go again.'

'Perhaps she likes my company.'

'That's another thing I can't understand. Anyway, it's time to meet your father. Take your hands out of your pockets.'

Marion's teashop was further down in the same street as the butcher's, overlooking the meadows and therefore practically out of town. It had been converted from an old mill and was quite ugly from the outside, but having one's afternoon tea there was considered a special treat as the place was patronised by the more affluent townspeople. Once inside, you could almost lose yourself among all the pot plants, and Marion must have been a vain woman judging by the number of mirrors around the walls. I certainly didn't enjoy catching sight of myself in the detested hat and coat every time I moved.

The place was quite busy that afternoon and I recognised one or two people I knew by sight, but Dad hadn't arrived yet and Gran and I sat down self-consciously at a corner table.

'Your father was never punctual,' Gran complained. 'I don't think he realises how I feel in a place like this when I have to explain that I'm waiting for someone.'

'You'd feel a sight worse if you had to wear this square old coat and a baby's hat.'

Gran obviously didn't feel that one was worth an answer. 'Get your elbows off the table,' she said automatically.

I hadn't asked her why Dad had chosen to spend the previous night in town instead of coming home; I was too busy worrying about The Welsh Connection. Not for one minute did I imagine my dad had anything to do with Margie's disappearance and the other girl's death, of course; but I knew suspicion was bound to fall on an Upper Grisham man who had recently spent some time in Wales. Finally I decided the best thing would be to have a word with him privately as soon as possible. If he kept quiet about Wales, nobody would be the wiser – and I would be spared acute embarrassment. I had overlooked one thing, though; Dad's companion.

My heart didn't skip a beat when I saw my dad; it somersaulted. At least, that was how it felt to me when I saw him, twenty minutes late as usual, pausing in the doorway to seek us out with those steady blue eyes. It wasn't just my pride – though I couldn't help but feel proud when everyone else in the room turned to look at him and his gaze swept over their insignificant heads to rest upon me. No, there was something more. Because, in his letter, Dad had told us he would be bringing a friend, and that could only mean one thing: a woman. I was prepared to test her, to show myself up in the worst possible light so that she would give Dad up completely rather than take on an obnoxious eleven-year-old stepdaughter. So I met my Dad's smile with a stubbornly bovine expression, though it cost me more pain than I would have admitted to anyone. I suppose my mother's return had made me insecure.

Behind him was a young man, no more than twenty or twenty-two I thought, very fair, very pale-complexioned, and with a physique bordering on the puny. He followed my dad as I might have done myself in a strange place, uncertain and dependent.

'This is Jeff,' Dad said when he had kissed Gran and me, rather formally, I thought. 'Jeff is an artist. He's eager to see Constable and Gainsborough country.'

I smiled broadly then, and Gran shook his hand.

'Pleased to meet you, Mrs Wade,' Jeff said. 'You too, Cassie. You're just as your dad described you.'

'Am I?' I realised what I had overlooked. Dad's friend had a beautiful, strong Welsh accent.

Wherever they went together, Jeff would advertise The Welsh Connection and bring suspicion on Dad as well as himself. But serious as this was, my greatest feeling at that moment was one of relief. There was no woman, no potential stepmother to take the place of Gran and myself in Dad's life. Only this young man, who probably looked on my dad as a kind of uncle or guardian, an older friend who was in a position to encourage him in his career and show him the countryside he longed to see. Yet even as I gave Jeff another broad smile, hoping to communicate my whole-hearted approval, I saw that there was a certain self-consciousness about him. About them both.

'We met a friend of yours on the way here, Cassie,' Dad said, turning to the door and beckoning. 'So we invited her to join us.'

Mrs Thoroughgood, I thought, forgetting Dad couldn't have known of my new friendship with Margie's mother.

But it was Dawn who walked in. Or rather, she slunk in, her huge eyes a mixture of uneasiness and the typical hostility she displayed whenever faced with more than one adult.

'Hi, Cassie,' she mumbled.

'Hi.'

Dad organised us all, grabbing a spare chair from another table to make up the five and ordering a pot of tea with scones, strawberry jam and cream. But he was too cheerful, almost desperately so, and I wondered if he had only dragged Dawn along to act as a kind of buffer between us.

'So you're an artist, Jeff?' said Gran in her gracious hostess voice.

'That's right, Mrs Wade. At least, Arthur seems to think so.'

Of course, we all looked at Dad then. He was occupied with searching through his jacket pockets, just as if nobody had spoken, which I thought strange.

I watched Jeff closely. His features, taken individually, were exceptionally handsome. Viewed as a whole his face was rather odd: certainly not ugly, but ill-balanced, as though only the eyes were really his and the nose and mouth belonged to someone else. He had an artist's hands: soft and supple with long, tapering fingers and short, well cared-for nails. They were expressive hands, too, and he held them clasped in a 'church steeple', which gave him a thoughtfully pious air.

'What do you paint?' Dawn asked. 'Trees or people?'

'Oh, people. Certainly more interesting than trees.'

'Trees are prettier,' I said, 'and they don't keep moving when you're trying to draw them.'

Dawn gave me a look that told me I had said something absolutely wet, as usual. So to redeem myself I suggested Dad take Jeff to visit Gainsborough's house in Sudbury one afternoon the following week.

'We've already planned a visit,' Dad said. 'Why don't you take the afternoon off school and come with us? You as well, Dawn. I'm sure Mr Riordan won't mind now the eleven plus is over. And it is educational, after all.'

'Great! Can I, Gran?'

Gran supposed she had 'better say yes' for the second time that

70

day, though she couldn't see why I was so eager to visit somewhere I'd already seen three times with the school.

'We'll say Tuesday, then,' said Dad. 'We can have tea somewhere afterwards. There's a rather nice little place along Friars
Street, I believe.'

'Oh, Dad! Not Tuesday! I'm going to tea with Mrs Thoroughgood on Tuesday!'

'Mrs Thoroughgood?' He looked questioningly at Gran, then
back at me. 'You mean the mother of the little girl who went
missing last year?'

'Margie's mother. Yes.'

'How did all this come about?'

I explained about the exercise books and how she had invited
me to take tea with her then, all of which was news to Dawn as
well. One thing I didn't mention was the promise I had made to
Mrs Thoroughgood in Margie's room. Dawn wouldn't have believed it, and anyway, instinct told me it was something Mrs
Thoroughgood wanted me to keep a secret.

'So you actually knew this little girl, Cassie?' Jeff asked.

'Yes. She was in my class. Our class, wasn't she, Dawn?'

Dawn nodded. 'I think she's dead. Like Myfanwy Davies.' She
glanced at Jeff when she mentioned the Welsh girl. 'They looked
a bit like each other, too. Didn't you think so, Cassie?'

Dad, Gran and Jeff said the sort of things people usually
say under such circumstances – it was too bad to bear contem-
plating and you could never be sure your kids were safe these
days, could you? – and I know they were sincerely meant. But
nobody mentioned the other similarities of the two cases, although the television and press coverage dwelt on them
constantly.

When we had finished the scones, Dawn got up and fastened
her jacket, saying that she had to meet her older sister in Woolies.
'And you can meet me in the churchyard after *The Comedy Hour*
tonight,' she added to me in a whisper.

She thanked Dad in the sugary way normally reserved for
Father Steven and left, looking more adult and self-assured in her
blue slacks and jacket than I ever could in my Sunday best.

Gran nodded at Dad, a signal that often passed between them
when I was due to be scolded, interrogated or merely 'told
straight'. She then gave Jeff her full attention, willing to flounder

in a subject she knew nothing about – art – so that her son and granddaughter could have the necessary talk.

'I hear your mother came to visit you at Easter,' Dad began.

'I didn't invite her, I promise you.'

'Now then, Cassie.' He lit a cigarette, which seemed to aid his thought processes. 'I'm not saying I don't think what your mother did all those years ago was wrong, because I do. Very wrong. There's no excuse for a woman who just walks out and leaves her child. But people can admit they've made a mistake, Cassie. They can be sorry and try to make amends. Hasn't it ever occurred to you that your mother may be sorry? May regret it very much, in fact?'

I shrugged. 'I don't know.' The impression I got from my mother's behaviour at Easter didn't suggest regret, or even a vague desire to do better by her child. 'I don't know, Daddy,' I said again. 'She was on her high horse all the time, I know that much. And she wants me to go and stay with her for a whole week during the school holidays.'

'I think that would be a good idea, Cass.'

'Daddy! The holidays are only seven weeks. And I'd planned to do ever so much!'

'Such as?'

'We-ell, I planned to go swimming every day. I want to be the youngest at the new school to have a mile certificate. Then I'm going to start another wild-flower collection. A proper one this time with the Latin names written in. And then . . . ' I looked hopefully at Gran, but Jeff was entertaining her so well that there was no chance of catching her eye. 'Oh, you know what I mean, Daddy. I can't leave Gran for a whole week either. What on earth would she do?'

Dad's eyes twinkled. 'I think your Gran would welcome a week's rest.' Then he suddenly became serious again. 'You know, Cassie, it wasn't all your mother's fault things didn't work out between us. I'm still not excusing her for walking out on you, you understand. But sometimes things go wrong between a husband and wife because they were never right in the first place.' He gave Jeff a quick, sideways glance which struck me as odd. Nothing he had said as yet could have been news to his friend.

'I don't want to go and stay with her, Dad,' I said.

72

'We can't always do what we want, Cassie. You're a big girl now, and you should have learned that already.'

'But I don't even know her. Not really know her.'

'That's another reason you ought to go, Cassie. A mother can teach you the sort of things a father never could. There are things you'll need to know about in a few years' time, when you make the transition from child to young woman.'

I was about to point out that Gran could teach me just as well when Jeff leaned across the table and touched my arm.

'Is it true what your gran tells me, Cassie? That you have no ambitions?'

'What? I mean, pardon?'

'You've no idea what you want to do when you leave school?'

'Not really, no.'

'Wouldn't you like to be a nurse or an air hostess? Most little girls do.'

'Not this little girl.' I was a bit mad at him for interrupting our conversation. 'I'd like to work in Madame Tussaud's, in the Chamber of Horrors.'

I still hadn't warned Dad to keep quiet about his stay in Wales. And I hadn't asked him if he thought my mother could force me to leave Gran and go to live with her, either.

The churchyard had once been a favourite playground of ours, but this was the first time we had been there – apart from going to Sunday school, when we kept strictly to the path – since gathering conkers on the day Margie disappeared. The sun had already set, but the gloominess and slight air of menace Dawn and I so enjoyed about the place were still a good half-hour away.

'We didn't go and see Keith last Remembrance Sunday,' Dawn said. 'It's the first time since we started. Let's go and see him now.'

'Okay, but not for too long. I want to read the notices in the porch before it gets too dark.'

Keith's was the only military grave in the churchyard, and we were in the habit of going to look at it every so often. He had died, aged eighteen, a few days before the nineteen-eighteen Armistice, a fact which appealed to our sense of romantic tragedy, and I had a strong mental picture of him as being rather like my Dad, only less robust and having freckles.

'I wonder how come they brought his body home when everyone else got buried in France,' I said.

'I expect he was shipped home injured and then died of his wounds.'

We had wondered about it before, but no one was able to enlighten us. For myself, I would have preferred to think he died instantly and in the act of saving his CO's life.

'I wonder if he had a girlfriend?'

'You wonder too much, Cassie. *I* wonder if that Jeff has a girlfriend. I bet he doesn't.'

'Why not?' I said indignantly. 'He's not bad-looking. I wouldn't mind being his girlfriend if I were a bit older.'

'You'd be lucky. C'mon, Cassie, I thought you wanted to read the notice-board?'

I gave Keith a last look, wishing I was brave enough to come this far back in the churchyard on my own or, failing that, I had the nerve to suggest we bring our soldier some flowers.

We walked through clumps of the long grass that was always damp due to this part being shaded by the horse chestnuts, and my socks were quite wet before we reached the porch. A mist was starting to rise from the nearby river, bringing with it an earthy smell that could just as easily have come from a newly dug grave.

'Did you know Mrs Fisher's dog won't come by the side gate after dark?' I said in what I hoped was an awful voice. 'He gets right off the pavement and into the road.'

Dawn didn't answer. She sat down in the porch, taking a cigarette from her jacket pocket and lighting it inexpertly.

'I'm dying for a fag,' she said, hooked after only a fortnight from first learning to smoke. 'Want one, Cassie?'

'Better not. Spoil my supper.'

'Chicken.'

'Why shouldn't Jeff have a girlfriend?' I asked, eager to get off the subject of smoking.

'Because –' She took a deep pull on the cigarette, partly inhaled the smoke, then blew it out with what sounded very much like a stifled cough. 'Because he's a moffradite.' At least, 'moffradite' was what I thought she said.

'Oh? How do you know that, then?'

'Well, it's obvious, isn't it?'

'Is it?' I should have kept quiet then, not pursued the subject any further and made out I shared her views completely. But I was desperate to know the meaning of the word 'moffradite' – without displaying my own ignorance, if possible.

'Why is it obvious?' I demanded.

'Well, the way he moves and that. The way he moves his hands when he speaks. The way he actually speaks, even. Just like a girl.'

I was more mystified than ever. 'So what?'

'*My* dad knew a moffradite once. *My* dad gave him a good thumping.'

I didn't like the way she stressed *her* dad, as though mine were inferior.

'You do know what that is, don't you, Cassie?' Her large, beautiful eyes scowled at me through the shadows. 'It's a man with a woman's bits inside him. He likes to do the sort of things with other blokes that normal men do with women.'

She couldn't mean sex. She *couldn't*. I felt my face starting to burn and was glad of the darkness in the porch.

'S-so what?'

'Oh, Cassie! Honestly! He's a friend of your dad's, isn't he? That must mean something.'

I gripped the stone seat. It was cold and damp under my fingers, slightly slimy.

'You made it up!' I screamed. 'How could my dad be like one of them – what you said – with women's bits? He had me, didn't he? You're a liar, Dawn!'

'Please yourself.'

I got up and stalked off down the path – I would *not* run – leaving her there alone in the dark. She was wrong, of course. Like the time she confidently told me you got pregnant by letting a boy pee inside you. Undiecause, she'd called it. But then, it was only half wrong. I recollected that everything Dawn ever told me turned out to have some truth in it, and her sources were generally reliable. She asked her older sister, who received the most interesting part of her education in the school lavatories, in between eavesdropping on her parents' private conversations. It was just that Dawn sometimes misheard, or put two and two together and got a vulgar fraction. But that she could even hint at my dad being like that . . .

I started to run. I would go straight home and check that word in Nuttall's Standard. And if it wasn't there it would prove she'd made it up.

'All right, all right. Where's the fire?'

I'd run smack into a hard, muscular chest, was trapped against it by equally muscular arms.

'Trust you, Cassie Wade. Why don't you look where you're going?'

'Let me go! Let me *go*!' I opened my mouth for one tremendous scream, only to have a hand clapped across it. When I looked up I saw Jack Knowles, who drove the grocery van, squinting down at me, his rabbit teeth thoughtfully embedded in his lower lip.

'There, that's better,' he said, removing his nasty-tasting hand. 'Now perhaps you'll tell me where you're off to in such a hurry?'

'Home. I'm late as it is. Gran'll go spare. Let me go, Jack.' He still had a hold on my arm. 'Let me go.'

'What, let you go running half-way across the village in the dark? Do you want to end up like poor little Margie? I bet your gran doesn't know you're right down here. Well, does she?'

'No-o, but – '

'Where does she think you are, then?'

'At Mary Thorby's.'

Jack shook his head and tut-tutted me. 'You're a naughty girl, that's what you are, Cassie. Come on, now. I'll run you home in the van.'

He took my hand before I could protest and began to pull me along to where the van was parked. I supposed it was all right; after all, Jack could more or less be counted one of Gran's friends.

'What are you doing here so late on a Saturday?' I asked.

'Special delivery to the pub. They've got a do on tomorrow.'

He made me sit in the front with him. Probably he didn't trust me in the shop part, where I might – and would – have been tempted to help myself to the Penny Arrows.

'I saw your dad in town this afternoon. How long is he home for this time?'

'I don't know.'

'Wonder he doesn't find himself someone nice and settle down. That would be a good thing, don't you think?'

'I don't know.'

'You don't know much.' Jack looked at my knees. Because they were scabby, I thought, hurriedly pulling my skirt over them.

The van was old – held together by rust, Dad used to joke – and it shook and rattled its way along Joshua Road until I wondered why the fruit and vegetables didn't fall from their shelves at the back. Immediately behind me, where Jack kept the bread and cakes, something heavy was sliding about and I was afraid it would fall on my head.

Although Jack kept turning to look at me with his rodent-like squint, I felt safe with him. I wouldn't even have minded him asking the same old questions he always asked when Gran and I went out to buy our groceries. But Jack didn't speak until he stopped the van outside my house. He turned the headlights off, the way they do in the films when the man wants to kiss the girl and she pretends she doesn't want him to.

'I hope your gran isn't cross with you,' Jack said. 'I could always come in with you and make up some excuse. If you want, that is.' Something about his face glittered in the darkness. I wasn't sure if it was his eyes or the protruding teeth. And he smelled of vegetables: cabbage boiled for too long and forgotten, moulding carrots.

'No, that's all right.' I fumbled for the door handle. 'She won't mind too much because Dad's home.'

Jack leaned across to open the door, briefly resting his free hand on my knee, which I didn't care for at all. To distract him, I said, 'Did you see Dad's friend this afternoon as well?'

'The fair-haired chap?'

'That's him. What did you think of him?'

Jack made a funny noise, like a suppressed chuckle. 'Bit of a nancy, isn't he? Still, I suppose your dad meets all sorts in his line of work. Off you go now, Cassie. And tell your gran I'm having a fridge put in the van, so I'll be selling meat and frozen foods in future. Save a trip to the butcher, won't it?'

I jumped down and ran indoors, not even stopping to wave goodbye, and certainly not caring that Jack must have thought me rude and ungrateful.

Gran was making cocoa in the kitchen, minus her apron for once, it being a Saturday night. Dad had gone to the pub with Jeff, she told me.

'He will be here tonight, won't he?' I asked.

'Of course he will.'

'What about Jeff?'

'He's staying in town. Cassie, what are you doing with that dictionary?'

'Just looking something up.'

I found 'moff' and 'mofussil', the meanings of which I didn't bother to read, and the next entry was 'mogul'. So Dawn must have made the word up, I told myself. And when I came to think about it, it actually sounded like a made-up word.

But Jack hadn't made up the word 'nancy'. I knew what that meant well enough.

Dawn must have told somebody about Jeff being from Wales because two policemen came to talk to Dad the next day. One of them was the same Detective Sergeant who had questioned us at school, and when Gran let them in I tried to catch his eye. I thought maybe I could somehow communicate to him that my dad didn't have anything to do with Margie's disappearance. But he didn't seem to recognise me.

Gran and I waited in the living-room while Dad and the two men talked in the Best Room. I thought it would be a good idea to make them a pot of tea, but Gran wouldn't hear of it. You didn't make refreshments for anyone who had the gall to suspect your only son of murder, she said.

An hour later the police left, satisfied that Dad's alibis could easily be checked. He had been in Germany when Margie vanished, on an internal flight from Hamburg at the precise time. But news travelled quickly in Upper Grisham, and when they left I saw that a small group of villagers had gathered outside our house. The DS spoke to them and they dispersed, but several of them cast hostile looks back at us.

I could understand their feelings; all these months gone by and the police were no nearer to finding Margie now than they were at the start.

8

The second time I visited Mrs Thoroughgood was the only occasion I ever saw her husband at home. Like her, he was very fair, and I supposed the double dose of blonde genes was responsible for Margie's beautiful colouring. He had a loud, unmelodic voice and what I believe is termed a mid-Atlantic accent, dressed in casual American styles and even drove a Galaxy. Although I hardly knew him and on the few occasions we had met he was always pleasant to me, I felt awed by him. I shrank from men with booming voices anyway, being used to my softly spoken dad, and I didn't like the way he had of talking to you as if you were an equal; it made you uncomfortable and uncertain. But I had to admit that he and his wife were a handsome pair. The couple who had everything – until last October.

I felt no more confidence as I knocked on their door now than I had the first time. She might have forgotten she'd invited me, I thought. Or worse, she might even have heard that the police had been to question my dad. The weather had turned warm at last and Gran let me go without a coat that morning, for which I was thankful. I would have hated to have to turn up in my Sunday best. Instead, I wore a blue dress, the latest of several presents that had recently arrived from my mother. It was fashionable and expensive, and because she had taken the trouble – surprisingly, I thought – to enquire of Gran my exact measurements, it fitted perfectly. The white cardigan Gran had insisted on my taking, 'in case it turns chilly', rather spoiled the effect, but I planned to remove it once inside the house.

It was Mr Thoroughgood who answered my knock, and although he didn't actually look displeased to see me, there was a certain resigned air about him, as though by admitting me he was giving way to some peculiar whim of his wife's. And perhaps he was.

'Come in, Cassandra,' he said, and I didn't bother to point out that I was actually christened 'Cassie'. I'd corrected that particular misapprehension too many times before.

'I think Mrs Thoroughgood is expecting me,' I told him.

'She's talked of little else all afternoon.'

'Oh?'

'You did want to come, didn't you?'

'Of course.' I followed him into the sitting-room.

'That's all right, then. Because if you ever feel uncomfortable here you can always make an excuse, you know.'

I hardly caught the implication that these visits might become a regular affair just then. Instead, I wondered if I looked bored or ungrateful enough to warrant his remarks and set about trying to smile, which was not easy to achieve with nothing to smile at and must have made me look rather idiotic. I sat down when he gestured me to do so, hoping Muffin was around somewhere.

'I'll tell her you're here,' said Mr Thoroughgood, and he left the room.

In a few moments I heard his raised voice coming from the kitchen, something about 'a substitute'. Then Mrs Thoroughgood's angry answer. 'That's rubbish! I like the child for her own sake.'

I was shaken, naturally. That she could be using me as a Margie-substitute would never have occurred to me. And because I had a childishly simplified view of things – Margie was blonde with blue eyes, while I was dark and brown-eyed – I had to agree that the idea was 'rubbish'.

Muffin strolled in and made straight for my lap, so that when Mrs Thoroughgood entered the room it was fairly easy to pretend I was fully occupied and hadn't heard anything. She wore a dark green blouse with a frill down the front and cream slacks, an outfit of which Gran would have thoroughly disapproved – and which therefore made her doubly attractive to my eyes.

Before I had thought of a suitable compliment, however, she was admiring my blue dress and saying what good taste Gran had.

'It was a present from my mother,' I said. 'She knows a lot about clothes. She has a dress shop in Ipswich.'

80

'Really?'

'I've got to go and stay with her during the summer holidays. I don't want to, but Dad said it would be a good idea.'

'And he's probably right.' Mrs Thoroughgood sat down opposite me and I wondered if she had set her husband to preparing the tea. I was hungry, having only picked at my school dinner in order to leave plenty of room for cakes and buns.

'It would be a good thing for you to spend some time with your mother,' Mrs Thoroughgood resumed. 'And an education for you to see her shop. Are you interested in clothes and fashions, Cassie?'

'Sort of.'

'Most young girls are. It's healthy and natural to care about one's appearance. I know my Margie had a very sophisticated approach to dress, and very good taste.'

My stomach growled and I had to cough to cover it. I thought it was all very well to say Margie had good taste when she would have looked great in anything – and had the money and a free rein to choose her own clothes.

'So she does,' I said, refusing to speak of her in the past tense. 'But any colour at all suits her. I look awful in yellow or red.' It was a remark I was very soon to regret.

'Oh, I don't know, Cassie. Come with me, dear.' She rose decidedly and I followed her into Margie's room, where she opened the wardrobe and took out a red dress from among the three dozen or so that were hanging in there. I shivered without really knowing why; I couldn't remember ever seeing Margie in that particular frock. Mrs Thoroughgood held it against me, the wooden hanger directly beneath my chin. It was of a darker red than my detested Sunday coat, which was pure pillar box red, and had pink broderie anglaise collar and cuffs.

'It's beautiful,' I said.

'It's a party dress really. I bought it for her to wear last Christmas, at the school party. She never did wear it, except to try it on.' She brushed the skirt out, not even flinching when her hand touched the half-crown-sized scab on my left knee. 'You wouldn't like to try it on, would you, Cassie?'

I thought she might give me the dress if it fitted, so I said yes.

'All right. You put it on. But don't leave the room. I'll be back in

81

a minute.' She left me alone, closing the door behind her as though she were afraid her husband might see me.

The dress was a little longer than was fashionable because Margie was taller than me, but apart from that it fitted quite well. I admired my reflection in the full-length mirror for some moments, then, as Mrs Thoroughgood hadn't returned, I went to study the paintings Margie had pinned up on her wall. They were mostly of trees, for which Margie had discovered a good technique; she would mix the paint thickly, then splodge it on the paper with rapid, dipping movements. The result was that the paint dried in little peaks and swirls and made the trees look lifelike. Mrs Thoroughgood had filled in the dates underneath; she had been proud of Margie's talent for art.

Ten minutes passed and still she hadn't returned, so I went and sat on the edge of Margie's bed to pick at my scabby knee. I was too warm in the red dress; it was meant for winter-time. And I felt embarrassed and ashamed, just as if Margie could see me. I could imagine her saying, 'Take my dress off this minute, Cassie Wade!' In a while, I heard the front door slam, and I guessed Mr Thoroughgood had gone out, so I got up and hid myself behind the cupboard in case he went by the window and saw me. It was a fearful game of Hide and Seek, and I wished with everything in me that I had never mentioned looking awful in red.

When Mrs Thoroughgood finally returned she was pushing a trolley laden with tea things: the rose-patterned china, a plateful of sandwiches, and a silver cakestand loaded with Danish pastries.

'I thought we might have tea in here,' she said. 'Wouldn't that be nice?'

If I hadn't been so hungry I might have said no, I didn't think it very nice at all. Apart from the fact that Gran had told me only ill-bred people take food into bedrooms, I felt it was a morbid thing to do. But I nodded meekly as my stomach growled again, and Mrs Thoroughgood explained.

'I feel her presence more strongly here than in any other part of the house. We often used to take afternoon tea in here. Margie would make a game of it, sending me a proper invitation. Do you ever do things like that, Cassie?'

'Sometimes. I used to write letters to my gran, even though she was sitting right next to me. I suppose it was because I didn't have anyone else to write real letters to, except Dad.'

'Poor Cassie.'

Her eyes scanned the room restlessly. To distract her, I said, 'You haven't told me what you think of the dress on me yet.'

'The – ? Oh, yes.' Had she really forgotten I was wearing Margie's dress? 'It fits quite well, doesn't it? And red does suit you, Cassie.'

'Well, this particular shade perhaps.' I hoped she would tell me then that I could keep the dress, but she didn't. 'Shall I take it off now?'

'No, keep it on while we have tea.'

'I don't want to get it dirty.' I held the hem up and away from my scab, which was oozing tiny droplets of blood where I had been picking at it. Mrs Thoroughgood noticed.

'You know, Cassie, if you're going to make a habit of falling out of trees and off walls you mustn't be surprised when you grow up with ugly scars on your knees.'

'I can't help it. Gran says I was born awkward.'

'You should try moving more slowly. I was a clumsy child myself at your age. Until I learned to move slowly. That's the secret, Cassie.'

She sounded like my mother. But I had the feeling Mrs Thoroughgood would only be amused if my shortcomings remained short, whereas my mother would become exasperated. I tried to follow her advice, starting with eating, and chewed slowly, the way she did. I noticed also that she didn't extend her little finger when drinking tea, as Gran, Mrs Woodruff and a few other ladies I knew did in company because they thought it was posh. So I didn't do it either. I followed her exactly, hoping to please her so that she wouldn't compare me too unfavourably with Margie. At that stage, I believe being a part-time Margie-substitute rather appealed to me.

When we had eaten, Mrs Thoroughgood saw me looking at one of the stuffed toys that were scattered around the room. It was a donkey, about a foot high, grey, with a scarlet saddle and reins and a mournful look in its eyes.

'That was Margie's favourite,' said Mrs Thoroughgood, picking it up and placing it in my lap. 'You can hold him for a while if you like. Margie called him Donkey Hoty. I think that's rather a clever name, don't you?'

'Donkey Hoty. Yes.' It wasn't until later I saw the play on that other name, Don Quixote.

'She used to sleep with him until she was eight, instead of a teddy bear. Margie never had a teddy bear.' She said this last as if she felt guilty. As if Margie's not having a teddy bear was some sort of disgrace, evidence of parental neglect.

'Eight?' I said. 'I still sleep with my best doll even now.'

'Don't worry, Cassie. My cousin took her golliwog on honeymoon with her.'

'Served her right if her husband had taken his Meccano.'

Mrs Thoroughgood looked at me for a second, then threw back her head and absolutely laughed. I had never heard her laugh before, even when Margie was there and still safe, not really laugh. It made me feel very pleased with myself.

'Oh, Cassie! You're such a funny child! What are you going to be when you grow up?'

'A writer,' I said emphatically.

'A writer? Well that's quite an unusual ambition for a little girl of eleven. Or a little boy of eleven for that matter.' She was still flushed from laughing and had to dab at her eyes with a tissue. 'Has that always been your ambition?'

'Oh no. Only since I was about seven. Before that I wanted to be a film star.'

'Like Marilyn Monroe?'

'No, like Celia Johnson.'

'How peculiar. And now you want to be a writer.'

I wriggled forward on the bed's edge and closer to her. 'I've never told anyone that before, not even Gran. Dad's friend from Wales asked me what I wanted to be and do you know what I told him? I said I wanted to be an assistant in Madame Tussaud's, in the Chamber of Horrors. I suppose he thought I was being cheeky, and I was too, but he shouldn't have – what's the matter, Mrs Thoroughgood?' Her face had turned pale and she was staring at me through large, unblinking eyes.

'Your father's friend is from Wales? Do you mean that horrid little man I saw him with last Saturday?'

'Jeff. Yes. But it's all right, Mrs Thoroughgood. Jeff has never been to Grisham before, and he and Dad were both in Germany

84

when – last October.' I thought I was going to start crying, or be sick or something, so I forced myself to finish my cup of tea until the feeling had passed and I could explain. 'Someone must've told the police Jeff was Welsh and they must've thought there was a connection. But Dad told them all about it. It would be easy to check because of Dad's job, don't you see? Anyway, Jeff is from Swansea, not Pontar – wherever Myfanwy was from. And there's a lot of Welsh people round here who still go back to Wales for visits. I suppose the police just have to check every tiny little thing like that to be sure.'

'Of course, of course. You're right, Cassie.'

'You didn't really think my Dad had anything to do with it, did you?' I asked anxiously.

'No, Cassie. Such a thing never entered my head. It's just that – well, his friend is a little odd. And when you said Wales – '

'Jeff's an artist,' I said, eager to defend Dad as much as him. 'That's why he's a bit odd.'

Mrs Thoroughgood gave me an indulgent smile. 'Indeed? Do you like this young man, Cassie?'

'He's very nice, Mrs Thoroughgood. And anyone my dad likes just has to be all right deep down. My dad's a good judge of character, you know.' She was looking at me earnestly, giving me the undivided attention other adults seldom did, so I decided to trust her.

'Mrs Thoroughgood, is a nancy the same as a . . . ' The colour must have been flooding my face like a wash of crimson paint. ' . . . a moffradite?'

'A hermaphrodite? Well, no, not really. Cassie! What a question to ask anyone.'

'So Dawn was wrong, then.'

'I'm sorry, dear?'

'Dawn Holgate,' I explained. 'My best friend. Ex-best friend, I should say. She said Jeff was a moffradite. I knew she'd got it wrong. She even hinted that my Dad . . . ' I couldn't go that far, even to Mrs Thoroughgood.

'Cassie, haven't you heard the saying that it's wrong to judge by appearances? It seems to me that that was what Dawn was doing. You wouldn't assume a man was a bully because he had large muscles, or stupid because he spoke with a heavy accent, would you? And even if your father's friend was . . . ' She studied

85

her fingernails, out of her depth for one of the few times in her life. ' . . . that way inclined, it certainly does *not* mean that your father is too. You mustn't listen to Dawn, Cassie. She obviously doesn't know what she's talking about.'

I smiled at her gratefully. Everything she said made sense. Even Gran was always telling me not to judge by appearances; a rule in her book that came second only to 'Coughs and sneezes spread diseases.' I was ready to confide it all to Mrs Thoroughgood just then: my fears that my mother could insist on me going to live with her and that Gran and I would be parted, that I was afraid of the new school, and that Jack Knowles had touched my knee. I wanted to say how nothing in life was ever as simple as it seemed, and if this was growing up, you could keep it. So many things I wanted to confide – and I probably would have done so had she not suddenly stood up.

'You'd better take the dress off now, Cassie. Patrick – Mr Thoroughgood – wouldn't understand. You'd better take it off.'

She helped me with the buttons of my own dress, then put the red one back on its hanger in the wardrobe. I was disappointed that she hadn't given it to me in one way; strangely relieved in another. We put Margie's Donkey Hoty back in his place on the bedside table and wheeled the tea trolley from the room together.

It had turned chilly by the time I left, just as Gran said it would, and I was glad of the white cardigan. But as I hurried along Joshua Road I suddenly felt happy. It was something I couldn't have explained, not merely a feeling prompted by Mrs Thoroughgood's opinion of my dad, or her apparent need of me, but the state of mind that sometimes washes over a person for no logical reason and leaves them full of well-being and optimism.

The body of a child was found in a wood on the Suffolk-Essex border a few days later. A female, aged between ten and thirteen years, the police said, but so badly decomposed that identification would take some time. The village seemed to come to a standstill. Everyone was so sure of the child's identity that everyday matters had to be put aside while we awaited confirmation.

I badly wanted to discuss it with Dawn, but I hadn't spoken to her since the evening in the church porch and pride forbade me to forgive her until some sort of apology had been offered in my direction. Instead, I chose Jack Knowles, running out to his van in an unusually helpful mood to buy Gran's vegetables for her.

'A sad end to it,' Jack said. 'A sad end. But there, when you come down to it, wasn't this what we expected all along?'

I nodded wisely. 'Poor Mrs Thoroughgood. I feel so sorry for her. But Jack, why can't they say for sure?'

'Well, I read in the paper that the remains are little more than a skeleton.'

'Already?'

'It all depends on the type of soil. One type will preserve a body, another will eat it right away.'

I shuddered. He made it sound as though clods of earth could attack one's flesh, like piranha fish. 'So I suppose they go by the teeth,' I said, having watched a great many murder mysteries on the television.

Jack's own incisors slid over his lower lip. Purposely or not, I don't know. 'I reckon.'

It should be fairly straightforward then, I thought. Margie had never had a filling, and she used to boast how her dentist told her she had the most perfect teeth he'd ever seen in a ten-year-old.

I never did find out how the police went about identification in this case, but next day we learned for certain. The remains found in a shallow grave in that remote wood were not Margie's.

9

The last day for Class Six at Upper Grisham County Primary. It was hot without being sunny, and Mr Riordan took the morning assembly with his shirt-sleeves rolled up to his elbows. Across the road outside two workmen were using an electric saw on an ancient tree which had been threatening to topple for some weeks, and our headmaster was forced to shout the prayers.

'Amen!' he bellowed finally, casting an irritated glance at the window. 'Now for some of you, today will be your last day at this school. When the holidays end you will begin at one of the senior schools in town; a big step on the way to your life as adults. We try, at Upper Grisham County Primary, to give our boys and girls –' His voice was momentarily drowned by the crash of the falling tree and several boys giggled. 'And I have the satisfaction of knowing that no child has ever left this school illiterate, innumerate, or wanting in good manners and consideration for others. When you go to your new schools, meet your new teachers and make new friends, all I ask is that you don't forget us and what we have tried to teach you here. Make us proud of you.'

Dawn scowled at the yawning Petey Scammel. Sylvia Tanner, a keen ballet student, put her feet in fifth position and made a demi-plié, for which she was promptly nudged to attention by Miss Saunders.

'Moving on can often be a little sad,' Mr Riordan continued. 'But for Class Six this year it is especially so. When you take your place in your new classrooms, one of your number will be missing. I think this would be an appropriate moment for us all to offer a silent prayer for Margie Thoroughgood. Then we will end this final assembly with the hymn, "Lord, dismiss us". Hands together, eyes closed.'

I prayed that Mrs Thoroughgood would give me Margie's red dress before I grew too big for it.

I seemed to be growing at an alarming rate; so much so that I was beginning to feel like Katy in *What Katy did*. Gran said I was just one of those people who grew in fits and starts; staying exactly the same height for over a year, then adding four inches almost overnight. Growing didn't seem to do much for my general health, though. I started having bouts of tiredness and irritability, often accompanied by dull, heavy stomach aches. Sometimes I thought it would help if I could only talk things over with Dawn as I used to do. But she and I hardly exchanged a glance any more. This morning she was standing as far away from me as it was possible to be and, I imagined, planning all the things she was going to do over the holidays – without me.

It had been arranged that I should stay with my mother for the second of the seven weeks' holiday. Afterwards, Dad would be home to take Gran and me for days out, possibly the odd weekend too, he said. That still left the first week empty. I would have liked to go swimming, but to me the worst thing in the world was having to stand alone in the queue waiting for the pool to open while everyone else had their friends with them. It never occurred to me to ask another girl to come swimming with me; Dawn had been my best friend for too long and nobody else could really take her place. Nor, I noticed, had anyone else taken my place with her. I told myself this was because no one else was stupid enough to trot meekly after her whenever she issued the order to 'C'mon'.

So now it was end-of-term, and the day had come upon me without the usual impatient countdown and taken me unaware. I'd had a lot to think about over the past few weeks and hardly noticed the days going by. Mrs Thoroughgood and I had a regular date for tea now, every Tuesday, and Gran – persuaded by Dad – accepted it as a sort of Christian duty I had undertaken. I never told them what we talked about, or how Mrs Thoroughgood sometimes made me wear the red dress. Nor could they know how I still marked off the days in my diary; allowing for my miscalculations, it was now over two hundred and eighty days since Margie disappeared.

The child found in the wood – 'The Babe in the Wood' as the newspapers called her – still hadn't been identified. Her remains

89

had lain in the shallow grave for approximately four years, and the files on every girl between the ages of seven and fifteen who had gone missing in the past ten years were carefully studied. But her identity remained a mystery. I saw Mrs Thoroughgood the day after we heard the body wasn't Margie's, and she cried. 'If only I knew what had happened to her!' she said. 'If only I knew!'

We were being watched again as carefully as when Margie first disappeared. There was a maniac on the loose, they said, and no child was safe until he was caught. And although the fields, meadows and woodlands around the village had already been searched, the police came to scour them again, this time with the help of hundreds of volunteers and several dozen sniffer dogs. I sat with Mrs Thoroughgood on the day of this search, and she said, 'They'll find her this time. I know they will.' But they didn't. Over the next few days the search widened, covering ground beyond Sudbury and right into Essex, with the same negative result.

The other things on my mind included the new school, of course, and especially Myrtle Baines, resident bully. Would she have remembered my face, I wondered? And would she be merciful if she knew that Dawn, sister of her old enemy, was no longer my best friend? Then there was Dad's friendship with Jeff: a tasty piece of gossip, should Dawn decide to use it. Perhaps the worst thing of all, though, was my mother's letters; always accompanied by an expensive gift, they hinted too boldly that she was not living alone. Not that I felt any jealousy the way I sometimes did when I thought about my dad having found himself a girlfriend. My attitude to my mother was that she could have any boyfriend or husband she chose and, like Aunt Betsey in *David Copperfield*, to hope he turned out to be 'a poker husband'.

We always had our favourite lunch for end-of-term: fish and chips with baked beans, followed by chocolate crunch and thick, lukewarm chocolate custard.

'I'll bet we don't have chocolate crunch at the new school,' Sylvia Tanner said glumly. 'The end of an era, as they say.'

And that just about sums it up, I thought. There were to be great changes at Upper Grisham County Primary, and for that reason I was almost glad not to be coming back. The old coal stoves that had warmed these classrooms since the school was built were to be taken out and replaced with modern radiators. There would be new lavatories, a climbing frame for the playground, and even the large globe in our room was to be thrown out as hopelessly antiquated. The biggest change – truly the end of an era – would be the retirement of 'Nana Bear'. She was our favourite of the three dinner ladies and had worked at the school for so long that nobody could remember how she got her peculiar nickname. Even Mr Riordan was known to call her by it, or sometimes just 'Nana', and he had organised a collection that was so successful we were able to buy her a magnificent silver tray, sherry glasses and a decanter for a leaving present.

Nana Bear cried when he handed our gift over after lunch.

'Even I have trouble remembering the names of every child in the school,' said Mr Riordan. 'Nana Bear not only knows every child, but also whether he or she refuses to eat their greens.'

We could tell by the tone of his voice and the expectant pause that followed that we were supposed to laugh, and we did so dutifully. Nana Bear dabbed at her eyes, lost for any words but 'Thank you', which she kept repeating until it made everyone feel uncomfortable.

Later in the afternoon I saw her crossing the playground alone, the silver tray, decanter and glasses carefully packed into her wicker shopping basket. Her moment of glory was over; ahead lay a lonely retirement. I imagined her coming back to stand outside the railings and watch all the playground activity – only to find that they had all forgotten her.

Poor Nana Bear. The Indispensable Gravy Dispenser, as Miss Saunders called her, had aged quickly over the past year. Her hands were not always steady these days, and she found standing at the serving hatch tired her. I think this change really began with Margie's disappearance; Margie had been her pet, and as the weeks passed and the chance of her being found alive and well grew slighter, Nana Bear seemed to go into a rapid decline. She never ceased her many little kindnesses toward us, but somehow the old vitality had gone. Where once she had doled out boiled sweets with an air of mischievous conspiracy – as though she were liable to punishment from Miss Saunders – now she offered the bag as one might offer condolence.

She had loved Margie, and it seemed Margie loved her back. She would twine her arms around Nana's neck and whine, 'Have you got a sweet for me today? Have you, Nana?' Or, 'Nana Bear, if there's any chocolate crunch left over today, please, please, *please* will you save it for me?' She would smile her winning smile and Nana found her irresistible. The chocolate crunch was usually forthcoming, and Margie, having paid for it with a kiss, was quick to share the treat with her close friends. There was no doubt of Margie's affection for Nana Bear.

And yet, as I watched our favourite dinner lady pass through the school gates for the last time and plod wearily toward her tiny cottage, one particular incident came into my mind and made me wonder.

A button came off Margie's frock one day, and because she was too idle to sew it back herself she ran to Nana Bear. When the job was completed, she returned with a handful of sweets to share with Mary Thorby, her current favourite. Patty, Dawn and I were with Mary.

'See? Good as new,' said Margie, triumphantly showing the resewn button. 'I can get Nana to do anything. Daft old bag.'

Dawn turned away, snapping a bit of twig into tiny bits and scowling toward the road outside. Mary and Patty looked stunned. Margie had called Nana Bear – our own Nana Bear, of all people – a daft old bag. It was like calling your grandmother names.

Straight away, Margie realised her mistake. 'There, now. I didn't mean that.' She tried to laugh it off in the awful silence. 'I think she's gorgeous really.' That afternoon she drew a picture for Nana, and she made sure Mary, Patty, Dawn and I were there when she presented it to her.

The other three soon forgot the incident. But for me it was just one of many that added up to another side of Margie. The darker side of The Girl Who Had Everything.

'Cassie Wade! Why aren't you in your classroom? I know it's end-of-term, but that doesn't mean you can do as you like, you know.'

I looked up to see Mr Riordan, and shamefacedly handed him the class register, which I had been on my way to deliver. 'Sorry, sir,' I said. 'I was just watching Nana Bear leave.'

'Yes, well. It's the last day for you, too, Cassie. How does it feel?'

I shrugged. How could he expect me to answer a question like that?

'Pretty exciting, I suppose?'

'Sort of, sir.'

'And how is Mrs Thoroughgood these days? I understand you see quite a lot of her.'

'She's not too bad, sir. Under the . . . ' I couldn't think of the word 'circumstances'. I used to muddle it with another word, which made Dad and Gran laugh for some reason. 'Well, you know, sir.'

'Yes. It's good of you to visit her, Cassie, and I know how much she appreciates it. But are you sure it isn't too much for you?'

'No, sir. We only have tea. Then we chat a lot. I love going to see her, really I do, Mr Riordan.' Which was basically true. I didn't like the way she sometimes asked me to put on Margie's red dress. I would have liked the dress to be my own, but not to wear in the Thoroughgood house – and especially not in Margie's room, where we sometimes had our tea. But Mrs Thoroughgood was a beautiful, sophisticated woman, as well as being someone I could talk to and even confide in. I was flattered that she looked forward to my visits and wanted them to continue.

'Because I saw Patrick Thoroughgood the other day,' Mr Riordan continued, 'and he seemed to think these visits might be unsettling for you. Do you have any idea what he could mean, Cassie?'

'No, sir.' My face began to burn, as it always did when I told a lie. 'I don't know why he said that, sir. I haven't misbehaved or anything.'

'He wasn't implying that you had.'

'Oh. Well then, sir. I really don't know . . . '

'Is your gran coming to collect you this afternoon?'

'I think so, sir.' It was usual for parents and guardians to turn up at the last day of the school year, especially those whose children were leaving for good. They liked to chat with the teachers, ask if there were likely to be any problems at the new schools, and sometimes enquire where they might buy the uniforms on the cheap.

'Good. Perhaps I'll get the chance to speak with her.'

'About me and Mrs Thoroughgood?' I asked anxiously.

'No, no. Of course not. Off you go now, Cassie. Have a nice

holiday, don't wander off or speak to strangers. And good luck at the new school. I'm sure you've done well in the exam.'

I thanked him, taking a last look along the road, but Nana Bear was no longer in sight.

At half-past three Gran arrived in Mrs Woodruff's car, which meant I would have to ride back in it and I was annoyed. After all, you only left junior school once in your life and it was an occasion to be savoured, cried or rejoiced over, depending on the type of child and scholar you were. I'd looked forward to walking home, calling in at the village shop to say goodbye to Jean and buy one last Jamboree bag. I would see Jean again, of course, and there would be more Jamboree bags in the next month, but it wouldn't be the same. Jean and the sweets were part of my school day and therefore couldn't be enjoyed to the same extent at any other time. Dawn and I used to go into the shop every afternoon, choose what we wanted and assure Jean – who only worked there after lunch – that we would pay the following morning. I suspect the poor woman rumbled us and paid from her own pocket.

Thinking of Dawn, I looked around for her before I could stop myself. She was with her great aunt, a diminutive woman dressed in grey and with a face like wrinkled toffee. This lady had a knack of saying the wrong thing at the worst possible time, had a reputation for it, in fact. Today, she stalked over to where Gran and I were standing and said, 'It's going to be very hard on you little girls, going from the head of the school right to the bottom again. I wouldn't be in your place for anything. By the way, Mrs Wade, did you know Dawn's older sister's going to have a baby?'

Dawn had just one sister older than herself, the celebrated Julie, only girl at Wickstead High School bold enough to tackle Myrtle Baines. Why did she have to get herself a packet now, when we needed her?

'How unfortunate,' said Gran, using her gracious hostess voice but with ice-like undertones. Unmarried mothers were a taboo subject with her.

'And I suppose you two will be down that swimming pool every afternoon,' Great Aunt went on, oblivious to Gran's expression and making it sound as if the pool was where everyone got pregnant. She looked at me, then at Dawn, who was – as usual – scowling. 'Well? Don't tell me you've gone off swimming, the pair of you? It was all you ever thought about last summer.'

'I expect we'll go,' Dawn mumbled. 'Won't we, Cassie?' It was the first time she had spoken to me since the evening I ran away and left her alone in the dark church porch.

'Yeah, I expect so.'

'I don't know,' the old lady grumbled. 'You girls never seem to stick at anything for long.'

It was because of her I forgot all about Mr Riordan wanting a chat with Gran, and the moment she saw him – seeing an escape from Dawn's aunt as well – Gran hurried over, hand extended ready to be shaken. I watched them while the old lady began on reminiscences of her own school-days, how she once got her knuckles rapped with a ruler for daring to touch the teacher's desk while something was being explained to her. 'I only put my fingertips on the edge, just leaning to see better, and all of a sudden – wham!' Dawn and I made the sounds of horror and sympathy automatically (we heard this account roughly once a month, and I think it was meant to illustrate how lucky we were to be modern schoolchildren), but my eyes were on Gran and Mr Riordan.

Gran looked troubled on the way home in Mrs Woodruff's car, and I knew it was because of something my headmaster had said to her. As if it was anyone's business but mine and Mrs Thoroughgood's, I thought angrily. But I didn't dwell on it just then. Before we left the playground, Dawn had hesitated, then come up to me and said, 'Swimming Monday afternoon then, Cass? Meet you on the quarter to two bus as usual.' 'As usual' meaning as we did last summer holiday.

'All right,' I'd agreed. 'See you.'

She hadn't apologised for that evening in the churchyard, but I wasn't going to hold out for it after all this time. Besides, no one knew better than I that a person could be sorry, and show they were sorry, without actually saying so. Dawn and I were friends again and I was happy for that, though I sensed a certain reserve on her part. But once we were splashing around in the pool on Monday, fooling around on the diving boards and seeing which boy had the best tan, things would be back to normal. We had such a lot to catch up on. I thought I might even confide a little of what Mrs Thoroughgood and I talked about; though I knew I could never tell her about Margie's red dress.

After tea, once Gran had gone through her little performance of

95

switching on the television, she began, 'I'm glad you and Dawn are friends again,' thereby telling me she knew of the split, though I hadn't said anything. It was a small exhibition of Gran's power – she was always saying I couldn't 'diddle' her – and a prelude to more serious matters.

'Mm?' I pretended to be busy with my entry for the *Tuesday rendezvous* competition – first prize a large, illustrated book on dogs.

'She's not a bad girl, young Dawn, whatever that sister of hers has been up to.'

'Mm.'

'Cassie, I've been thinking. Perhaps it would be a good idea for you to stop these visits to Mrs Thoroughgood.' She raised her hand to silence me before I could protest. 'I've been talking to Mr Riordan and he's worried that she may be – not quite well.'

'Aw, Gran! She's all right! Only the other day she said she'd been up to London to buy a new dress. And she ate two Danish pastries with her tea. I saw her. An ill person wouldn't be able to do that.'

'I don't think Mr Riordan meant that kind of ill.'

'What kind, then?'

'Well, she's still very upset about Margie, of course. Does she – does she talk about her a lot?'

'Not much,' I said, which was a lie. Sometimes our conversation – at least, Mrs Thoroughgood's conversation – was all Margie. Margie did this and Margie said that, until I began to wonder if there were two Margies: the one I remembered and the one her mother spoke about. Later, I realised Mrs Thoroughgood was idealising her daughter, recalling her brilliant moments and forgetting the not-so-nice bits in between. For although Margie had shone at sport, art and social skills, I knew now that she'd had a cruel streak, a meanness in her that would almost certainly have developed and turned her into an unlikeable teenager.

'Well, what do you talk about?' Gran wanted to know.

'Oh, this and that.'

'Cassie, if there's one thing you've inherited from both your parents it's evasiveness.'

'Well, what can I say? We talk about so many things.' Gran pressing the point by her very expression, I added desperately, 'The weather, school, clothes, Muffin the cat. All sorts.'

'Anyway, it doesn't really matter because I want you to write her a letter to say you won't be able to see her any more. She'll understand, what with having to stay with your mother and the new school to think about. You can tell her I thought it would be best if you like.'

'I will!' I shouted. 'I'll tell her you forbid me to see her any more because Mr Riordan says she's mad!'

'Cassie! He said nothing of the sort! And I didn't actually forbid – '

I ran out of the room and slammed the door.

I could get around this by writing one unsuitable letter after another until Gran gave in, I thought. The week after next, I would be staying with my mother, and I couldn't go through that without first seeing Mrs Thoroughgood. Perhaps I needed her then as much as she seemed to need me.

It wasn't a good time to be away from Upper Grisham, that second week of the holidays. Gran used to say things happened in threes, and two occurred on the Friday before I was due to be handed over to my mother. The first was the news that the Babe in the Wood had finally been identified. She was a fifteen-year-old London girl, missing since Christmas 1958. A man had been questioned about her disappearance at the time, but he had been released and a few days later had killed himself. The police were not looking for anyone else.

The second piece of news came on the later bulletin. After fresh evidence in the Myfanwy Davies case, South Wales police issued a description of the man they wanted to question. He was a forty-three-year-old civil servant, David Davies; Myfanwy's uncle.

10

My mother's house was not in Ipswich, as I had supposed, but a tiny village called Willingswell five miles outside the town.

'I could never live in Ipswich,' she explained, driving along with her head tilted back as though the steering wheel was in her way and she had to crane her neck to see over it. 'Oh, no. It's much too noisy.'

I thought about how she used to complain of Upper Grisham's being too quiet, but said nothing.

'Is it an old house?' I asked.

'Georgian.'

'Oh. That's pretty old. Is it haunted?' I asked this more to make conversation than with any real interest or concern, but my mother snapped, 'Don't be so childish, Cassie! It's a charming house; red-brick and full of character. And there's a fair sized garden, so you can run about as much as you like.'

It was easy to see that the residents of Willingswell were affluent, a cut above the Grisham people. The houses along the main street were all large, some Tudor, their top storeys jutting out over narrow pavements and casting angular shadows on the dusty road. The heat was making me very thirsty. My mother had refused to open the car windows because of the farmyard smells along the way to the village, which she feared would stick to her clothes, and by now I felt half-baked and quite dehydrated.

'Is it much further?' I asked, trying to sound bright. But no one can ask such a question and make it sound anything other than impatient and petulant, and my mother snapped again.

'I hope you're not going to spend the entire week moping and whining, Cassie.'

It wasn't a very promising start, I had to admit, especially as one of the bouts of lethargy I had been experiencing lately was threatening to spoil the rest of that day. I had a stomach ache, too; a heavy ache alternating with a peculiar sort of cramp in the base of my abdomen. The aspirin Gran had given me in the morning (given reluctantly as she thought I was shamming) was wearing off, and I fidgeted in my seat.

'I'm making a special effort to please you, Cassie,' said my mother, noting my squirms, 'and the least you can do is make the effort to be appreciative.'

Why was it she made me feel I ought to respond with a dutiful 'Yes, Mother'? Everything she did 'for me' seemed like a great favour, bestowed after terrible inconvenience to herself.

The house came as a surprise after all the mental pictures I had conjured up. It was large and typically Georgian, orange- rather than red-bricked, situated at the bottom of a winding hill at the tail-end of the village. Impressive, certainly, but where was the garden? The front door opened directly on to a pavementless road, and the strip of earth under one of the windows was so narrow that the dead rose trees in it appeared to sprout like brown stalagmites from the tarmac.

'The largest part of the garden is at the side,' my mother said, indicating a tall privet hedge to the left of the house. 'It gets all the afternoon sun, so you'll have to mind you don't get burned. We have a garden table and chairs in the shade at the back, and I thought we could all take tea there this afternoon.'

'All?'

'Yes. You, me and Uncle Ray. All together. Won't that be nice?'

I remembered the card she sent me the first Christmas after she had walked out on us, the one signed *Mummy and Uncle Ray* which Gran had thrown out.

'Is Uncle Ray your boyfriend?' I asked.

'No, darling. He has an interest in the shop, that's all. I told you I planned to expand, didn't I? Well, Uncle Ray handles the financial side of things for me. Running a business is very complicated, Cassie, and your Uncle Ray is indispensable.'

'But he does live with you?'

'I couldn't afford to keep this house on my own,' she explained severely. 'It needed a lot of repair work. Again, simply a business arrangement.'

She couldhave bought a smaller place, I thought, but – typically of my mother – had to have it all at once. I couldn't forget the way she constantly nagged Dad for all the things her socially superior acquaintances had and we could never afford.

'Actually, Cassie . . . ' She paused at the front door. 'I've told your gran that Ray is a cousin of mine. She has a narrow mind, I'm afraid, and simply wouldn't understand. Or she'd think the worst and refuse to let you stay with me again.'

This last I could believe, anyway.

As soon as my mother inserted her key in the lock, there came a tremendous barking from the rear of the house. Two dogs, by the sound of it. Large ones.

'Are they Alsations?' I asked. Gran had a fear of Alsations – they were 'liable to turn' – which she had passed on to me.

'No. They're greyhounds. They used to race, but they're retired now and Uncle Ray bought them for guard dogs. Don't worry, Cassie, they won't hurt you.'

She led me into a hallway that was bright and modern in décor, but struck me as chilly after the heat outside. The barking persisted, and it sounded as if the dogs were using their bodies as battering rams against the door. I was eleven years old, and the dignity of being that age prevented me from running away wailing that I wanted to go home, so I forced myself to be calm. I caught a glimpse of the dining-room as we passed: six highbacked chairs around a long table so highly polished even Gran would have been impressed, with a silver candelabra as centrepiece. To my eyes, it looked like a dining-room from the Regency period.

My mother showed me into the sitting-room, which was at the back of the house and in shade, and there, at ease in front of the television like the master of the house, sat 'Uncle' Ray. He rose to greet me, and for a moment I thought of little David Copperfield coming home from Yarmouth to be greeted by his new stepfather. But there was nothing grave about Uncle Ray, no cast in his eye, and his hair – what there was of it – had auburn highlights in the sparse brown curls.

He *did* say, 'Cassie, gal. How are you?' But he smiled hugely and his eyes twinkled, robbing his words of any Murdstonian threat. Perhaps it was with that same scene still in my mind that I approached him and offered my hand. His grasp was reassuring: firm but not painful, cool but not clammy.

'Hello – ' I looked to my mother for guidance, but she appeared uninterested, flipping through a pile of letters that had arrived during her short absence. 'Hello, Uncle Ray.'

'Well, well. I've been looking forward to meeting you for a long time, Cassie. Tell me, is it true you were christened Cassie and not Cassandra?'

'Yes, quite true. Cassie Jane Wade. I'm glad it's not Cassandra. I think that's too – oh, I don't know the word.'

'Pretentious?'

'That's it.' It sounded right anyway.

I liked him. Despite all my preconceived ideas, my plans to make myself disagreeable, I liked him and wanted him to like me.

He wasn't very tall, only about three inches above my mother in her flat heels, nor was he exceptionally handsome. Instead of combing his hair over his bald spot, he let it shine like a little pink moon, as if he was proud of it and wanted to display it. He had a neat, thin moustache over his rather serious mouth which didn't really suit him but was grown, I assumed, to hide a slight hare lip. Perhaps the greatest thing in his favour was the way he nodded toward my mother when she wasn't looking and winked at me, telling me we must present a united front and were in cahoots from now on.

It soon became clear that Uncle Ray was useful for other things apart from financing my mother's projects. He showed us the big box of groceries he had just bought, gave my mother the shopping list to check, then went to prepare the afternoon tea.

'I never could abide getting meals ready,' my mother said gaily. 'Your Uncle Ray is a real treasure.'

Later, she told me he did all the cooking and was never happier than when in the kitchen with a vegetable knife in one hand and a rolling pin in the other. Once I learned that the dogs were generally kept in the kitchen it wasn't long before I began to wonder if Uncle Ray favoured the place because he found more respect in there.

We had tea in the garden in the shade of the house, which would have been enjoyable had my mother not requested me to 'go and explore' within two minutes of sitting down. I was tired and hot, and exploring the garden was something I would have preferred to leave until evening. But to say so might have been interpreted as 'moping and whining', so I got up as if it were a

101

great thrill and ran the length of the lawn to what promised to be a handy retreat, the garden shed.

It was a shack, really. The last coat of creosote had been applied so long ago that the wood had faded through every shade of brown to a pale grey, and the one window was broken and patched with cardboard. A shack is preferable to a new shed, however. New sheds seldom harbour anything of real interest and tend to be used regularly, which is no good to a child hoping for a retreat. As I pushed the door open the top hinge fell to the ground, and on the floor inside several large spiders were panicking at the sudden intrusion.

'Cassie! Cassie, don't go in there, darling!' my mother called. 'It's all nasty and dirty in there. You'll spoil your nice dress.'

I came away with only a glimpse of the piles of magazines – magazines with unfamiliar names and pictures of ladies in their underwear on the front covers – old books and, curiously, a darts board. Never mind, I thought, it would keep for another day.

There was virtually no shade in the garden, the sun not being far enough across the sky to cast shadows from the three small apple trees. Dutifully, I 'explored'. That is, I stood for some moments looking at the lawn, which I suspected had never seen a lawn mower but was kept in check by the services of someone's pet goat. The other half of the garden was taken up by Uncle Ray's attempts to grow things, but the only successes as far as I could see were the tomato plants. Some few lettuces thrived among others that had wilted or been savaged by slugs, though because he had planted them willy-nilly the best ones were all too close together and would have to be thinned out. I guessed he would get about four decent heads from the four dozen I counted there.

After that, there was nothing more to see and I went back to the table to finish my lemonade.

'You look pale, Cassie,' said my mother accusingly.

When I thought about it later, I couldn't believe I actually apologised for it, but that was just what I did do. I certainly wasn't going to 'whine' that I had a stomach ache.

'She's tired,' said Uncle Ray. 'Heat is tiring for a highly strung child, Isabel. You should know that. Have some more lemonade, Cassie.' He refilled my glass, winking at me. 'You're not afraid of dogs, are you?'

'N-no. Only Alsations.'

'That's all right, then. I can let Bertie and Amaryllis out.'

'Is that their names? Didn't they have proper names for racing?'

'Well, yes. Let me see ... They were Bertie-Why-Do-You-Bound and Lady Amaryllis of Toadspit Hall.'

'Ray.' My mother didn't seem amused, though I was giggling. 'You made that up. Finish your lemonade while I fetch your case from the car, Cassie. Then I'll show you your room and help you unpack.' She stalked into the house, letting the dogs out and slamming the door behind them. I didn't understand why she was angry, but it was a display I would become quite familiar with as I gradually got to know my mother. Eventually, I came to the conclusion that she was jealous. She had to be the centre of everyone's universe and couldn't bear to think two people might find something in each other that she couldn't give them.

The dogs, one black and one brindle, hurled themselves at Uncle Ray, gave me a perfunctory sniff, and, having judged me a harmless person and approved guest, bounded away up the garden.

'Which is which?' I asked.

'Bertie is the black one. They're affectionate dogs, Cassie, and they make good companions. You'll like them.'

'I can't imagine my mother keeping dogs in the house. I wanted a puppy once, when I was about four, but she wouldn't let me. She said it'd get hairs all over the place.'

Uncle Ray looked at me steadily, in rather the same way Mr Riordan had looked when deciding my punishment after the broken milk bottle incident. I felt I was being judged and didn't like it.

'Your mother is an unusual woman,' he began carefully. 'No one knows that better than I do. She's tried to make a nice little room for you here, but – well, I'm afraid she had no idea of what an eleven-year-old likes. Not that I'm an expert myself, you understand. I suppose eleven is a difficult age to be, really. No longer a baby, eh?' I must have looked confused because he added, 'You'll see what I mean when she shows you the room.'

I nodded, expecting I don't know quite what. But I made up my mind to like the room, for Uncle Ray's sake, if not for my mother's. The longer I looked at him, the more I liked him and was sure Gran and Dad would like him too. He was quietly spoken, like Dad, and had the same way of picking around words until he was sure he had the right one. I guessed he was well educated and, though not classically handsome, charming enough to attract most women, which made it hard to understand his devotion to my mother. Because as I saw it she was utterly selfish, using him as she used my father; as she would use any man to promote her own interests.

She returned with my case and we went upstairs, one of the greyhounds, Amaryllis, sneaking up behind us. The room that was to be mine whenever I stayed with her was at the front of the house, giving me a pleasing view over the village. At first glance, I was thrilled; the room was just like Margie's, blue and white, and straight from the pages of a glossy magazine. Then I saw the wallpaper design – fluffy lambs jumping over blue hurdles – and the little table loaded with colouring books, crayons and plasticine. The books she had provided were children's classics I had already read several times over, except that these were from the 'Retold for Younger Readers' series. There were dolls as well. Not the teenage dolls I was already beginning to discard, but the chubby-faced sort which are roughly modelled on, and meant for, the five to eight age-group. Incongruous amid this nursery setting was the dressing-table cluttered with creams and lotions, a make-up bag, a manicure set, and all the other aids to personal grooming that I didn't want or yet know how to use.

Perhaps even my mother realised her gifts had been ill-chosen because she almost blushed as she looked around the room, and she rubbed the palms of her hands together as if she was cold.

'It was so difficult to know what to buy you,' she said. 'You're at an awkward age; a child one moment, a young woman the next . . . '

Suddenly, I felt sorry for her. She had done her best to please me, after all. And maybe I was wrong to judge her any differently from the way I'd judged Dawn. A person could be sorry for the past, and show it without needing words.

'It's lovely, Mummy!' I said. 'Thank you.' I was genuinely happy to see the relief on her face.

But the day ended badly, as some instinct had told me it must. Uncle Ray and I were watching *The Comedy Hour*, laughing at Lucille Ball and Desi Arnaz, when my stomach ache returned and

I was forced to excuse myself. I thought maybe the prunes I had eaten the previous day were beginning to have their effect, but when I got to the lavatory and found what the trouble really was I almost fainted. Gran had forewarned me, of course, but she'd led me to believe this wouldn't occur until I was at least thirteen, so I'd thought nothing of the stomach cramps and was totally un-prepared. I used the last of the bathroom tissue, cleaning myself up as best I could, then went downstairs.

I found my mother in the sitting-room, scribbling in a thick notepad while Uncle Ray was still chuckling at Lucille Ball. Be-cause I liked to think of myself as being well brought up, knowing which subjects were all right in mixed company and which were not, I approached my mother and bent to whisper. She brushed me away angrily.

'Don't you know it's rude to whisper, Cassie?'

'I have to tell you something.'

'Then tell me properly. Don't whisper.'

'But it's private.'

'Cassie!' She flung her pen on to the notepad and glared at me. 'I won't have that sort of nonsense here. If you can't say what you have to in front of Uncle Ray, then it obviously isn't worth saying. Now, either you come in and sit down or go to bed. Take your choice.'

'But Mummy –'

'Cassie, that's *enough!*'

I gave up, deciding I'd just have to deal with it myself, and set about searching various cupboards around the house for tissues or old rags. After ten minutes of this I had found nothing more suitable than a pile of face flannels in the airing cupboard, and by now I was getting desperate. So I chose the softest of these, folded it into a rectangle and stuffed it in my knickers. It wasn't very comfortable, being bulky, but was absorbent enough for the purpose.

Just before my bedtime, it occurred to me to use a couple of the dozen or so handkerchiefs Gran had packed in the case, so I took the soiled face flannel to the bathroom and tried to wash it. That was when my mother came in, took one look at the stain and slapped me, hard.

'You *dirty* little beast!' she screamed, her face crimson with fury. 'You filthy, dirty, dis-*gusting* child!'

Her hand struck my thighs repeatedly until I started to grizzle. 'You wouldn't listen! You wouldn't listen!'

'My face flannel! My *best* face flannel!' Her hand took one last swipe at my leg, then she grabbed my shoulders and began to shake me. 'Is this how you behave at home? *Is it?*'

'You wouldn't listen!' I screamed back at her. 'I tried to tell you! It's not my fault!'

Suddenly, she let go of me – I think it was because of Uncle Ray calling up the stairs and demanding to know who was killing who – and made a peculiar, snorting sound, as though the sight of my menstrual blood repulsed her.

'Is this your first time?'

'Yes, and I didn't know it was going to happen! It's not my fault!'

'But a *face flannel*, Cassie! Couldn't you have found something else?'

'There wasn't any toilet paper left. I couldn't find any. And you ... ' I wanted to hurt her. She had hit me for something that wasn't my fault. 'You didn't listen when I tried to tell you.'

'Well, how was I to know? Take your clothes off, Cassie. I'm going to give you a bath.'

'A bath?' If that wasn't adding insult to injury. 'But – I had a bath last night. I'm not dirty.'

'Please, just do as you're told, Cassie.' She put the plug in the bath and turned on the hot water tap. 'You'll feel much better after a bath, I promise you. It will help you sleep. Besides, you must get into the habit of taking a bath every day now. Your body is beginning to change and you'll soon be a woman, physically at least. That means bathing regularly, Cassie. Grubbiness is all very well in a little girl, but not at all nice in a woman. Take your clothes off and hop in. Then I'll find you something to wear.'

I stared at her, amazed that she could be shaking me in an almost uncontrollable fury one minute, calmly lecturing on personal hygiene the next. I wiped my eyes and started to undress, though I was still trembling and my fingers fumbled with my buttons. My mother appeared not to notice.

While she was out of the room I sat down in the warm, comforting water and glared at the offending part of me. So this was what it was all about: 'visitors', 'the curse'. Where was the pride and dignity one was supposed to feel at reaching the menarche? I hated the smell of blood, the sight and stickiness of it, and I didn't feel at all different in myself. I'd supposed I *would* feel different somehow – more sophisticated and independent – and that people would look at me with a new respect, treat me as if I did have a mind of my own and a little common sense after all. The trouble with childhood wasn't the Six Impossible Things one was expected to believe before breakfast, but the six disillusionments one had to endure before bedtime.

Bathed, kitted out with the necessary protection from my mother's supply, and put into my pyjamas, I allowed myself to be escorted severely to my room. Uncle Ray passed us on his way to the bathroom, stopping briefly to pat my head.

'Never mind, Cassie,' he said cheerfully. 'Boys have their growing-up problems too. Don't worry about it.'

She had told him. I couldn't believe it, but she had actually *told* him.

I turned on her when he was out of earshot. 'Gran said it's common to talk about things like that with other people.'

'Good Lord, Cassie! It's not as if you were fifteen; it would be quite improper then, yes. But you're a little girl, and this is 1963, not the Victorian age. Besides, if you're going to feel unwell I have to give some explanation or Uncle Ray will think you're sulking, and we don't want that, do we? It's no different from your gran mentioning it to your father.'

'Gran wouldn't do such a horrible thing. And Uncle Ray *isn't* my father.'

She sighed. 'You're overtired, Cassie. Go to bed. I'll see you in the morning.'

I *was* overtired, as she said, so it took me a long time to fall asleep in the unfamiliar room. I didn't get into bed straight away, but wandered about looking at everything by the light of the street lamp just outside the house. All of these things would have to be used in order to please my mother. The colouring books could be filled in when I didn't have anything better to do, the strips of plasticine could be kneaded together to a grey-brown ball, which would make it look as if it had been played with, and I could keep moving the dolls around and swapping their clothes. I found the bottle of hand lotion and applied rather a lot of it to my hands and legs, then sprinkled some of the talc powder inside my pyjama jacket. Satisfied with that, I climbed into bed.

Downstairs, Uncle Ray was laughing, rather an alarming sound after I had got used to his soft speaking voice. I wondered if my mother was talking about me, or Dad and Gran, saying disparaging things, perhaps, or whether he was just laughing at the television. Anyway, my mother had told me one lie already when she said Uncle Ray wasn't her boyfriend. While I was searching the cupboards I had found her bedroom, and some of his clothes were draped over a chairback. Gran, who was religious (or 'God-fearing', as she often described herself) and had high morals, would have thrown a fit. I imagined my mother applying for custody of me and my having to go to court where I would tell the judge confidentially, 'I don't like her very much, Your Honour, but the chap she's living with is okay.' That thought amused me and eventually helped me to fall asleep, but I couldn't bear to think I'd have to pass a whole week here. I'd be living in dread of spilling my food or breaking something, giving her an excuse to shake and slap me again.

I dreamt about Margie that night; not dead in her grave as the last time I had dreamt about her, but very much alive and so exactly as she used to be that I was afraid, even while the dream was happening. She wore a pale blue summer dress, the shade of her eyes, which had a full skirt and billowed about her as she stood before me, laughing.

'Oh, Cassie!' she said, half bending and clasping her hands between her knees. 'You are silly! Don't you know I'll see you on Saturday? Bring lots of crayons and paper – oh, and plasticine. Don't be late, will you, Cassie?'

'I beat you, Margie,' I said. 'I beat you. I've got my periods now.'

Margie laughed again. 'No, you didn't beat me, Cassie. You didn't beat me.' Her voice began to fade, along with her body, so that all I could see was her smiling face, like the Cheshire cat in *Alice*. 'You didn't beat me, Cassie. Oh, no, you didn't.'

11

A whole week with my mother; however would I be able to stand it? And why hadn't I simply refused to come in the first place? Gran would never have forced me to if she had known I would be unhappy here, and if my dad knew how I felt he would have Gran take a taxi and fetch me home straight away. So I told myself as I lay in my babyish room wondering whether I ought to get up or wait until I was called. The room looked much worse in the morning light. The lambs on the wallpaper weren't even realistic, but had eyelashes and smiles on their faces like something out of a Walt Disney film. The thought of what Dawn would say if she could see it made me blush.

But then, things always do seem worse than they really are first thing in the morning. I could have refused to come here, but greed — what my mother might buy me, where she might take me, and who she might introduce me to – made up my mind for me. Now I would just have to make the best of it.

In this optimistic mood, and at the breakfast table, I announced my intention to attend the morning church service. By the looks on their faces, I could tell that neither my mother nor Uncle Ray was accustomed to church-going; but they both agreed it was right and proper for me to go. They weren't to know how I usually dodged Sunday school by hiding on the steps of the Boy Scout hut, eating the sweets I had bought with my collection money. The question was, who took me and who stayed at home to start preparing the Sunday lunch.

'I'll take her,' said my mother.

I enjoyed her obvious discomfort when the vicar addressed her as Mrs Masterton (Uncle Ray's surname), and said it was a pity he didn't see very much of her. I told him I was from Upper Grisham, but he didn't recognise the name even though it had been mentioned so much on the television, and I was disappointed. It made me feel important when people said, 'Upper Grisham, that's where the missing girl came from, isn't it? Did you know her?' And if there was no danger of my being found out, I used to answer, 'She was my best friend.'

In the afternoon we took the dogs for a long walk; *miles*, my mother complained when we reached the neighbouring village. Uncle Ray remarked that we hadn't forced her to come, which didn't go down too well.

'This will be a nice little job for you if you get bored in the afternoons, Cassie. You can walk the dogs,' said my mother, sitting down on a tree stump to massage her feet. But Uncle Ray wouldn't permit it, and it was one of the few times I was ever to hear him lay down the law to her.

'No, Isabel. She's not to take the dogs out on her own. If they saw a rabbit they'd try to bolt and she'd never be able to hold them. No, I absolutely forbid it.'

'They obey the order to heel, don't they?'

'Yes, but I doubt very much if they'd obey once they saw a rabbit. You have to remember, greyhounds are trained to chase small furry objects –'

'Damned dogs!' My mother got up and started walking on ahead, limping slightly in her unsuitable shoes.

This was to be the pattern of things all week. Mother would complain about something, Uncle Ray would try to reason with her, and it would end with her stalking off in a huff. Perhaps this was how they carried on all the time, but I couldn't help thinking my presence somehow aggravated matters.

I was taken to see the shop on Monday. It was larger than I had supposed from looking at the photograph, but was not in one of the main shopping streets. It was sandwiched between a butcher and a café which seemed to cater exclusively to layabouts. At first, I wondered that my mother ever sold anything with her premises on such a poor site. But I'd underestimated her clientele, women like herself and Mrs Thoroughgood who would gladly walk ten miles to be first with every 'New Look'. She made me sit in a corner, out of the way, while she attended to the morning's most urgent business, and I watched a steady stream of customers come and go. Some bought, some didn't, but all of them knew my mother by her Christian name.

It was dull in the shop, both dimly lit dull and deadly boring dull, and I spent most of the time stifling yawns. Nobody took any notice of me, except that my mother, in between greeting the more valued customers and attending to business over the telephone, kept saying, 'All right, Cassie?' If I got up and went to look at something, Mother's assistant would hurry over to guide me away with, 'Don't touch that, dear,' as if my hands were dirty. At last, I was given five shillings and told to go to the newsagent's a few doors down and buy myself sweets and comics. I spent the rest of the day reading *Bunty* and *Schoolfriend* and sucking sherbet fountains.

At the dinner table, my mother told Uncle Ray it was 'gratifying' I had been so impressed and delighted with everything. He looked up at me and nodded, giving just a hint of a grin.

Uncle Ray was at home most of the time, and when he wasn't, the woman who cleaned for my mother was there to prepare my meals. In the evenings we drove out to little country pubs, where I was invariably dumped in the garden with a bottle of Vimto and a bag of crisps.

The afternoons were the worst. Once or twice, I ventured into the village but the other children were unfriendly, even hostile, and after several of my overtures were snubbed I gave up. Mostly I just sat around the garden with the colouring books, waiting for the next meal or Mother to come home. I think Uncle Ray felt rather sorry for me, but he couldn't do much to help. On the one occasion he suggested taking me to Walton for the day, Mother suddenly remembered there was something of the utmost importance she wanted him to attend to. Instead, he bought me sweets and two books, *Shadow the sheepdog* and *The young Victoria*, both of which I enjoyed very much, though my mother had to find fault even with that. We'd had quite enough of dogs already, she said, and what did he have to go filling my mind with useless history for? I stood up for Uncle Ray.

'It's not useless,' I told her. 'We learned about Queen Victoria at school, and I think it's great!'

She went off in a huff.

Only one other episode stands clearly in my mind before the events of that Thursday overshadowed the rest. Unable to bear

111

another hour without hearing a sympathetic and truly understanding voice, I plucked up the courage to telephone Mrs
Thoroughgood.

She seemed pleased to hear me, perhaps a little too pleased,
and it made me uneasy.

'I've spoken to your gran,' she said, 'and everything's all right
again, Cassie. You can still come to tea with me on Tuesdays. If
you want to, that is.'

'Of course I want to. I've missed seeing you, Mrs
Thoroughgood.'

'Have you? Really?' Her voice was strange, childlike. 'Are you
having fun, Cassie? Does your mother take you out a lot?'

'Not really. She took me to see her shop on Monday, but it was
dead boring.'

'I'll bet.'

'She made me sit in a corner and watch everyone coming and
going, and I didn't have anything to *do*. Every time I moved they
told me not to touch anything.'

'Poor Cassie!'

'They take me out in the evenings,' I said, not feeling a grain of
disloyalty. 'But only to little pubs out in the back of beyond. They
leave me ouside in the garden and come back acting like it was a
bloody great joke. Only it isn't. And they squabble –'

'"They", Cassie?'

'My mother and her boyfriend. He lives here too. But it's all
right, Mrs Thoroughgood. He buys me sweets and things. He's
not a bit like Mr Murdstone.'

'Mr – ? Oh, yes. I see. Are you fond of reading, Cassie?'

'Yes. But there's not much here to read that I haven't already
read.'

There was a slight pause, and I heard her sigh. 'Margie had a
good many books, some of them not even glanced at. She wasn't
a great reader, I'm afraid. When you next visit, we can look
through them together if you like. Then you can take any that you
haven't already got.'

'But Mrs Thoroughgood, what will Margie say?'

Another pause. 'Cassie, Margie has been gone over ten
months. She isn't coming back, dear.'

The way she said that, as though she felt sad for me as much as
herself, made me want to cry. I knew Margie wasn't coming back,

we all did deep inside, but somehow I'd imagined that the mother of a missing child never gives up hope.

'Aren't you well, Mrs Thoroughgood? You don't sound it.'

'I've not been sleeping much lately. I've been having night-mares this past week, awful nightmares.'

'Oh, I'm sorry. I – ' I was going to say I had dreamt about Margie last Saturday, then thought better of it. 'I have bad dreams too, sometimes.'

She made a curious sound; not a sigh, nor a gasp, but the peculiar little intake of breath one makes when trying not to cry.

'Cassie, do you remember how you and Margie once started a wild-flower collection?'

'Yes. Margie had trouble with the scabious because they're bulky and she couldn't press them properly.'

'That's right. Well, couldn't you use the time to add to your collection? You may find wild plants there which don't occur here, you know.'

'All right, that's what I'll do. Most of the flowers I pressed last year went wrong, anyway. I wasn't using the right paper, I suppose. Or I didn't put enough weight on them.'

The suggestion fired me with enough enthusiasm to get me out of the garden and the whole picturesque, sunny and to me totally boring village. I followed the path we had taken with the dogs, sometimes leaving it to investigate a promising field, hedgerow or ditch, and eventually gathered a bagful of wild flowers. As far as I could tell without my *Observer's* book, I had found nothing that wasn't in last year's brown, crumbling collection. I did find a quite perfect toadflax, however, and because it reminded me of the day Margie found one and thought it was an orchid, I deter-mined to press it beautifully, to show Mrs Thoroughgood.

On Thursday morning Uncle Ray went to Ipswich with my mother, leaving me in the care of the cleaning woman once again. When he came home at lunchtime he brought with him a thou-sand-piece jigsaw of Constable's *Haywain* and gaily proposed we 'rattle it off' that afternoon. So we cleared the kitchen table, which was seldom used for meals anyway, and carefully emptied the pieces into a pile in the centre.

'Don't you think it might take a bit longer than one afternoon?' I asked doubtfully.

'Not with two of us, Cassie. Jigsaws have to be set about

methodically; do the frame first, then sort out according to colour.'

Ninety minutes later, when I had completed the top and sides of the frame and he was still struggling with the bottom, he said optimistically, 'The frame is always the hardest part.'

'Do you do a lot of jigsaws, Uncle Ray?'

'I used to, when I was a little boy. Don't have the time these days, of course. How about you?'

'Sometimes. My gran likes doing jigsaws. Jigsaws and Patience. I don't know why she likes playing Patience, though; she hasn't got very much of it.'

He laughed. 'You shouldn't say things like that about your poor gran. I'm sure she must have a lot of patience to take on a little horror like you.' We knew each other well enough by then for him to say things of that sort to me without my taking offence, and I laughed too.

'She's nice, my gran. I wish you'd come with us when Mother takes me home on Saturday, then you could meet her.'

'I don't know. We'll see. You like living with your gran, don't you, Cassie? I mean, you wouldn't be as happy here, would you?'

'N-no. Uncle Ray . . . ' Perhaps I could have confided in him then; perhaps he could have reassured me on the custody point. But there was a knock on the front door and the time for confidences passed us by.

I heard his voice in the hallway, even above the noise of the dogs barking. 'Yes, yes, she's here, but what's all this about?' A pause, a man's voice, indistinct. Then, 'Of course, Sergeant. Come in.'

Several minutes went by before Uncle Ray returned, during which time I trembled, wondering if the Ipswich newsagent had seen me slip the Blackjacks into my pocket and, if so, how they had managed to trace me. I didn't think of Margie at all until Uncle Ray came and said, 'There's a policeman to see you, Cassie. He wants to ask you about the missing girl.'

'They haven't found her, have they?'

'No, but I think – you'd better come and see what he has to say, Cass.'

He led me into the sitting-room, his hand protectively on my shoulder. I felt proud and important.

'Hello, Cassie. I believe we've met before.' It was Sergeant

Jordan, who had interviewed us all at school and who had questioned Dad about his trip to Wales. He sat at his ease in Uncle Ray's chair, smiling, overdoing the Just-Routine act the way police, like doctors, invariably do when something is wrong.

'So, your mother has a dress shop in Ipswich?' he said, baring yellow, nicotine-stained teeth at me.

'That's right. She's there now.'

He turned to Uncle Ray. 'I'm sorry, sir, I didn't get your name?'

'Masterton. Raymond Masterton. I'm a business associate of Mrs Wade.'

'I see. And you're looking after Cassie this afternoon, are you?'

'That's right.' He looked slightly miffed. 'In loco parentis, as you might say. We were just doing a jigsaw together, weren't we, Cassie?' He smiled at me reassuringly, his hand still on my shoulder.

We sat side by side on the sofa, facing Sergeant Jordan, who was in his shirt-sleeves, and I stared at the damp patches under his arms.

'Cassie, there's a little dell behind your house, isn't there?' His tone was light, conversational.

'Colonel Cartwright's dell, yes.'

'Your gran tells me you play in there quite a lot.'

'Yes, sir. But it's all right. Colonel Cartwright never used to mind, and the new people – '

'I know, Cassie. That doesn't matter. But you do play in there?'

'Yes, sir.'

'And the other children, they play there too?'

'Some of them. All the boys, and most of the girls.'

'Margie Thoroughgood?'

I didn't have to think about it. 'No, sir. Not Margie.'

'You seem pretty sure about that, Cassie.'

'She never played there.'

Sergeant Jordan shifted in his seat, and I felt Uncle Ray become tense beside me. 'How often do you play in the dell, Cassie?'

'I don't know. Whenever I feel like it, I suppose.'

'When you see the other children playing there?'

'Yes.'

'So Margie could have been there without your knowing?'

I shook my head. 'No, sir. Margie was afraid of the dell.'

'Afraid of it? Why?'

115

'Because the trees touched overhead. It made her feel as though she was suffocating.'

'Margie told you this, did she?'

I glanced at Uncle Ray. The dell had been searched when Margie first went missing. Why had it suddenly become so important that Sergeant Jordan had come here to question me?

'Yes, several times. Dawn – she's my best friend – she often used to ask Margie to come with us. But she never did.'

'She was afraid of the trees?'

'Because they grew so close together and their branches meet overhead so you can't see through them. It's a bit like being closed up in a house made of trees. That's what she told me. She even went – well, she sort of trembled just thinking about it. She said the doctor told her mother it was a phobia. Claustrophobia.' I remembered how proud Margie had been of that word, pronouncing it carefully and distinctly, as though it were something rare and special. (I soon looked up the word 'phobia' in my dictionary, and finding it to mean 'a morbid fear or aversion', decided I had one or two of those myself.) 'Yes,' I said. 'It was a phobia she had. Didn't her mother tell you?'

Sergeant Jordan answered matter-of-factly, too cheerfully. It was a tone any child over the age of six would recognise, and I knew something had happened that I wasn't going to be told about.

'I haven't had a chance to speak to Mrs Thoroughgood yet, Cassie. I thought to ask you first because you live so near the dell and must know it better than anyone.'

'Well, she never played there, sir. I can tell you that much'

'All right, Cassie. You've been a big help. You can go back to your jigsaw now.'

Uncle Ray signalled me to leave the room, but made no move himself. I closed the door quietly behind me, took a few steps down the passage, then tiptoed back to listen.

'The hairslide was caught in a low branch of a tree,' Sergeant Jordan was saying. 'And it's her hairslide, there's no doubt about it. But because it's brown we must have missed it when we searched the dell before. There was a chance it caught there while she was playing, you see.'

'And now Cassie says the girl never went into the dell,' said

Uncle Ray, and as I listened my knees began to tremble. 'I can see the significance.'

'The branch was quite low. It could have caught when the child – her body – was being carried along the path.' He cleared his throat. 'You get a feeling about these things sometimes, Mr Masterton, and I feel we're close now. Very close.'

I felt it, too.

12

Uncle Ray presented Gran with an enormous bouquet, which immediately made her suspicious, and I knew I could look forward to an interrogation the moment we had waved him and my mother goodbye. I supposed the bouquet was a little over the top when a pot plant would have done just as well, but Uncle Ray boasted that he 'never did anything by halves', and insisted on buying it despite my protests. Gran arranged the flowers in a cut glass vase that had been a wedding present to my parents; deliberately, I suspected, as that particular vase had always been considered too good to use and was normally stored in a cupboard, well away from my clumsy hands.

'I hear there's been a new development in the Thoroughgood case,' said my mother. 'Have you any idea what's happening, Lilian?'

Gran looked at me as though wondering if what she had to say was suitable for my ears. Then, probably deciding I would only listen at the door anyway if she sent me from the room, she told us how one of the village boys had found the hairslide and recognised it as Margie's.

'Who found it?' I wanted to know.

'The Scammel boy. The one you say smells.'

'He does smell. He smells of guinea pig's muck. I don't know, some people have all the luck. I suppose it'll be fourpence to speak to him from now on. I wish it'd been me who found it.'

'Strange no one's found it before,' Uncle Ray said. 'You don't think it could have been put there deliberately, do you?'

Apparently Gran hadn't looked at it in that light before; she was apt to take everything at face value and wouldn't, I thought, have made a very good detective.

'Well, they said it was stuck quite fast,' she said slowly, then hinted at Divine Intervention, a favourite explanation for the otherwise unexplainable. 'And from now on Cassie is going to keep out of that dell. I've told her time and time again, it's on private land and she's not to assume the new people don't mind children playing there just because they haven't said anything yet.'

'I shan't want to rotten well play there any more now, anyway,' I said.

'That's all right then, isn't it? The police are up there this morning, and this time they're going to go over every inch.'

'With dogs?' I hoped to watch from my bedroom window.

'I don't know, Cassie. They've been waiting for some specialist chap from London; they say he can tell by the growth of the plants whether the soil has been disturbed in the past year. It's marvellous what can be done these days.'

'Modern science!' remarked Uncle Ray affably and to change the subject. 'It'll be men on the moon next, and before the decade is out, I'll bet on it.'

Mother gave him one of her withering looks – she specialised in them – and told him he was being ridiculous.

Gran served tea with a plate of her home-made biscuits, which I'd missed very much while I was away, then put the dreaded question: Had I behaved myself?

'Oh, she was as good as gold, Lilian,' my mother gushed. 'I'll be only too pleased to have her stay again whenever you like. We had *such* fun, didn't we, Cassie?'

My smile must have been a bit sickly.

'Oh, there's a letter for you, Cassie,' said Gran. 'It came last Wednesday. Postmarked Germany, so it must be from your father.'

It was the first letter I'd ever had all to myself, apart from that Christmas card from my mother, which didn't really count, and I would have liked to open it casually, as if letters to me were everyday occurrences. But Gran and Mother came to peer over my shoulder, turning it into a Big Event.

'Let's see what he has to say for himself,' said my mother contemptuously.

It was a disappointingly short letter.

Dear Cassie,

Just a line to let you know I'll be home Monday. I thought we might visit Southend sometime next week. I know how much you and Gran enjoy the Kursaal.

Jeff sends his love to you both. Enclosing a photo of us taken outside the Beethovenhaus.

See you soon.

Love, Daddy.

'Never much of a letter writer, was he?' Mother remarked. 'Who's this Jeff? Let's see the picture, Cassie.'

I felt as if several internal organs were sinking in company with my heart when I saw the photo. Dad and Jeff stood side by side, grinning at the camera, the lovely old house in the background. Dad, posing rather woodenly, looked handsome and muscular, but Jeff was as puny as ever. His hair almost reached his shoulders now, longer than the Beatles wore theirs; his shirt could well have been a woman's blouse. But worst of all was his stance, so girlish and silly that I cringed.

'He stands there as if he's messed himself,' said Gran, embarrassingly blunt as ever.

My mother couldn't bring herself to say anything but 'Well!' as she showed the picture to Uncle Ray, who was at least more tactful.

'Your father's friend certainly looks a lively character, Cassie.'

'Oh, he's very nice. He's an artist.'

'An artist?' Mother snatched the photo back and studied it again. 'Well, that explains a lot, doesn't it? Has Cassie actually met this person, Lilian?'

'He came with Arthur last Easter – '

'You mean to say you allowed that – *fairy* to stay here?'

'*Isabel!*' Gran signalled Not-in-front-of-the-child with her eyes. 'Jeff stayed in town. And as Cassie said, he's a very nice young man. After all, there may be nothing in that appearance of his; it might be just his way.'

'I suppose you have to say that, Lilian. It's your son he's friendly with.'

'I hope you're not implying – '

'Which would also explain a lot.'

'Isabel, *please!*' Uncle Ray tried ineffectually to silence her, while Gran rose as if to slap her face.

'Well, whatever Arthur's relationship with this alleged *man* – ' Gran interrupted her here to order me from the room. 'I don't want Cassie exposed to that sort of thing. She's eleven years old and has no business knowing there are such perverts in the world.'

It occurred to me that I'd known about a worse kind of pervert for nearly ten months. Now Margie's hairslide had been found, the biggest break the police had had since she first disappeared, and all my mother could think about was condemning a friend of Dad's whom she had never even met. I'd expected her to have something to say on the matter as soon as she saw the picture, but couldn't have imagined such a violent reaction. I wanted to run back into the room and scream at her: You don't know Jeff! You don't know him!

Slowly, the anger in their voices subsided and they were talking normally, but I didn't go back into the room. I waited until my mother called me to say she and Uncle Ray were ready to leave, then Gran and I went to the front gate to wave them off. I had the colouring books, crayons and plasticine in a bag in one hand and the two ten-shilling notes they had given me, one from each of them, in the other. The dolls I'd thankfully managed to leave behind.

'Your mother,' said Gran when their car had disappeared down the end of Joshua Road, 'sinks to new depths every time I see her. She's trying to make out bad things about your father, Cassie. Things which are totally untrue. And I should know; I'm his mother.' She muttered something under her breath, which I didn't quite catch but which sounded very much like a swearword. 'And she's got no sense of decency whatsoever. Well, I always did say she was dragged up – for all her airs and graces. Fancy mentioning a woman's periods in mixed company! Remember, Cassie; that's something that's never, ever done. Honestly, I didn't know which way to look. And neither did that poor devil.'

'Oh. She told you about me, then?'

'Yes, she told me. Good Lord, Cassie! You're only just turned eleven. I'll have to have a word with the doctor, see if he can't give you some iron tablets or something.'

I laughed and put my arms around her neck, which she didn't understand at all.

Dawn came to call for me after lunch. That is, she waited until Gran went out to the garden – Dawn knew Gran liked to do a spot of weeding on a fine Saturday afternoon – then she sneaked in through the back door.

'The police are in Colonel Cartwright's dell,' she stage-whispered. 'Coming to watch, Cassie?'

'Don't be stupid. They'd never let us watch.'

'I didn't say we were going to ask, did I? They're searching along the right of the path. There's a hedge to the left, remember? If we're behind that, we'll see them without them seeing us. Aw, c'mon, Cassie. It'll be fun.'

'I don't know – '

'I've already been up there once. It's all right, I tell you.'

'Okay. Might as well. Though I reckon it's a waste of a good afternoon. We could have gone swimming.'

Dawn helped herself to a biscuit from our tin. 'The pool's too crowded on Saturdays. C'mon, Cassie. Get a move on or we'll miss it.'

'Miss what?' Gran stood in the doorway looking suspicious. 'Where are you two going?'

'To Mary Thorby's house,' Dawn said without hesitating.

'And what don't you want to miss?'

'The afternoon film. Margaret O'Brien's in it.' I was a convincing liar, too.

'All right. But just stay away from the dell, do you hear? I don't want you brought home in a police car.'

We knew she would be watching from the front-room windows, so we went down Joshua Road as though we were on our way to the Thorby house, but cut straight through the side of Mrs Woodruff's and into the field instead. We had to crawl along on all fours to avoid being seen by anyone in the back gardens, then sprint along a rough track until we were on the road again. Joshua Road became narrower the further up you went, then there was a sharp bend and you were in Potter's Lane. This went on for about four hundred yards, then there was a group of houses known as The Potteries – Cyril and Conny Jennings lived in the last one, a tumbledown place that hadn't seen fresh paint since Conny's mother died. In between was The Red House, where Colonel Cartwright used to live, and beyond that was the dell.

The New People – we still called them that because the Cartwrights had owned The Red House for so long – must have been away on their holiday. There were no cars in their driveway and the curtains were partly drawn at the downstairs windows, so we had no qualms about cutting through their garden. Dawn stopped to look at the orchard, once so carefully tended by the Colonel and now so shamefully overgrown, and I wondered if she was getting cold feet.

'Guess what, Dawn?' I said. 'I've got my periods.'

'Don't shout. They might hear us.'

'Dawn, I said I've had my first period.'

'Big deal.' She picked an apple, though they were nowhere near ripe, and bit into it.

'You're jealous.'

'No, I'm not. Anyway, I don't believe it. A little weed like you? Nobody has their periods until they can wear a bra. And you're as flat as a board.'

'All right. You ask my gran.' I looked back at the old house. It was red-bricked, like my mother's, but Victorian, and with creeper all over the walls. It made me feel gloomy, even in broad sunshine. 'I thought we were going to see what's happening. Not scaredy-cat, are you, Dawn?'

'Of course I'm not. C'mon then, and keep your voice down.'

I allowed her to lead the way; which meant we took a complicated route, involving much ducking, creeping and darting, all of which was unnecessary as no one appeared to be about. I had imagined there would be ropes around the dell and uniformed policemen posted at the perimeter to keep the inquisitive away; but we saw nobody, so we crossed the path and crouched among bushes, feeling something of an anti-climax.

'I thought you'd already been up here today,' I said.

'I have.'

'Where are they, then?'

'In there somewhere. Can't you hear them?'

I listened. There *were* voices and not too far away, but they were subdued, like daylight poachers who couldn't remember

123

where they had set the traps. Occasionally, a twig snapped, or there was the sound of someone lighting a match, then we saw a curl of cigarette smoke away to our right, blue in the shafts of sunlight that broke through the trees overhead.

'Down there,' Dawn whispered. 'We can get much closer, Cassie. C'mon, I want to see what they're doing.'

We crawled through the undergrowth, catching our clothes on hawthorns and grazing our knees; mishaps that wouldn't be noticed until much later.

There were six men. One was the Detective Sergeant who had come to question me at my mother's house, four others I remembered from when police activity had been at its height in the village, and the sixth I assumed to be the 'specialist chap from London' Gran had heard about. He was casually dressed, in the American style Mr Thoroughgood favoured, and was laden with notebooks; the others were listening to what he had to say and looking gloomy.

'They haven't found anything yet, then,' I said.

'I don't suppose they will.'

'Why did we bother to come, then? We could have gone swimming.'

Dawn began to edge closer, flat on her stomach because it was still a game, and I followed, pretending we had just uncovered a plot to kidnap Princess Anne and we had tracked the perpetrators here in a desperate bid to save her.

'Where does that path lead?' asked the man with the notebooks.

'Back to the field behind Joshua Road.'

'And it was ploughed – when?'

I didn't catch the answer, but it was obviously unsatisfactory and the men started to move further into the dell where it was shady and dark and always smelled damp. We had to leave the cover of the bushes in order to follow, but they had their backs to us and we were able to dart from one tree to another without being seen. My knee was bleeding where I had grazed it crawling through the bushes and I tried to wipe it on some leaves. Dawn had a handkerchief tucked in her shorts and when she unfolded it, ordered me to 'gob on it' and wiped my knee with uncharacteristic gentleness, I trembled without knowing why.

'Oh, Christ! You're not going to faint, are you?' She looked me over with her scowling, speedwell eyes. 'It's only a little graze, Cassie.'

'No, it's not that. I'm frightened, Dawn.'

'What of, for God's sake?'

I couldn't tell her because I didn't know myself.

'Can't we go back now?'

'You can if you want, Cassie. But I'm staying here. And if you go now they're sure to spot you, then we'll both be for it.'

I looked up to where the men were standing, then back to the bushes that had hidden us so well a few moments before, and I realised she was right. The only possible way was forward to the next clump of bushes, where we would be even closer but perfectly hidden providing the expert's eye had already covered that spot. We crawled forward slowly, and suddenly I didn't feel frightened any more; it was a curious release.

'We should have brought a picnic,' Dawn whispered as one of the men surreptitiously drew a sandwich from his pocket and bit into it. 'Or at least something to drink. I'm thirsty, aren't you?'

'No.'

'Cassie, what was it like?'

'What?'

'You know.' She patted her stomach.

'Nothing to it. My mother walloped me for using a face flannel instead of a whatsit.'

'Walloped you?'

'*Thrashed* me. Ssshh!' The DI, whose name – Washkansky – had reminded Miss Saunders of a Polish soap powder, turned and for a moment I thought he had heard us.

'Fancy using a face flannel! You are *dirty*, Cassie!'

'I couldn't find anything else. Her boyfriend thought it was funny.'

'She's got a boyfriend?'

I nodded, trying to look suitably ill-used. I was going to pretend Uncle Ray was a brute, but I found I couldn't bring myself to tell a lie of such magnitude and told the truth instead.

'He's really nice. He's got two greyhounds called Bertie and Amaryllis. And he bought me loads of things – '

'Well,' said Washkansky loudly, making us both jump, 'I think the only course now is to bring the dogs in.'

'Again, sir? We drew a blank with them last time.'

125

'What else is there, short of digging up the entire dell? And I'm beginning to think it might just come to that.'

'There's that last section, over there, sir,' a third man hinted respectfully, but the one with the notebooks shook his head.

'Can't tell much from – ' Here he said some Latin name, unfamiliar to me with my elementary knowledge of botany, as were the actual weeds he indicated. 'Those little bastards spread like wildfire. There'd be no difference in the growth of a patch on soil disturbed last autumn than the rest. But let's look at the ground itself – '

Just then, an old man who lived in one of the houses called The Potteries came hobbling along the path and caught their attention.

'I don't know if it's important,' he began, panting as though he'd been running some way, 'but there's a well here, you know.'

Dawn and I looked at each other. It was the first we had heard of it and, picturing a fairy-tale wishing well, I put my index finger to my forehead. 'Must be batty!' I whispered.

But the detectives were taking him seriously.

'I'd forgotten about it until today. My brother and me were talking over the old days, the way you do, you know?' The old man rambled semi-coherently. 'He's down from London for the weekend, you see. I haven't seen him for ten years. Ten years! Would you believe that?'

'Yes, sir. And you were saying about a well?'

'We grew up here. Used to play in here as lads. Our mother was always going on about that well; what happened to boys who played near wells and how the devil lived in them.'

The DI nodded patiently. 'And you can show us where it is?'

'I reckon so. It isn't very deep as wells go, but it's still pretty dangerous. Old Colonel Cartwright was always meaning to have it filled in properly. That was twenty-odd years ago. He had it covered with a great slab of concrete "in the mean time" as he used to say. But he never did get around to having it filled in. The new people in the house probably don't even know about it. Nor many others, for that matter. Like I said, if it hadn't have been for my brother I wouldn't have given it a thought myself.'

'You were going to show us, sir.' The DI's voice had the slightest crack of impatience in it now.

'Yes, of course. The memory's not what it was, but I'm sure I can find it for you.'

He led them to the edge of the dell, to the path and the old stone wall that enclosed Colonel Cartwright's orchard. Ivy clung to the wall and spilled over on to the ground like a heavy splattering of green paint from a huge paint tin; tendrils snaked and twined about the broken pieces of statue that had once been the pride of the Colonel's garden. As we crept closer, sheltered by the first clump of bushes once more, we saw the man in the casual dress, the 'specialist from London', bend over something.

'I'd say this has been disturbed sometime within the past year,' he pronounced.

'Oh, Dawn!' I grasped her wrist. 'Have they found it? Is it the well?'

'I don't know. Shh!' Her face was abnormally pale.

The man knelt down and began pulling away the ivy. 'Yes, this was certainly disturbed fairly recently. There's an iron ring, but . . . ' He was panting with exertion. 'We might need a rope.'

The policemen tactfully persuaded him that this was where they took over, if he didn't mind. Apparently he did mind, and stepped back looking offended. I heard, or thought I heard, the DS say, 'Is it my imagination, or can you smell . . . ?'

My heart began to race and I felt very hot, unreal. 'Dawn, let's go!' But I was as unable to move as she was, and we crouched there, holding hands and staring at the little group as they struggled to remove the concrete cover. Their voices were jumbled now, soft but unmistakably urgent.

'Shall I get a rope, sir?'

'Would a crowbar be any good?'

'No, no. Hold on.'

'I think it's coming! Out of the way!'

We saw the cover rise, then fall back. The men stood very still in a semi-circle a short way away, waiting for the DI to make a move. He approached the well, looked down for about three seconds then turned from it with the back of his hand to his mouth, nodding slightly.

'John, you know what to do. And let's have a cordon around this place.'

Dawn got up and, still holding my hand, began to lead me away. Though we walked softly, we made no attempt to hide; it wouldn't matter now if they did see us. Dawn's face was the colour of suet pudding, and as I was trying to keep up with her I watched her suddenly stumble, then fall to the ground.

'*Dawn!*' I screamed, and the DS heard me and came running over.

'Cassandra Wade! What the devil are you doing here?'

I felt so small in front of him. Overhead, I could hear the flurry of dozens of birds in the treetops, startled by the shouting. 'My name's Cassie,' I said stupidly. Then I looked down at Dawn. 'I think she's fainted.'

Mrs Thoroughgood had been waiting just over three hundred days.

13

The days that followed hardly seemed real. Perhaps it was something to do with seeing Upper Grisham on the television news so much, or the fact that nobody scolded me for having been in the dell – they were all unusually kind to me. Or maybe it was the many police, reporters and even morbid sightseers that swarmed the village. It was as if Margie had died twice but her disappearance had merely been a dress rehearsal for the real thing.

Dad and Jeff had only just heard about Margie when they arrived, and straight away Dad began to make plans for the days out I had been promised.

'Unless we could squeeze in somewhere last-minute for a week,' he suggested. 'I could phone around the hotels on the south coast; one of them might have had a cancellation.'

'I'd rather not, Daddy,' I said, idly flipping through the pages of the *Bunty Summer Special*. 'There's the funeral, you know.'

'The funeral? Oh, I'm not sure if it's a good idea for you to go, Cass.'

'But I must!'

'All the children are going,' Gran told him. 'All those from her class and the teachers. It's been agreed, Arthur. But I don't suppose it will be yet a while, anyway. The body has to be released officially.'

'Well, I'm still not sure it's a good idea. You say she's been having nightmares as it is.'

This was true. Three times on Saturday night and twice the previous night I had woken myself and Gran up, screaming out about Margie. I'd dreamt of her body, all broken up in the bottom of the well, with moss growing in her platinum blonde hair and over her wide-open eyes. But I knew if I didn't go to the funeral

129

the nightmares would be worse. I would see her standing before me, asking me why I hadn't been in church; or even putting some sort of curse on me for prancing around in her red dress while she lay alone and cold in the dark.

'I must go, Daddy! Whatever will Mrs Thoroughgood think if I don't? Besides, I've never been to a funeral before.'

'It's not a pleasure outing, Cassie. All right, if your friends are all going I suppose I had better say yes.'

Sometimes he sounded just like Gran.

There was an atmosphere in the village similar to that which hung over us when Margie first disappeared, but more intense, to the point of being menacing. The men gathered on street corners to talk, an occupation usually reserved for their wives, and I knew that anyone having the slightest suspicion upon him would not be safe. They looked to people regarded as 'outsiders', and that meant anybody who had lived in Upper Grisham less than ten years, or whose livelihood was not the Wickstead factory or the land. So the list of unofficial suspects included the pub landlord, who had a crippled, bitter wife, Jack Knowles, the coalman's red-haired, truculent son, and my dad. Nothing was actually said, or even implied, at first. But we knew by the way these men gave sideways looks at Dad whenever we passed. Perhaps Jeff suffered most. The Welsh Connection, broken when Myfanwy Davies' uncle was charged with her murder, was still evidently in the minds of the local men. So Jeff avoided the village as far as possible, driving straight to our house from his hotel in town, politely declining all my invitations to picnic by the river. Gran became very fond of him, and he of her – despite the innocent little remarks she made about his appearance: 'Doesn't that long hair get in your way?' and 'Isn't that shirt rather loud?'

We learned a little about his family. His mother had died when he was ten and he was brought up by an overbearing, short-tempered father whose life was given to chapel-going alternated with pub-crawling. There was a sister, Olwyn, not yet twenty-one and currently nursing the father in his terminal, alcohol-related illness. I thought Dad had a rather strange expression on his face when Olwyn was mentioned, but because my mind was incapable of sustained concentration on any subject at that particular time I soon forgot all about it.

130

I spent most of the time worrying about Mrs Thoroughgood. Keeping our usual Tuesday tea date was out of the question, of course, but I felt I should write her a letter of condolence, as that was the normal procedure among adults after somebody's death. Gran, however, said that this was an entirely different thing and as I was a mere child I ought not try to make any contact with her until at least a fortnight after the funeral. Margie's body would not be released for burial for another week, we were told. Then, when everything was arranged, Mr Riordan would contact every member of Class Six himself. We would assemble at the school and walk quietly, in a crocodile, to the parish church and take our places behind Margie's family. We were not going on to the burial, which was to take place in the village cemetery instead of the churchyard; that was considered unsuitable for eleven-year-old eyes.

I looked forward to the funeral with all the innocent callousness of my age. And Margie had been gone so long now that I had some trouble picturing her face without the aid of the photograph in Mrs Thoroughgood's sitting-room, so that the occasion seemed quite unconnected with her. It was simply something that would have to pass before I could see Mrs Thoroughgood again. One big event closely followed by another; the way Christmas is followed by the New Year.

Dad kept his word and took Gran and me for day trips to the coast, always accompanied by Jeff, who shared my fascination for the sea. At Southend, he and I chose to walk the length of the pier and back, while Gran and Dad opted to ride the little train. We stopped often to gaze over the railings; not speaking, just gazing down into the water or across its choppy expanse to the horizon. I loved to breathe in the sea air and dream of being a pirate, like *Anne of the Indies*. We watched a jellyfish, no more threatening than a plastic bag caught on the tide, as it drifted along and finally vanished under the pier. How strange that they should have that fluent quality in the water, like a sea-ghost, yet be reduced to a gelatin pancake when stranded on the beach.

Gran loved the amusement arcades and she must have spent at least seven shillings' worth of pennies in them that afternoon. We came away with our pockets full of those cheap plastic trinkets won on the penny cranes – the machines you were supposed to 'pay to see operate' with no thought of prizes – feeling skilful and pleased with ourselves. After a lunch of plaice and chips, eaten with our fingers and from a newspaper, Gran demanded her usual treat of jellied eels.

They were all making the effort to take my mind off Margie and what had happened last Saturday, which I half resented as I wanted to think about it. I couldn't picture Margie's face any more, or recall her voice, but there was still the idea of her. When I ate doughnuts and candyfloss I thought, Margie'll never do this again. I led the way to the Kursaal, eager because I knew Margie had been there too, and more recently than my last visit. I wanted to go on all the rides I thought she might have liked best: the big dipper, the caterpillar, the awful ghost train called 'Laff in the Dark'.

'I'm not going on that thing with you,' Gran said when I pointed to the dancing skeletons above the waiting cars. 'The last time I went on a ghost train with you you screamed right in my ear and deafened me.'

And every time we fell into conversation with someone, I waited for them to ask where we were from. Everyone had heard of Upper Grisham now, and I would feel important when I told people I knew Margie.

I hardly thought about anything else that afternoon, and it helped me stay awake on the return journey when I would normally have fallen asleep after a good dose of sea air. Besides, Jeff was with us and I had to show him how adult I was. I determined to keep my eyes open. First, we examined one of the little toys I had won on the penny cranes. It was a plastic pig with legs and ears that could be removed. The instructions were unbelievable – and impossible, as I later discovered. You were meant to remove one of the pieces, insert a live fly, then put it back together. The legs and ears were then supposed to twitch and jump comically. Jeff said it was disgusting. After that we told each other jokes, but mine were not too successful as the only good ones I knew began with 'There was an Englishman, a Scotsman and a Welshman' and I didn't want Jeff to feel insulted.

Eventually, I did fall asleep and didn't wake until we were in Upper Grisham and Dad's voice, cursing uncharacteristically, disturbed me.

'What is it, Dad?' I said, rubbing my eyes and looking over his shoulder at a group of village men at the bottom of Joshua Road. 'An accident?'

'I don't know, Cass.' He hooted at them sharply.

They turned at once, but made no effort to clear the road, and I saw Sergeant Jordan in their midst. It appeared that the men had been heckling him, and when he saw Gran, who had made him several cups of tea last Saturday when he brought me home, the relief on his face was obvious.

Dad wound down the window and asked – none too politely – if they wouldn't mind getting out of the way as he had a home to go to if they didn't.

'You ought to be here with us, Wade,' said Mr Woodruff, 'and never mind about getting home. This concerns you as well, you know.'

Shouts of 'That's right!' and 'Hear, hear!' surrounded our car. Through the open window I could smell the perspiration of hot, angry men.

'What concerns me?' Dad asked.

'We want this copper to tell us what the hell he's doing about finding the Thoroughgood girl's killer,' an anonymous voice shouted. 'And it concerns you because you've got a kiddie of your own, Wade.'

Then Cyril Jennings pushed his way to the front, and straight away I knew he was sober. Cyril, unlike Upper Grisham's other well-known tipplers, generally held his tongue when he'd had a few pints and even became quite courteous. Without his 'medicine', as Dawn's father called it, he was sour-tempered, always ready to start trouble, but quick to run if the argument looked like coming to blows. Some people felt sorry for Cyril – a widower of many years with a backward son to care for; it was enough to drive anyone to drink, they said. But I didn't feel sorry for him at all. I couldn't because I'd seen him hit poor Conny.

Now he was glaring at my dad with the same look of contempt he used on his son. 'I'd like to know where Wade was on the day the kid went missing,' he said, and I felt Jeff, Gran and myself tense with anger and disbelief.

'I don't see why I should have to account for my movements to a grubby odd-job man,' said Dad, who was not usually given to insults. 'But I was in Germany, as a matter of fact.'

'Can you prove that?'

133

'I don't have to prove anything to you, Jennings.'

The others muttered angrily. This wasn't the attitude to take; didn't Wade know they were talking about murder?

Sergeant Jordan looked ready to intervene, but Gran, who had miraculously kept quiet until now, suddenly launched her attack.

'You want to guard your tongue, Jennings. You've no right to go around hinting and accusing without reason – '

'Without reason? I'd like to know why the law were three hours questioning him that time. And why they were around your house again last Saturday when the kid was found. There's no smoke without fire is what I – '

'Do you want me to come out there and give you what you're asking for? I'm not afraid of a lout like you, so don't you think it. You want to keep tabs on that boy of yours – always roaming around all over the place, he is – you want to watch out for him before you start on someone else.'

'You old – ' Jennings clenched his fists, and for a moment I thought he was going to reach inside the car and hit Gran. But then Sergeant Jordan did intervene, seizing Jennings by his shoulders and pulling him away.

'Now that's enough! You too, Mrs Wade. If you men aren't on your way in two minutes flat I'm going to call the station and have you all taken in for a breach of peace. That includes you, Jennings.'

'What about him?' Jennings pointed to Dad. 'Can you be sure he was where he says he was the day the kid disappeared?'

'Mr Wade was on an internal flight in Germany that morning. There's no question of him being involved. Now will you please all clear the road and let these people get by?'

They did so, but slowly and insolently. Cyril Jennings was the last to move, and as we drove away I looked back to see him still staring after us.

'Well done, Mrs Wade,' said Jeff. But Gran suddenly looked tired and barely managed to return his smile.

Once indoors we bustled around in the usual way of a family returning home after a day out. Gran put the kettle on – a cup of tea being the most urgent requirement – and cut sandwiches while Dad, Jeff and I brought things in from the car, took the washing off the line and laid the table.

'Well, did you ladies enjoy yourselves?' Dad asked when,

relieved of our shoes and pocketfuls of cheap trinkets, we were sitting at the table.

'I did,' I said. 'When can we go again?'

'Oh, I don't know, Cassie. How about Walton next time? They have a good beach there.'

'Sand's for babies. I wouldn't be seen dead with a bucket and spade.'

'I like a good beach,' Gran said. 'Give me a nice stretch of sand and a deckchair and I'll be quite happy. I don't know, I enjoyed myself today, but I think I must be getting too old to traipse round fun-fairs.'

Dad advised her to have an early night, but he looked a little worried; it wasn't like Gran to feel tired at eight o'clock in the evening, even after a dose of sea air.

'I'll be as right as ninepence after a cup of tea,' she said.

In a while I began to feel sleepy myself, but as my official bedtime wasn't until nine nothing would have persuaded me to go before then. So I picked up last week's *Bunty* and tried to concentrate on 'The Four Marys'.

'Mum, I don't think that was very wise of you just now,' I heard Dad say.

'What wasn't?'

'Making those hints about the Jennings lad.'

'Well, he asked for it in the first place. Besides, you must remember all that trouble with the boy a few years back? That's why I don't like Cassie having anything to do with him.'

I sensed her looking at me, and expecting her to say, Cassie, go and get ready for bed, I pretended to be chuckling at poor Miss Creefe in the *Bunty* story.

'Of course I remember,' Dad said. 'But he didn't know any better at the time. What do you expect with a boy like that and only Cyril Jennings to guide him? Young Conny should have been put in a special school years ago, then perhaps he would have stood a chance. He might even have had some sort of job by now, instead of roaming over the fields all day. After all, he may be backward, but he's not completely un-teachable.'

'That's a matter of opinion,' said Gran with a little sniff.

'But who is this Conny?' Jeff wanted to know. 'And what was the trouble?'

I sensed more sidelong glances and I bent my head lower over my comic.

'They say every village has its idiot,' said Gran, 'and Conny is ours.'

But Dad was more charitable. 'Hardly an idiot when he can tell you the name of practically every wild flower there is, Mum.'

'He's not all there though, is he, Arthur? I mean, would you trust him alone with Cassie?'

I could tell Dad was unable to say yes with any conviction; if he couldn't answer honestly he always remained silent.

Jeff was still curious, however, and as I listened to the story Gran had to tell I wondered what they would say had they known I'd been talking to Conny only the previous day.

Cyril Jennings was a loser; that was one thing everyone who knew him was agreed on, whether they pitied or despised him. He had failed at school – through indolence rather than a lack of intelligence – and then lost a string of jobs because of his inability to get on with others. He married a pretty but dull-witted village girl, who was actually first cousin to both himself and Jack Knowles, a union that was short and unhappy. In 1939, Cyril suddenly found himself with strong moral and religious convictions and went to work on the land. Six years later, after the birth of his only child, he conveniently abandoned these convictions and took to the odd-jobbing way of life, plus a little poaching in between, which he still pursued today.

At this point in the story, Gran allowed that Conny may have been born with his handicaps; but she couldn't help her belief that they were the result of Cyril's rough treatment. Whatever the truth of this, Mrs Jennings never fully recovered from the birth, and after two years as a semi-invalid she died suddenly while Cyril was out on one of his night-time jaunts; and it was well known in the village that Cyril took the loss out on his son.

Conny went to Upper Grisham Primary School for six months, where he either hid under a table or screamed himself to exhaustion, until he was finally pronounced 'educationally subnormal'. So he began to accompany his father on the jobbing round, and when he tired of that he would roam off across the fields to collect wild flowers, stones, odd-shaped bits of wood, or anything else that took his fancy. Quite often his father forgot to provide him with a midday meal, then he would knock on someone's door and ask for something.

My first memories of Conny were of him sitting on Mrs Woodruff's doorstep eating bread and dripping or bread and sugar. Gran used to give him biscuits as well – until about two years ago when she suddenly began to shoo him away. When I asked why, she said he was getting 'too much of a good thing', by which I understood her to mean he had tried her patience with his scrounging. Now I heard the real reason.

'It was bad enough at the Flower Show,' said Gran, her voice lowered to almost a whisper. 'I mean, there's a lavatory behind the pavilion, so he had no excuse. He didn't even go right behind the hedge but did it where everyone at the coconut shy could see. And at sixteen – well, it was like a man. Luckily Cassie wasn't nearby, so she didn't see. But other kiddies did. Someone went and got his father and he gave the boy a hiding. But instead of curing him it seemed to have the opposite effect.'

Dad started to laugh, then checked himself. 'I suppose the poor boy thought he'd found a great way of attracting attention.'

'Maybe, but it was no joke to anyone with young children. Anyway, the last straw was when Pam Grundy went home in tears because he'd chased her and tried to kiss her. Constable Seagle had to give him a good talking to; he told him he'd be put away if he didn't behave himself.'

'And has he behaved himself?' Jeff asked.

'As far as I know. But he *will* hang around the little girls, and I don't like it. I think it was very lucky for him that Jack Knowles had him helping load Carson's vegetables on the van the day Margie Thoroughgood went missing.'

I didn't sleep for a long time that night, tired though I felt. Poor Conny. He'd had a rough time when Margie first went missing. The police were satisfied with his alibi, even impressed by his bewilderment and his tears, his readiness to describe past misdemeanours that had brought him to Constable Seagle's notice. So much I'd overheard Father Steven telling Miss Game, the Sunday school teacher. He knew Conny well and he'd told them, 'I don't believe that boy is capable of a violent act, or of telling a lie.' But it was some of the villagers who gave him a hard time, until they realised that if Margie was dead (this was back in November) whoever killed her must have concealed her body very cun-

137

ningly, which ruled out poor simple-minded Conny. Yet I sensed
the police were still keeping an eye on him. What would they –
and Gran and Dad – have said had they known of the conversation I'd had with Conny only yesterday?

Dawn had gone to the dentist, Dad and Jeff were busy with
some CSE business that had cropped up and were gone to
London, and Gran had the weekly wash to do. So I wandered
over the field with my sketch book. I wasn't really defying Gran's
order to stay where she could see me, because she could have
seen me very well from the main bedroom window.

Conny was sitting in the long grass, the old biscuit tin he used
as a kind of travelling home for his white mice beside him. He was
eating a shilling bar of Cadbury's and getting smears of it all
down his shirt.

''lo, Cassie,' he said, his deep voice made even thicker with
chocolate. 'D'yer wanna see me pet mouse?'

'I don't mind.'

The tin was lined with bits of torn-up lavatory paper, and I
couldn't see more than a pink, worm-like tail.

'Asleep,' Conny explained. 'I got some babies at home. D'yer
want one?'

'No, Gran won't let me. She says they smell. Besides, I
wouldn't like a pet that doesn't live very long. Mice don't live
much longer than two years, do they?'

Conny looked at my drawing pad. 'What yer gonna draw?'

'I don't know yet.'

He stared at the blank sheet of paper very hard for a minute.
'Draw Margie.'

'Margie?'

'Yeah. Draw Margie on 'er bike.'

'I'm not very good at drawing people. And anyway, I can
hardly remember what she looked like now.' I tried, but his
peering over my shoulder and sucking chocolate next to my ear
made me nervous, and after a while I gave up.

'It don't matter,' said Conny cheerfully, ''cos I got loadsa
pictures of Margie what I cut from the papers.'

'Isn't that a bit morbid?'

'Whass that mean?'

'Well, you know; not very nice. Because Margie's dead and it's
not nice to keep thinking about it and cutting out her picture.'

'I fink it's nice.'

I shrugged. There was no reasoning with someone like Conny.

After a while, he said, 'You was there when they found 'er, weren't yer? You an' that Dawn. She was down the old well.'

'You knew the well was there?'

''Course! I bin an' looked down it.'

'I mean, you knew about it before Margie was found?'

'Yeah, 'course!' He looked surprised, as though I were the dim-witted one.

I couldn't help thinking about this later. They'd said few people knew about the well because Colonel Cartwright had covered it over with that concrete slab years ago.

But Conny knew.

And then we heard something which made us all feel that not only was the police investigation getting nowhere, but that perhaps Margie's killer would never be caught.

Sixteen-year-old Pamela Grundy, who lived at the bottom of Joshua Road, walked into Wickstead police station with her extremely nervous boyfriend to make a statement. A year before, Pamela's parents had forbidden her to see this lad, a trainee mechanic from Colchester and – according to Mrs Woodruff – 'not good enough' for their daughter. But she had defied them, and whenever the boy could wangle a day off work he would drive over to Grisham and take Pamela out.

Pamela had almost platinum blonde hair and was small for her age; Margie had been quite tall. Therefore it was possible that one could be mistaken for the other from a distance, which was exactly what had happened that Monday last October. Petey Scammel and the short-sighted Mrs Rabbs had seen Pamela getting into her boyfriend's green car, and because the couple had arranged to meet on the other side of the village, well away from the Grundy house, the two witnesses assumed the girl was Margie.

The reason Pamela hadn't come forward before was plain enough; she feared her parents' anger. And later, when Mr and Mrs Grundy accepted the boyfriend, she was far too frightened to go to the police, fully understanding she had allowed them to begin the investigation on a false trail.

So why had she come forward now, Gran wanted to know?

'She hoped Margie was still alive,' said Mrs Woodruff, who was a close friend of the Grundys. 'And as she knew the truth about the green car it seemed possible to her that Margie could simply have run away. It happens all the time, after all. But then when the child was found – well, she knew she had to go to the police. And I think it was brave of her, too, after all this time. That Inspector Washkansky read her the riot act, of course. But they've asked her parents not to punish her. I suppose they think she's had her punishment in one sense.'

At this point, Gran and Mrs Woodruff both glanced at me. But I was pretending to be engrossed in a book, and Mrs Woodruff went on in a whisper.

'Have you heard the latest? They say she was strangled, but not – you know – interfered with.'

'That's a mercy,' said Gran.

'And they say – I don't know how they can tell these things, mind you – they say she'd been lying somewhere for several hours before she was put down the well.'

I sensed another glance at me and I mouthed the words on the page in front of me.

'She's reading *Jane Eyre*,' said Gran proudly. 'Go on. What were you saying?'

'It's something to do with the blood and rigor mortis. And there were seeds sticking to her pullover. But it's a fact; she'd been lying in another part of the dell for some hours before. I can't understand why no one found her.'

'It's possible, I suppose,' said Gran. 'The children were all in school, and the only other people likely to go there are folks taking a short cut into Joshua Road, and they would have kept to the path.'

Another thing Mrs Woodruff couldn't understand was the description Petey had given of the man driving the green car. It might well have fitted a thousand average men, she said, but not a nineteen-year-old lad.

I couldn't keep quiet any longer. 'Petey Scammel? I wouldn't trust him to describe his own back door. He never gets anything right.'

'Cassie,' said Gran, 'take your book outside, there's a good girl.'

As I stood in the passage turning back the pages of my book to the place where I had stopped reading and started eavesdropping, I heard Mrs Woodruff say, 'Well, I still think it's someone local, someone Margie knew well. What's more, I don't believe she planned to go to school that morning, either. If she'd been in Old Mill Road at half-past eight to twenty up, someone must have seen her.'

'Someone local,' Gran repeated. 'And until he's caught no child is going to be safe. I'll be afraid to let Cassie out of my sight.'

I don't think I'd realised just how much responsibility Gran felt for me until that moment when I heard the anxiety and weariness in her voice. And it was no comfort to know that this time it wasn't actually my fault.

14

The first person I spotted in church was not Mrs Thoroughgood, her husband, or my gran, but Jack Knowles. He was standing just inside the door as we entered, looking uncomfortable in his black suit and the only tie I had ever seen him wear. He held his hat in both hands, as though it was more respectful that way, and fidgeted from one foot to the other. I tried to catch his eye and would have whispered, Why didn't he go and sit down, but although there were twenty-four of us entering in a crocodile Jack didn't appear to notice us.

We had assembled quietly in the school playground, dressed as far as possible in the dark skirts or trousers with white tops that Mr Riordan had suggested. Then, boy partnering girl, we moved slowly away from the school and down Laurel Road to the village church. I had hoped people would be at their gates to watch us pass – it would have been solemn and important, like the old soldiers at the cenotaph on Remembrance Sunday – but we saw no one. It wasn't until we arrived at the church that I realised why; they were all here. The entire village, whether they had known Margie or not, came and gathered in the churchyard.

As Margie's classmates, we had to sit immediately behind her family, and I felt a great satisfaction knowing all those other people were watching us. The rest of the class felt the same, I could tell. After all, Margie had been gone eleven months, and at our age that was a long time. It would have been different had the interval between the last time we saw her and now been a few weeks, I supposed. As it was, we sat down with an air of expectancy and alertness, as if we were going to be entertained. Most of Class Six had never been to a funeral service before.

Dawn and I had even discussed the possible condition of the

body. I thought it would have to be wrapped in a polythene sheet before they put it in the coffin because of the smell.

'No, they won't,' Dawn said knowledgeably. 'It'll be past the smelling stage by now. Bodies dry up, like meat. Then they don't smell any more.'

'Well, if it's all dried up, how come they could tell she was strangled but not had anything else done to her?'

'How should I know, stupid? I'm not a scientist.'

No one listening to Dawn would have believed she was the same girl who fainted in the dell that Saturday.

This afternoon was hot, so hot that we felt it even through the thick, ancient church walls. It seemed unnatural to feel hot in church, and perhaps it was that as much as the sight of the coffin which resulted in three girls having to be taken out. I turned to watch and saw Jack Knowles still standing at the back. Several people were forced to stand because there wasn't enough room, but there had been when our class entered, and I wondered again why Jack hadn't found a seat earlier. Many of the police, both uniformed and CID, were present, but I couldn't see the Jennings though I kept looking for them until Miss Game, the Sunday school teacher, nudged me and ordered me to sit still.

Father Steven had a lot to say that afternoon, much more than he usually did on Sundays, but at least he managed not to get sidetracked for a change. On it went, until I became aware of the surreptitious nail-biting, foot examinations and, in the case of Petey Scammel, nose-picking. Margie would have yawned.

I only looked at the coffin once; the first time I had seen a coffin close to, and it was strange to think that, in a way, Margie was here with us again. Mostly, I kept my eyes on Mrs Thoroughgood's back. Her husband had his arm around her, supporting her, though it didn't look to me as though she needed much support. She was very poised and dignified; 'brave', as Mrs Woodruff put it later. Even when the service was over and she followed the coffin, borne by Margie's four uncles, down the aisle she kept her head at a proud tilt.

We were supposed to assemble in the churchyard and wait until the hearse and limousine had gone on to the cemetery before we went to our homes. I was watching the people still filing out of church and having a little bet with myself that Gran would be last, as she usually was on such occasions. I felt a hand touch my shoulder, lightly, but enough to make me jump.

'Cassie, I'm sorry. I didn't mean to frighten you.'

I looked up at Mrs Thoroughgood. She had raised her black veil, which to me was shocking enough, but far worse was the beautiful, but sad smile she gave me.

'My dad sends his . . . his . . .' I couldn't think of the word I needed. 'He's really sorry he can't be here, Mrs Thoroughgood. He's gone abroad again, you see. But he sent some flowers . . .' Somehow that didn't seem quite the right thing to say.

'That was kind of him. You must write and thank him on my behalf. Cassie, will you come to tea with me as usual on Tuesday? I've missed you so much, dear.'

I was stunned. How could she be thinking of such a thing on the day of Margie's funeral? If I ever lost a child, I thought, I should want to shut myself away for weeks and not see anyone. At last I nodded, and she seemed relieved.

'That's a good girl. I knew *you* wouldn't let me down.'

Gran came out of the church just then and she wanted to know what Mrs Thoroughgood had said, so it wasn't until later I recalled the peculiar way she had stressed the word 'you'.

'She thanked us for the flowers,' I told Gran. 'And she said to write and thank Dad, too.'

After tea, Dawn and I walked past the cemetery. We didn't go in; Dawn said someone might see us and think we were being morbid, and I agreed, but we both knew we were really too frightened. Somehow the cemetery, which was fairly new and only had a dozen graves, was more frightening than the churchyard, full up as that was with centuries of death.

'I'm glad she wasn't buried in the churchyard,' I said, meaning that adult disapproval of anything translatable as 'morbid' would have deprived us of a favourite playground.

'I don't know.' Dawn peered through the cemetery fence at the colourful mound of roses. 'I think she would make a lovely ghost. I read about the ghost of a beautiful girl once. Her father flung her out of the house for getting pregnant and she died in the cold. Her ghost used to come back and knock on the kitchen door, pleading to be let in.'

'You made that up.'

144

'No, I didn't. It was local, too. Sometime in the eighteenth century.'

Wanting to change the subject, I said, 'How's your sister? Julie?'

'Okay. Why?'

'Well, she's pregnant, isn't she? Everybody knows that.'

'So what? How's your dad's friend? The fairy?'

'He's not a fairy. He's coming here again soon and he'll show you who's a bloody fairy when I tell him, so there. Just because everyone's talking about your rotten sister getting up the spout.' That wasn't true. Nobody dared say anything about Julie's pregnancy in case her fist-happy dad went after them.

'You mean everyone's talking about your father, Cassie Wade. They say he must be one of them. A pansy, like his mate.'

I stared at her. 'Liar! Bloody liar!'

'Am I? All right, you'll see.' She turned and walked away, humming to herself. I thought of picking up a stone and aiming it at her back, then decided against it. I knew Dawn; that was just what she wanted me to do. She specialised in goading people to fight so they'd get all the blame.

So I let her go, knowing this was the real break. The row we'd had before in the church porch had only been the start and things were never really the same between us, but this was the final split. Too much had been said on either side. In a way it was a relief; Dawn was so exhausting. She knew far too much for her age and insisted on trying to educate me in things I'd rather not have known about. And she asked me so much about Mrs Thoroughgood that I began to be afraid she would simply make up stories and spread them around as 'Cassie said's.

But I wasn't worried that she'd spread lies about Jeff. He had written to say his father was now very ill, and as soon as it was over and the old man respectably buried, Jeff would bring Olwyn to meet Gran and me. This was puzzling. Why on earth would Olwyn, who was probably sophisticated and worldly-wise, want to meet us? Or, indeed, we her? I didn't puzzle about it for very long, though. Providing Olwyn didn't resemble her brother too closely people would assume she was Jeff's girlfriend, and that would put an end to the gossip.

I went home feeling suddenly light and happy. I had Mrs Thoroughgood for a friend, and now it was all over I felt sure she

145

would begin to recover and take her place as a leading lady of village society once more; a good friend to have. It didn't yet occur to me that, for Mrs Thoroughgood, it was far from over. The question was no longer where? but who? and why?

I'd never seen Mrs Thoroughgood looking so beautiful before. Even her black mourning, which had contrasted so perfectly with her pale skin, couldn't match the kingfisher blue silk she wore that afternoon. I had to look closely at her face before I could tell she was wearing make-up, and that, I realised, was the secret: to apply the cosmetics so carefully that people thought you were quite natural. My mother could have learned from her.

'It's such a lovely day,' she said, guiding me through the house with her hands on my shoulders, 'so I thought we'd have tea in the garden. Would you like that, Cassie?'

'Yes, please.' Anything was better than having tea in Margie's room again. Yet I wondered, would that room feel different now? The last time I had been in there Margie was still a Missing Person. Now she was a murder victim and already buried. Surely the atmosphere in her room would be changed in some way?

I paused at the door, which was ajar, and peered in. Everything was as before; the portable typewriter, the dressing table set, the soft toys with Donkey Hoty in place of honour. It was still very much Margie's room, with a feeling of living and being lived in.

'I was there,' I said. 'You know, that day. Dawn and I went to the dell and we saw them.'

'I know. It must have been awful for you. Poor Cassie!'

'Dawn fainted.'

'But you were very brave.'

'I thought about you. That's why I didn't faint.'

Mrs Thoroughgood closed Margie's door. 'You're a good girl, Cassie.'

I remembered what she had said to me after the funeral service; *I knew you wouldn't let me down.*

'Go through into the garden, Cassie, I'll be with you in a minute.'

The last time I had seen her kitchen was when Margie took several of us in there for orangeade. But my Margie-connected thoughts were beginning to fade now. I no longer looked at things or scenes and thought, The last time I was here, Margie was still alive. Even in the garden, where Margie used to organise writing and drawing for the magazines we were always starting, I didn't automatically think of her. It was only when Mrs Thoroughgood came out with a tray of lemonade and sandwiches and said, 'I miss her poppies,' that I remembered. Margie had used to gather poppy seeds to sprinkle on the flower beds – much to her father's dismay – because she loved their colour. Now everything was neat and tidy. No books and crayons scattered on the lawn, all the plants and flowers at a precisely measured distance from each other, like soldiers on a parade ground, and not a weed among them.

'You like the sumachs, don't you, Cassie,' said Mrs Thorough-good, looking at the trees at the end of the garden. 'Margie did, too. Why do you like them?'

'The fruits. They remind me of Gran's best tablecloth; all vel-vety, and just the same colour.'

'Do you know why Margie liked them? She used to like pulling the fruits to pieces.'

She had a strange look on her face, like someone who had lost the thread of what they were saying right at the most important part.

'I can tell you things, Cassie,' she said after a moment. 'I can talk to you when it's impossible to talk to anyone else. And I can trust you, can't I?'

'Of course you can, Mrs Thoroughgood.'

'You see, I want to talk about Margie. I need to talk about her.'

I didn't understand. Wasn't that what we had been doing on our Tuesday tea dates? We spoke about other things, certainly, but the conversation – or rather, Mrs Thoroughgood's conver-sation – generally turned to Margie.

'But they won't let me,' she went on. 'All my so-called friends. All they can say is, We know, Rochelle; we know. But they don't know. How could they? Margie wasn't their child.

'She was never easy, you know. Even as a toddler she was strong-willed and quick-tempered. But I always tried to be patient with her. I used to tell myself that she was highly strung and forward for her age, so I seldom punished her, even when she was really naughty and destructive. I tried to reason with her when she was older, old enough to understand; but nine times

147

out of ten I failed, and Margie went her own pig-headed way as usual. I failed, Cassie.'

I didn't know what to say, or what she expected me to say. Talking about Margie with Mrs Thoroughgood normally consisted of exchanged anecdotes: all the funny things Margie had said and done, her tastes in clothes and music, her love of animals, her occasional impulsive acts of kindness toward the school's youngest children. Until today we had always discussed Margie's brighter side, and it made me uncomfortable to think Mrs Thoroughgood could ever admit to that darker one.

'She was always talking about you,' I said hurriedly. 'Boasting, even. She'd keep on with, My mother this and my mother that, until we – ' I stopped short. She was giving me an impatient, almost angry look.

'Now, let me ask you something, Cassie. Did you like Margie?'

'We-ell, she was okay.'

'That won't do, Cassie. Did you like her?'

I remembered how Margie had treated poor Conny, the names she once called Nana Bear, and so many other incidents. Dad had often said you shouldn't just look at a person's bad side, but take their good points into account as well; everyone had their light and dark sides, but if you only thought of the good then it would often outweigh the rest. Yet somehow I just couldn't apply that rule to Margie. She had shown a great deal of kindness toward the smaller children, but even at the time I'd had the feeling it was all an act, a show put on for the adults' benefit. Perhaps Dawn summed it up the best when, watching the blonde figure cartwheeling across the playground one day, she said, 'Margie Thoroughgood just doesn't give a shit.'

I looked down at my fingers. 'No,' I said, 'I didn't really like her.' It seemed an unbelievably wicked thing – to tell the mother of your dead classmate that you hadn't liked the girl. But it was the truth. 'Isn't it the same for everyone, though?' I said, desperate to atone for the offence. 'I mean, some people like me and others don't. Gran says you can't expect everyone to like you.'

'What about the teachers? Isn't it true that while Mr Riordan made a pet of Margie, Miss Saunders felt rather differently?'

I thought about this for some moments. Margie had never idolised Miss Saunders the way the rest of Class Six did. In the two years we had been in that teacher's charge, Margie had never made a contribution to her birthday posy or the little Christmas gift, or even brought something for Miss Saunders' wonderful nature table. When we had birthdays, Miss Saunders always gave a card in which she'd copied an appropriate verse of poetry. We'd all treasured these cards. All but Margie, who'd muttered careless thanks and tossed it into her satchel with hardly a glance. I remember asking her why, and she'd said, 'Because I don't want her thinking I'm screwy over her like the rest of you twerps, Cassie Wade.'

At the time, I thought she was merely jealous of Miss Saunders. Margie liked having a fuss made of her, she was as hooked on attention as if it were a drug, and so she couldn't bear it when someone else won all the affection. Now I began to wonder if our teacher had had Margie 'taped', as Gran would say, and if Margie knew this and resented her for it.

At the time of Margie's disappearance it had seemed to me that everyone loved her. The Girl Who Had Everything. And it was only now, after all these months, that I could see it wasn't true. Perhaps Conny Jennings was one of the few people who had seen both sides of Margie's nature and still loved her.

'Perhaps it's my fault she turned out the way she did,' said Mrs Thoroughgood. 'I was trying to erase my own childhood through her.' And when I looked up questioningly: 'My father was a drunk, Cassie. And my mother, who married beneath herself in the first place, gradually got so that she didn't care about feeding us, washing our clothes or cleaning the house. I did what I could, of course, but with four younger brothers and so little money . . .'

I looked at the kingfisher blue dress, the rings on her fingers, the expertly applied make-up, and I knew she was speaking the truth. Gran had once said something about Mrs Thoroughgood's younger days, when she 'didn't have two ha'pence to rub together'. Now she had some fine things in her house, and it was obvious she knew their value and treasured them.

'I never owned a doll,' she went on, 'let alone a book. And I was seldom well, even in the summer. So as soon as I was old enough I packed my bags and left before they dragged me even further down. I managed to trace my maternal grandparents to Wickstead, and they were good enough to support me while I finished my education.

'That's why I determined everything should be different for

Margie. She would be loved and cherished: a sunny-natured, outgoing little girl who was always healthy and lacked for nothing. Instead, I raised a wilful, scheming girl who thought everything came for nothing. She came close to breaking up my marriage. You see, Patrick – Mr Thoroughgood – could never understand that I found Margie so unmanageable. She behaved quite differently with him; he could get her to do anything. But with me – well, Margie and I often ended up screaming at each other.'

'I screamed at my mother the last time I stayed with her,' I said. It was the most comforting thing I could think of to say, but Mrs Thoroughgood went on as though she hadn't heard me.

'We had a row that morning, the morning she went missing. Patrick had allowed her to buy nylons to wear on special occasions, but she wanted to wear them to school. I told her to take them off and put her socks on, and she threw a tantrum. The last I saw of her was when she flounced out of the house and slammed the door. I guessed she planned to give school a miss, but I didn't follow her or phone Mr Riordan before because I couldn't bear another scene so soon after the first. So I let her go.

'I loved Margie more than anything. When you grow up, marry and have children of your own, you'll understand, Cassie. If my daughter had been twice as spoiled as she was, twice the worry and trouble, I would still have loved her more than anything. She was my only child, and the faults she had were the results of my inability to cope as a parent. If I could turn back the clock to that Monday, Cassie, do you know what I'd do? I'd run out of the front door and call her back. I'd tell her she could wear the stockings after all. It was such a little thing to fight about, Cassie. Such a little thing. But then she would have gone to school to show them off, and she would have been safe.' She took my hand in hers and smiled. 'Perhaps it's just as well people don't encourage me to talk about her. Then it's easier to remember her good moments; to hold on to the girl she might have been.'

I walked home feeling suddenly depressed. I was fond of Mrs Thoroughgood and flattered by her attentions, but I wished she hadn't told me so much. It was as if she expected something in return. Something I was unable to give her.

15

Memory must be one of the human brain's weaker spots, I thought, looking up at Wickstead High School for the first time since February. Hadn't it seemed to be made all of windows then? And wasn't it much bigger?

Sylvia Tanner and I walked in together. Sylvia was my new best friend, for the simple reason that she had never liked Dawn, and we planned to present a united front at the new school. We looked smarter than we might have supposed in our grey uniforms and were actually quite proud of them, but one thing spoiled it for me. There was a choice of headgear: a beret, known by the girls as a 'pancake', or the St Trinian's-style hat called a 'pisspot'. Sylvia wore a beret – they were cheaper – but Gran had decided I looked the part in a pisspot. It was spoiled because I wanted Sylvia and me to look alike.

We had brand new satchels, large and stiff, which smelled horribly and were as yet empty but for our equally new pencil cases. Sylvia's, she being bone idle, was destined to remain empty, while it was only a matter of days before mine became a mobile rubbish tip. I had my hand in my blazer pocket, clutching the five shillings dinner money, threepence bus fare home and sixpence for sweets. Already I was wondering whether it would be worth my while to tell the teacher I had a packed lunch so I could keep the five shillings for comics.

I didn't see Dawn until we were in the assembly hall, and even then she pretended not to notice me. We had to sit on the floor – only sixth form prefects and teachers had chairs – and because the floor was stone it struck our bottoms cold and uncomfortable. The hall was also used as a dining-room, and above the serving hatches I noticed five wooden shelves bearing the names of long-dead Prime Ministers: Gladstone, Disraeli, Palmerston, Lloyd-George and Melbourne. Three of the shelves held trophies and shields, and I thought how marvellous it must be to win a cup for your house and have it up there on display.

In a while the headmistress, Mrs Barker, came on to the platform and we had to stand and sing 'He Who Would Valiant Be'. I sang loudly. Here I was at the senior school at last; part of it and proud to be so. I felt grown up and powerful. At four o'clock I would step off the bus and walk through Grisham in my new uniform and I would disdain to look at the babies still at the County Primary.

The great feeling was spoiled slightly when, sitting once more, we listened to Mrs Barker's Start-of-Term address.

'And I hope you will try to make these youngsters feel welcome.' Youngsters. She meant us. Then, echoing the words of Dawn's great aunt, 'I hope you'll remember, too, how hard it is to come from being top class at a small school to being the very youngest at a school the size of this one. Our new first years are always special and I would not normally single out one group. But as you all know, the children from Upper Grisham have had to face a sad and unpleasant ordeal in the past months.' She looked down at the front rows, her eyes magnified comically behind thick-lensed glasses. 'And so I'm going to break an old rule of mine. Upper Grisham, we're glad to have you here as part of our school. We hope it won't be long before you feel a part of us.'

We tried to look gratified, but as she had no idea which of us were from Grisham it hardly mattered.

After the traditional assembly, Mrs Barker read out the class lists, adding to each girl's name the house she would be joining. I looked up at the trophy shelves and prayed, Please don't let it be Melbourne or Lloyd-George. Those were the two with no awards at all.

We fidgeted a lot while the first list was read. This was 1A, the top stream, and no one from our village entertained serious hopes of getting into it, though we all agreed Carol had a chance of 'moving up' if she worked hard. The coloured girl sitting in front of me rose when Mrs Barker read out, 'Jennifer Unwin. Palmerston House,' and I was so busy staring at her frizzy hair and wondering how on earth she managed to get a comb through it, that I didn't hear what the headmistress said next. Sylvia nudged me.

'That's you, you nana!'

'Cassie Wade?' Mrs Barker peered around short-sightedly. 'Disraeli House, Cassie. And don't look so worried, dear.'

I tried to smile at her, but my lips trembled and it must have looked as though I were about to cry. Crying, in fact, was the last thing on my mind. The top stream and Disraeli House – it had so many trophies and shields that it was a wonder the shelf didn't collapse. I couldn't wait to tell Gran. She'd be so proud, and perhaps it would cheer her up so she would lose that tired look I'd noticed so much lately. I would be learning French now, and maybe I could even teach Gran. And I would study real science – not just growing silly little bean sprouts and crystals – and she'd be amazed at my knowledge.

With my head full of plans and daydreams I managed to follow the coloured girl out of the hall without a backward look at Sylvia or Dawn, or even wondering what class they'd been put in.

For the first few days at Wickstead High School our natural tendency was to seek out friends from our old schools at morning and lunch breaks and gather together in tight little groups. Then someone would say something like, 'That red-haired girl from Defford collects stamps too,' or 'The girl with the pony tail is a fan of Cliff Richard.' So we began to mix, and by the second week I found myself drifting further away from my old friends of Class Six.

Sylvia Tanner was in the next stream down, where most of the Grisham girls were placed, and Dawn in the one below that. We took different subjects now. I had French and Civics while they had cookery lessons. We grew further apart, and soon, when we passed each other in the corridors, we barely exchanged a nod of recognition. I never saw the infamous Myrtle Baines. Perhaps she had left school or been expelled. Or perhaps my memory was at fault again and the girl I remembered from February was quite different. At any rate, I no longer had my old fear of our paths crossing. I began to see Dawn in a new light, too. She smoked in the lavatories, was disruptive in her class, and had soon clocked up more detentions than any other girl in the first year. I found it hard to believe she had once been my best friend, or that I had ever liked her.

I should have been happy. The new subjects were easy and enjoyable, the teachers pleasant, the girls in my class friendly. The captain of Disraeli House made me first-year representative, which involved keeping an eye out for potential house champions on the sports field and reporting general trouble-makers – who could then be conveniently dumped on Melbourne with the excuse of 'balancing numbers'. I should have been happy. But there were too many shadows.

Gran worried me a lot. She had lost all her old energy, and sometimes even had difficulty getting to the village shop and back. I planned to discuss it with Dad as soon as he came home next time. Then there were the letters my mother had taken to writing once or twice a week. She was going to see a lawyer about getting custody of me. Gran wasn't getting any younger, she pointed out, and Dad, with his dubious Welsh friend, was hardly a fit parent.

And there was Mrs Thoroughgood. I still kept up my Tuesday visits, but it was no longer an occasion I looked forward to. Her behaviour was strange – she often forgot what she had been saying and stared out of the window – and she had become possessive of me. We talked a lot about my new school, but never Margie any more; and when I managed to peek into Margie's room I saw that the pretty bed had been stripped. Now the weather had turned quite cold she made me wear the red dress again. It became an important ritual to her, and I wondered what would happen when I grew too big for it to fit me.

Then one day I came home to find Gran lying on the bed, housework neglected for once and the smell of vomit in the room.

'Oh, Cassie! I think I'm dying!' she groaned, and I felt the back of my neck prickling hot with fear.

'Gran! What's the matter? Oh, if only you'd gone to the doctor when I told you!' I'd suggested this many times, and she – typically – had obstinately refused. Now it was plain there was something radically wrong and, terrified she was having a heart attack, I asked if there was any pain.

'No pain. I just feel awful. And I've been sick. Cassie, I think you'd better run and fetch Mrs Woodruff, there's a good girl.'

I made our neighbour telephone for the doctor before bringing her back and I think Gran was secretly relieved, although – again, typically – she said, 'You oughtn't to have troubled the doctor, Cassie. He's a busy man.'

'It's what he's paid for,' Mrs Woodruff told her. 'Cassie's perfectly right and sensible. Now, just try to rest, Mrs Wade. He'll be here directly.' She took Gran's hand and appeared to be checking her pulse. I doubted she actually knew how to do this, but supposed it all went to aid Gran's peace of mind. 'And while we wait for him Cassie can go downstairs and get her tea.'

'I want to stay with Gran.'

'No, you go and get yourself something to eat,' Gran said. 'I'll be all right with Mrs Woodruff.' She stuffed her handkerchief to her mouth, retching.

I ran downstairs to wait for the doctor, but I didn't eat anything; I couldn't. I wanted Dad, Mrs Thoroughgood, or even my mother to be here with me. Gran had hardly ever been ill in her life, and certainly I'd never known her to have anything more serious than a winter sniffle. So it came as a shock to think she was really ill, or worse, that she could be dying. How many times I'd heard her say, 'You won't always have your old Gran to look after you, you know.' And until now they'd been only words, just another of her pet sayings.

Our family doctor was a giant of a man with the encouraging name of Savage. We never saw him without his waistcoat and jacket, whatever the time of year, and he always smelled of tobacco, even his hands, which was particularly noticeable when he had to examine you. He could never remember children's names – he always called me Elaine – and if the television was on when he came to your house he would march in and switch it off, as if he didn't think you were well-mannered enough to switch it off yourself.

'Now then, Elaine,' he boomed before the door had closed behind him. 'What seems to be the trouble with your auntie?'

'My gran, Doctor.' I gabbled out a brief explanation and was about to lead him up to her room when he marched on ahead.

'Don't worry, dear,' he called back over his massive shoulder. 'Probably she's eaten something that didn't agree with her. We'll soon have her as right as ninepence.'

I went back to the kitchen, crumbled some breadcrumbs on to a plate and stuck the butter knife in the jam pot so it would look as though I'd had my tea. From upstairs came the interrogative rise and fall of Dr Savage's voice, and occasionally his lumbering footsteps as, I assumed, he moved around the bed examining Gran. Perhaps it was something she'd eaten, after all; one of Jack Knowles' meat pies, or the crab apple jelly Mrs Woodruff had given her.

But when Dr Savage came downstairs again he looked less confident.

'It seems your grandmother has been feeling poorly for some time and not told anyone,' he said, sitting uninvited at the table.

'It's not her heart, is it?'

'No. Her heart is pretty sound, I'm glad to say. Now, what I think we'd better do is have her in hospital straight away for observation. I have an idea – ' He broke off, realising he was dealing with a child. 'I'll arrange for blood tests in the morning, and they should tell us more. The question is, young Elaine, what are we going to do with you?'

'Cassie,' I reminded him. 'My name's Cassie.'

'Ah, yes. Cassie. Of course. I'm sorry. Well, you can't stay here on your own, can you? I hear your dad's away in Malta or Cyprus, or some such place. So, what are we going to do with you? Eh?'

'There's my mother,' I admitted reluctantly. 'She lives in Willingswell, just outside Ipswich. I'll have to go and stay with her, I suppose.'

'There's no need to make it sound like a prison sentence, dear. I'm sure you'll be well looked after while your gran is in hospital.'

'Will she have to stay in long?'

Dr Savage rose. He didn't like too many questions, especially when they came from females and those under the age of twenty-one.

'I can't tell you that, I'm afraid. But let's hope not. Now, I'll go and see what I can do about getting her a bed. Is your mother on the telephone?'

'Yes.' I tore the address and phone number from the top of one of her letters and gave it to him.

'And can she get herself here this afternoon?'

'I suppose so.'

'All right, Elaine. I'll have her contacted straight away. And don't you worry. I'm sure everything will be fine.'

He let himself out of the front door and I watched him away, humming to himself as though he was glad to have discharged a troublesome duty.

But what would I do if anything happened to Gran? I couldn't bear to live with my mother and have to begin again at a new school. Yet as Dad's job was so closely connected with the army I feared he might not be able to just drop everything and come home, so going to my mother's seemed the only realistic course.

I went upstairs and sat beside Gran. She looked so pale and bewildered; like me, she had taken her good health for granted. I tried to be adult about it.

'Dr Savage says he's going to have them do some blood tests in the morning,' I said. 'So perhaps it's nothing very serious.'

'I'm thinking about you.' Gran touched my hand. 'You'll have to go to your mother, Cassie.'

'I know. But it's all right, Gran, I don't mind. Really I don't, It won't be for very long, after all, and then everything'll be back to normal.'

'There's your schooling, too. I don't like to think of your missing too much and I can't see your mother driving you there and picking you up every day. It's a long way from Willingswell and I don't want you travelling alone on the bus. If I have to stay in hospital for several weeks you'll have to go to a school in Ipswich, I suppose.'

'Must I?' A new school, even on a temporary basis, was a horrible prospect. 'Gran, couldn't I just take my books with me? Then I'd keep up with what the others in my class are doing.'

'I don't think the authorities would allow it, Cassie. No, we'll just have to wait and see what happens. Look, Jack Knowles will be here soon with the van. I want you to cancel our regular order until further notice, and tell him I'd be grateful if he'd come in and turn off the water, gas and electricity – '

'I can do that, Gran,'

'No, you don't know where they are. Besides, the gas tap is so stiff you'd never manage it. Then you'll have to leave a note for the milkman. Write, "No milk until further notice, thank you", and put it in the empty bottle. Mrs Woodruff is packing a bag for me, but you'll have to get your mother to pack yours. Be sure to close all the windows, lock and bolt the back door. Lock the front when you leave and give the key to your mother. Can you remember all that, Cassie?'

157

'Get Jack to turn everything off, milkman, doors, windows, key. Yes, Gran.' I began to cry. I didn't want to be adult any more.

'Now, then! Stop that grizzling.' Gran reached for her handkerchief and held it to her mouth, shaking her head at me. Unable to finish the verbal admonishment, she pointed to the door, dipping her index finger sharply to indicate I was to go downstairs. But when I got to the landing she called me back, gulping against the rising vomit.

'I've been in hospital before, Cassie. When I had your father, and that damn near killed me. I'm not worried, so there's no need for you to be. Off you go now and wait for Jack.'

I passed Mrs Woodruff in the passageway and any courage Gran might have given me was undermined by her lugubrious tones. 'You'll have to be a brave girl now, Cassie,' she said. 'Old age and illness are facts of life, you know.' For a moment, I quite expected her to add some morbid quotation, such as, We are suddenly cut down like the grass. But even Mrs Woodruff wouldn't go that far.

Jack was more optimistic. As soon as I'd passed on Gran's request he locked his van and followed me back into the house, looking brisk and businesslike.

'I shouldn't worry,' he said cheerfully. 'It's probably just that she's run down. A bit anaemic, maybe; or diabetic. It happens a lot with older folk, but nothing to get alarmed about, Cassie. Now, do you think I ought to make a pot of tea before we turn off the gas? Perhaps your gran could manage a cup before the ambulance gets here.'

I sat down, letting him get on with it and thinking how peculiar it was to see him in our house. Somehow he looked much taller in his van, but I noticed for the first time how large his hands were. Not only large, but ugly, with knobbly knuckles, nicotine stains and hairs on the back of his fingers. They would have been sinister hands were they less clumsy.

'Jack,' I said when he had made the tea. 'If she's only run down or anaemic, why was the doctor in such a hurry to get her into hospital? Why couldn't he have waited till tomorrow?'

'Well, I suppose he wanted to be sure of her getting a bed.'

That sounded a rather feeble reason to me, but I hardly had the chance to start worrying again because Jack began inching his chair toward mine. I knew he was only trying to be chummy and confidential, but I still didn't like it, and to distract him I said, 'She's been feeling tired for ages. Ever since we went to Southend for the day. When we got home there was a crowd of men in the road pestering Sergeant Jordan, and Gran had a row with Cyril Jennings. It was an awful row and I thought Cyril was going to hit her. She looked really ill after that.'

Jack stopped fidgeting with his chair and stared at me. 'Cyril? What did they row about?'

'Well, he kept making hints about Dad; where he was on the day Margie went missing and that sort of thing. So Gran said he ought to look to his own before he started accusing other people. She meant Conny, you see, and Cyril got really mad. People were saying things about him when Margie first disappeared. Only he can't have had anything to do with it because he was helping you load vegetables on the van that morning, wasn't he, Jack?' Jack didn't answer, so I said, 'He was with you, wasn't he?'

'Yes. Yes, he was with me all right. Besides, you know Conny wouldn't hurt a fly. Not deliberately, anyhow. I'm not surprised Cyril was mad at your gran, Cassie. He's got a temper where that boy's concerned. Perhaps he's ashamed.'

'Well, I never thought he was proud of him,' I said, remembering how Cyril used to hit his son. 'But if he's ashamed – well, why does he lose his temper in defending him?'

'He's defending himself, Cassie.'

That didn't really make sense to me. But I didn't want to ask any more questions because I knew Jack was some sort of relation to the Jennings.

Gran, helped by Mrs Woodruff, came into the room and Jack set about turning everything off. He placed a tray in the fridge to catch the drips and was kind enough to store our frozen foods in his own freezer on the van. While he was busy, I took the opportunity to ask a favour of Mrs Woodruff.

'Could you let me telephone Mrs Thoroughgood from your house, please? I go to tea with her sometimes, you see, and she'll be worried if I don't turn up.'

'Of course you can, Cassie. As soon as the ambulance has taken your gran to hospital we'll give her a ring.' Mrs Woodruff had changed her opinion of me since she heard I was in the top stream at school. Poor Colin had failed his eleven-plus and now his mother liked to hold me up as an example to him. She couldn't do enough for me these days, and I tried to feel grateful.

The two ambulance men insisted that Gran let herself be carried on the stretcher, even though she said she could walk. 'I'm not dead yet,' she muttered, but gave in gracefully.

My last view of her was her hand feebly waving to me as they carried her into the ambulance. I was tearful, and trembled to think I might never see her again. And Mrs Woodruff ended up having to call Mrs Thoroughgood for me because she was afraid I would start crying and upset her.

We waited in the Best Room, Mrs Woodruff having a surreptitious look around while Jack tried to amuse me with awful jokes. Then my mother arrived, flustered and ill-tempered, and Jack made a hasty exit through the back door; those two had never liked each other.

'Poor Cassie!' my mother gushed. My nose was heading for collision with that brooch of hers as she flung her arms around me, and I braced myself. 'Poor child. All tensed up, and no wonder!' She went on complaining over my head to Mrs Woodruff: this was a fine state of affairs, but really no more than one could expect when a certain person left his family while he gallivanted across Europe. I thought it amazing that my mother, of all people, could make such an accusation, and I pushed her away angrily to defend Dad.

'He's not gallivanting. It's his job, and it's a very important job.'

'Yes, so damned important that any fool could do it.' She sat in the best armchair, primly smoothing her skirt. 'Well, don't just stand there, Cassie. Go and pack. Don't forget your underclothes and socks – and *don't* bring anything that isn't absolutely necessary. I don't know! What a time for this to happen! I'll have to cancel several appointments, not to mention a special weekend break.' As if Gran had deliberately become ill to spoil her plans.

I packed slowly, just to annoy her. Gran could be dying, and all she could think about was the inconvenience to herself.

And then I heard Mrs Thoroughgood's voice downstairs.

'Hello, Isabel. I came to see if there's anything I can do.'

'It's kind of you, Rochelle,' my mother answered, 'but everything's been arranged. Cassie! Will you hurry yourself up!'

I clattered down the stairs with my case. Mrs Thoroughgood

and my mother had known each other well a few years ago, and I had a vague memory of playing in a sandpit with Margie when we were both very small. But it was odd to see them together now, and I had the feeling that if they had met under different circumstances they would have had nothing to say to one another.

Mrs Thoroughgood was sympathetic and did all she could to reassure me, which didn't help my mother's patience.

'Yes, well, we'd better be going now, Cassie, or the shops will be shut and we'll have no dinner. I'll have to get some more food in tomorrow. What a nuisance this is!'

Mrs Thoroughgood repeated her offer of help, and my mother snapped at her. 'If you can keep several business appointments in my place next week then, yes, you can help.' The sarcastic tone was unmistakable.

'So it really is quite inconvenient to have Cassie staying with you at the moment?'

'That is an understatement, Rochelle.'

'She could stay with me if you like. There's plenty of room at Allgoods. Patrick would enjoy having her, and so would I.'

My mother looked at me eagerly. 'Yes, it's the perfect solution really. She wouldn't have to miss any schooling then. I'm sure I'd never have time to drive her there and back every day. But are you sure it wouldn't be too much trouble for you?'

'Not at all, Isabel. Cassie is good company.'

'What do you say then, Cassie? Would you like to stay with Mrs Thoroughgood?'

I nodded enthusiastically – not that I'd have dared say no after that. 'Yes, please.'

My mother's attitude changed immediately. She became tearful – probably with relief – and for the first time since I was five years old she invited me to sit on her lap. I felt slightly ridiculous, especially with Mrs Thoroughgood looking on. I was too old, too lanky and angular to make sitting on laps a very dignified or comfortable thing.

'Now, Cassie darling, you're not to worry about your gran. It's probably nothing very serious at all. Old people get these ailments from time to time. I'll make sure your father knows what's happened, and he'll come straight home, no doubt. So you be a good girl for Mr and Mrs Thoroughgood in the mean time and I'll keep in touch. I really would have loved to have you with me, Cassie, and so would Ray, but it's so difficult at the moment. Maybe we can arrange something before Christmas. Now, let's get your case and I'll drive you both to Allgoods.'

She gaily dropped Gran's front door key into Mrs Thoroughgood's hand, as if disposing of me at the same time. Mrs Thoroughgood smiled at me.

Why had I accepted her suggestion so eagerly? Actually living at Allgoods would be very different from spending an hour or two there in her company every week. Already I was beginning to feel I had made a mistake.

16

There had been a time when I thought I could never refuse Mrs Thoroughgood anything. She was such a beautiful, sad figure to my mind, and she had been so good to me that I believed no request of hers could ever be too much for me. But not this. Anything but this. Yet when I tried to explain how I felt, all that came out was a pleading, whining, 'No, Mrs Thoroughgood! No!'

'But Cassie, I thought you'd like it. I have lovely new blue sheets in the airing cupboard, all ready for you. And it's such a pretty room; it gets all the morning sun.'

'No!' I repeated. 'I'll sleep on the sofa, or even the floor, but please – not Margie's room!'

'All right, Cassie.' She made an impatient gesture with her hands, which reminded me of my mother. 'I'll make up the bed in the guest room. But it's cramped in there and nowhere near so pretty.'

'I don't mind.'

'It would have been lovely to see that room used again. Can't you tell me why, Cassie?'

Tell her why? I wouldn't have known where to start. The main reason was my fear of being alone there in the dark; I was afraid I'd feel Margie's presence once the light was out and Mr and Mrs Thoroughgood sound asleep upstairs. And somehow it would seem an act of disloyalty to Dad and Gran to sleep in Margie's room; perhaps because of what Mr Thoroughgood had once said about his wife wanting 'a substitute'.

'It's Margie's room,' I said, 'and it wouldn't feel right.'

She nodded. 'That's all right, Cassie. I understand.'

'Where's your husband? I thought he would be home by now?'

'Oh, didn't I tell you? He's away, visiting his mother.'

So Mr Thoroughgood didn't know I was here. She would have allowed her husband to come home and find me using Margie's room, when once she had been terrified he would see me in the red dress and made me stay out of sight.

'Shouldn't we have asked him if I can stay?'

'Of course not. He won't mind at all. Trust me, Cassie. Patrick will love having you here. I'll have to show you how he likes his whisky and soda, and how to put tobacco in his pipe. He loves being waited on when he comes home from work, and that will be a nice surprise for him.'

Did I really remember, or only think I remembered, Margie once saying she used to pour her father's drink and fill his pipe when he came home of an evening?

Before I went to bed in the spare room, Mrs Thoroughgood telephoned the hospital. Gran was comfortable, had stopped feeling sick and was settled down for the night; but she was very weak and tired. The hospital would start tests in the morning, but in the mean time, where could they reach the next of kin? Mrs Thoroughgood handed me the receiver.

'I'm not sure where my dad is right now,' I said. 'Gran can tell you how to get in touch with the CSE, but my mother's already promised to see to that. Is Gran very ill? When can I see her?'

'No children allowed, I'm afraid.'

So I couldn't even visit her. A terrible thought struck me – that the last time I saw her, bravely waving from the stretcher, really would be the last time ever. Then supposing no one told her children were not allowed to visit? She would die thinking I hadn't been bothered.

As soon as Mrs Thoroughgood closed the bedroom door, I began to cry into the brand new blue pillowcase.

Dad used to say troubles are lighter after a night's sleep, and although I knew this wasn't always true for me, I really did feel much better in the morning. Mrs Thoroughgood looked so lovely in her navy blue dress, which she had covered at the front with a white apron, her hair simply pinned back; so lovely that I got a peculiar, achey feeling in my chest as I watched her move about the kitchen. She was singing softly as she prepared the scrambled eggs and bacon – an aria from one of the operas she loved and had often played for me.

And every minute or so she turned to smile at me, and once again I felt I would do anything for her.

We had fresh orange juice with our breakfast, which was a novelty for me, and she made the toast exactly the way I liked it: very dark brown and spread thick with unsalted butter. While I ate, she read out one or two interesting little news items from the morning paper.

'You should always take an interest in what's going on in the world, Cassie,' she said, and of course I listened dutifully, to please her.

So the first few days with Mrs Thoroughgood passed well. She enjoyed cooking dainty little meals for the two of us, helping with my homework, and deciding which television programmes we should watch. Every morning we telephoned the hospital, and every evening I wondered again why Dad hadn't been in touch.

On the fourth day the hospital had some news for us: Gran was suffering from pernicious anaemia.

'Will she die?' I asked Mrs Thoroughgood, who had been on the phone for some time while I hovered anxiously in the doorway.

'No, Cassie, she won't die. A few years ago she might well have done, but it can be treated today and she'll be able to lead a quite normal life. She'll probably have to stay in hospital for some weeks until they're sure it's under control, though.'

I felt hot prickles of fear on the back of my neck. 'Weeks? But will she really be all right? What else did they tell you?'

'She'll have to have regular injections, Cassie. The district nurse will come to do it once a fortnight, or perhaps once a month. You see, her body is unable to absorb a certain vitamin – Vitamin B12 – the way we do, in food. So she'll be given it through these injections.'

'Like when someone has diabetes?'

'Very similar. Now, let's get you ready for school, Cassie. You don't have to worry about a thing now. And I'll see a message is sent to your father to ease his mind too. The ward sister told me your gran is anxious he shouldn't come home now that she's feeling so much better.'

That was typical of my gran, and at last I allowed myself to believe she would be well again.

But they still wouldn't let me see her.

Like Margie, Mrs Thoroughgood was used to getting her own way. And I soon came to realise it wasn't so much a Margie-substitute she wanted, as her husband had once claimed, but a second chance to erase her own miserable childhood – this time through me. Patrick Thoroughgood was still away, which left me exclusively in her care outside of school hours.

She was kind and considerate at first. One day she even managed to sneak me far enough inside the hospital to wave to Gran from the ward door, while she delivered a letter from me and the chrysanths we had cut fresh from the garden. It cheered Gran to see me, and I think she was happier knowing I was with Mrs Thoroughgood rather than my mother, who she believed was trying to turn me against Dad.

Yet although Mrs Thoroughgood was so kind, I felt uneasy with her. She gave up trying to persuade me to sleep in Margie's room after a while, but then she began moving things from that room into mine and encouraging me to use them. First came the typewriter, which I couldn't resist playing with. Then the transistor radio – complete with new battery and new earphone – and the soft toys, including Donkey Hoty. Finally, the dressing-table set. But much as I admired that silver-backed hairbrush engraved with dancing girls and its matching hand mirror, I could never bring myself to use them.

She tried to arouse my interest in Margie's hobbies; or rather, the hobbies she would have liked Margie to have. I was presented with a stamp album, and all the embroidery and tapestry sets that were unwanted, untouched Christmas presents. So I had to spend hours fiddling with foreign stamps, flimsy hinges, and skeins of silk and wool, just to please her.

Then came the clothes. Not just the red dress, but the best of everything in Margie's wardrobe which fitted me. Fortunately, I had grown so tall that these were all the very newest, and the dresses I remembered Margie wearing at school remained in her wardrobe.

'It would be a crime to waste them,' said Mrs Thoroughgood, presenting me with a white pullover and wine-coloured corduroy slacks. 'Patrick wanted to burn them, but I said no. I intended to give them to the charity shop in Wickstead eventually. But even now I can't bear the thought of a strange child wearing them.' She massaged her forehead with her fingertips, as if to get her thoughts in order.

Then, without warning, she grabbed my shoulders so hard that it hurt and reminded me of the afternoon last year in the playground when the Animal Defenders badge had been found.

'Cassie, promise me you'll always go straight to school – and come straight home? Promise me you'll never speak to strangers or go off with anyone, for whatever reason – even if you know them well.'

'I promise,' I said automatically. I'd had all this before, from Gran, Dad, Jeff and my mother – not to mention various teachers and our neighbours.

'And that if you go to play with your friends you'll always let me know where you are and what time you'll be back?'

I nodded, but it wasn't enough for Mrs Thoroughgood. She dug her fingernails into my shoulders so hard that I cried out. 'Yes, Mrs Thoroughgood! I promise, I promise!'

'Good girl. You must understand that you're my responsibility now, Cassie. I didn't mean to hurt you just then. It's because I want you to remember what I've asked of you, and that you'll keep your promise. Always.'

I assured her that I would with all the sincerity I could put into my voice. And I really did mean to keep that promise.

There was one afternoon that will always stay in my mind. It was a Saturday, the last really warm day we were to have that year, and Mrs Thoroughgood and I were sitting in the back garden. I had on the wine-coloured corduroy slacks and a white blouse she had bought for me that morning. In my hair I wore one of Margie's distinctive slides, the red one, shaped like a dragon-fly. We both had books on our laps, although neither of us was reading. It was what Mrs Thoroughgood liked to call a 'silence between friends'.

She stretched her legs, clasped her fingers behind her head and smiled at me. 'How's school, Cassie?'

'Great. Jennifer Unwin, that coloured girl I told you about, she's my best friend now.'

'Why do you like her especially?'

'I don't know. Because she makes me laugh. After gym she brushes her hair with a plastic brush, and it's all tight, wiry curls, so the sound puts your teeth on edge. She does it on purpose, but it makes me laugh.'

'You must invite her to tea one day. I'd love to meet her. And how's the French coming along?'

I pulled a face. We were taught from dull, repetitive little books similar to the *Dick and Dora* series of our first year at the junior school; except these featured a small French boy named Toto, who spent most of his time opening and closing doors and asking for more milk, *s'il vous plaît*.

'Never mind,' said Mrs Thoroughgood. 'You'll begin German next year, and I think you'll find that much easier. Do you like poetry, Cassie?'

I was going to say yes, but then I thought she might ask me to recite some, so I told her, 'No, not really.'

'Oh, that's a shame. I used to love it when I was your age. Housman, Emily Dickinson, Emily Brontë ...' I must have looked bored or something, because she stopped, smiling apologetically. 'I think the attitude of some teachers can put a child off poetry for life. So often a youngster is expected to go straight from *A child's garden of verses* to learning Wordsworth by heart.'

'I know. Miss Saunders made us learn that stupid thing about the daffodils. I hated it. My dad quite likes poetry.' Anxious to please her, I tried to remember a verse – any verse.

Mrs Thoroughgood was sitting with her back to the fence and didn't see Conny Jennings peering over. He was eating something made grubby from his hands, and I could only tell it was a doughnut when the jam spurted out and trickled down his chin. I thought he would speak or wave to me as usual, but he went on slowly eating, watching me all the time as though he didn't recognise me there in the Thoroughgoods' garden.

'I know,' I said. 'What's that one that goes:

'While I nodded, nearly napping, suddenly there came a tapping,
    As of someone gently rapping ...

'I can't remember any more.'

Mrs Thoroughgood finished the verse for me.

'... rapping at my chamber door,
"'Tis some visitor," I muttered, "tapping at my chamber door –
    Only this, and nothing more."

'That's "The raven", by Edgar Allan Poe, Cassie. Why do you like it?'

'I don't really know.' I had recited the two lines parrot-fashion, as most children reciting poetry will do; but Mrs Thoroughgood wasn't satisfied with my answer.

'Cassie, there's always a reason for liking – or disliking – anything. It's not good enough to say, Yes, I like it, but I don't know why. People will think you walk around with your eyes and ears half closed.'

'We-ell,' I said, aware that she was waiting – and that Conny was watching me with such admiration that I longed to show off. 'It's got a good rhythm in most parts. And there's a sort of – atmosphere. When he describes the bird,' – I remembered Dad once reading it to Gran – 'it's just as though you can hear the wings fluttering.'

'Good, Cassie. That's very good.' She began to recite the whole piece in her clear, cultured voice; but where her tones were normally light, she darkened them so that I shivered. I was impressed by her dramatic sense and her memory – she didn't falter once – and admired her more than ever.

Conny was listening too; his mouth open, the jam still trickling down his chin, the doughnut clasped very tightly in one grubby hand. I thought his face had turned pale, but it was hard to tell under all that grime.

> *'Take thy beak from out my heart, and take thy form from off my*
>   *door,*
> *Quoth the raven, "Nevermore."'*

Perhaps it was just as well that Cyril Jennings came along then and clipped his son around the ear, or Conny might have had one of his 'accidents' – the usual result of his being frightened. Conny couldn't possibly have understood the poem, of course, but I thought individual words and phrases, as well as Mrs Thoroughgood's voice, might have upset him. Conny was sensitive to that sort of thing.

The sound of hand striking head startled Mrs Thoroughgood and she turned around. 'You'll hit that boy once too often.'

'Got to keep him under control, ain't I? Got to keep him in check. I told him I wanted help with those brambles in the churchyard this afternoon – got to have the place ready for Remembrance Sunday – and here he is, prancing around like Joe Soap. You get moving, boy. D'you hear?'

Conny heard and went on his way, wiping his hands on the shiny seat of his trousers.

'It may be necessary to keep him in check, as you put it,' said Mrs Thoroughgood, 'but I don't think beating him around the head is the best way to do it.'

'You people just don't understand,' Cyril whined. 'I've reared that boy alone all these years, and I know what he's like. There's no reasoning with him. You can't sit down and explain things. You can't tell him to stop doing something that's wrong; it'll just go in one ear and out the other. The only way to make anything sink in is to send it through that thick skull of his with a clout.'

Mrs Thoroughgood still looked disapproving. For his part, Cyril refused to meet her eye and addressed himself mostly to me.

'And he's strong, that boy o' mine. Twice as strong as I am. Only he don't fully know his own strength, that's the trouble. And that's why I've got to show him who's boss. The minute I let him get the upper hand – ' He covered his mouth to hide a burp, which told us where he had just come from and why he was in a fairly good humour. Still, I thought I had never seen Cyril looking so ugly before. His beak of a nose was red and shiny, and his small round eyes, almost amber, reminded me of the knobs on Gran's knitting needles.

Mrs Thoroughgood rose. 'Yes, well, we'll leave you to get on with your work, Mr Jennings. Come along, Cassie.'

We began walking across the lawn toward the back door, and Cyril called out, 'Hope your gran gets well soon, young Cassie. That's a pretty hairslide you've got on.'

When I turned around I saw he was laughing. He must have recognised the slide as Margie's because it was so large and unusual; that meant other people must have noticed I sometimes wore Margie's things, too.

'Ignore him,' Mrs Thoroughgood told me. 'The man's a wastrel. The only reason he takes so much care with the churchyard at this time of year is his guilty conscience.'

'What do you mean, Mrs Thoroughgood?'

'He was a conscientious objector during the war, Cassie; a

170

conchie, as we used to call them. You know what that means, I suppose?'

'Yes. I've heard Gran talk about them.' Sympathetically too, I thought; but I couldn't tell Mrs Thoroughgood that. 'That's why he's never at the Remembrance service, then. It must be awful to be a conchie. Poor Cyril.'

Remembrance Sunday. How quickly it had come round again. Only this time, Dawn and I wouldn't be going together to see our young soldier, killed just days before the 1918 Armistice. Father Steven would never have to tell the pair of us not to play around the memorial again, and Miss Saunders wouldn't be asking us, the Friday before, if we all had our poppies. The only thing that hadn't changed was the familiar sight of Cyril Jennings, hacking away at the brambles and then laughing off Father Steven's advice to bathe the scratches on his hands with the words 'War wounds'.

The little episode with the Jennings didn't spoil the rest of our day, however; and I'll always remember it because it was the last time I saw Mrs Thoroughgood anything like her old self. We prepared tea together, a really special tea with cakes I had helped to bake and appetising open sandwiches that Mrs Thoroughgood said were Danish. And we talked all the time. We discussed school, clothes, food, music, how many children I planned to have when I got married – I told her how Gran would say, 'That's if anyone'll have you,' and she laughed.

Then, in the evening just before it started to get dark, she led me back into the garden.

'I know you object to using some of Margie's things,' she said, opening the garage door. 'But I think you'll like this. It's much newer than the one you already have, and therefore safer.' And she wheeled out the silver Moulton bike.

It was the first time I had seen it since Margie disappeared, but the old envy, the old desire to own this perfect bike, soon returned and gripped me so hard I couldn't say no.

'Already your own bike is far too small for you,' said Mrs Thoroughgood, wiping mudguards which didn't need wiping. 'You need an adult-size bike now, Cassie, and I want you to have this one. I've had the brakes checked, and everything's in good order, all ready for you to ride.

I looked at the bike longingly, still hesitating. Then I gripped the handlebars, just to get the feel of it, and turned once more to Mrs Thoroughgood.

'It's all right, Cassie. It's yours. Look, dear; Margie loved this bike and she was proud of it. It was the only one of her possessions she ever really looked after. She cleaned and oiled it every Saturday without fail, and I know you'll take the same care of it. Margie would have hated to see it rusting away there in the garage.'

That finally decided me. I had come to dislike Margie in the months before she died as a selfish girl who didn't care how much she put others out or hurt them so long as she was happy. Now she was dead and I had to feel sorry for her. Besides, there was always this thought at the back of my mind: that perhaps Margie, although in some strange and altered state, could still see and hear all that was going on. I was afraid not to accept and care for her bike.

So, because it was a Saturday, I cleaned and oiled the silver Moulton as she would have done while Mrs Thoroughgood watched, looking pleased. When it grew too dark to see properly, I wheeled it carefully back into the garage and closed the door. It was mine, and tomorrow I would ride it to church, not caring about who saw me on it or what they would say.

I wrote a full page in my diary that night. Margie had been dead over a year now, but I still entered the number of days at the top of the page. It had become a ritual that I was afraid to break, like the way I felt compelled to shut every cupboard door twice or look under the lavatory seat in case of earwigs before I dared sit on it. Unlike these last two habits, I realised there must come a day to stop counting, and I would know when it arrived.

But before I broke the ritual, I broke my promise to Mrs Thoroughgood.

17

Margie's clothes, books and toys, and now her bike. Somehow, this latest gift changed things between Mrs Thoroughgood and me, and I felt myself to owe an uncomfortable sort of debt to her. It was as if she had given the bike and expected me in return. She made so many plans – plans that would never come off because Gran and Dad would surely be home before the time came to carry them out: a birthday party for me, for instance, and a visit to her brother's home in Yorkshire for Christmas. When I tried to point out the impossibility of these schemes she grew very quiet and sat staring out of the window or sipping her brandy – which she seemed to drink rather a lot of. Then she would think up something new: a trip to London, perhaps, to do some shopping or see the ice show at Wembley. And she would become quite animated, jumping up from her chair and pacing about, her fingers locking and unlocking as she described the treats she planned for me.

I hardly dared protest or contradict her too often, so I would listen to these plans and smile, and pretend to be excited too. I didn't know what else I could have done. When I telephoned the hospital (unknown to Mrs Thoroughgood) the ward sister told me Gran would be home in a fortnight. But I still didn't know when Dad would be home, or if he knew I was in Mrs Thoroughgood's charge. I tried ringing my mother, but there was no answer. So I could only hope Mrs Thoroughgood's husband returned, and soon. When I asked her about him she became evasive, even angry, and I began to wonder if he were ever coming back.

Half of me still trusted and had confidence in her; she was Mrs Thoroughgood, kind, beautiful, and a highly respected member of the community. The other half knew the time for trust and confidence had long gone, and there was no one I felt able to confide in and ask for help. I did seriously consider approaching my form teacher, Miss Dear, who was a sympathetic woman and always found time to listen to her pupils' troubles. But she was *authority*, and I imagined myself ending up in the children's home on Lindley Hill and Dad having to go to court to get me back. So I decided I must hold on for as long as possible and humour Mrs Thoroughgood.

It was a tremendous relief to get out of the house and go to school in the mornings, but I had to be home punctually; not a minute later than ten past four, or I would find her in tears of anxiety. This meant I couldn't dawdle along with the other girls when we got off the bus, as I would have liked, and had to make some pathetic excuse to my friends, which they soon grew very tired of. Most of all, I resented the limit of one hour on my evening playtime and the way she would be waiting for me at the gate afterward. She seemed happy only when I was safely in the house with her, and although I understood why, I resented it more and more. It was only a matter of time before I had to rebel.

Jack was late that afternoon. Usually he would have finished serving Upper Grisham and been on his way home to Wickstead before I stepped off the school bus. Today, I'd already had my tea and was on my way to meet Sylvia Tanner at the rec. when I saw his van, still parked at the end of St John's Drive. I was curious enough to have stopped anyway, but as Mrs Thoroughgood had asked me to buy some apples from the village shop, and as I owed Jean for a quarter of sherbet pips, I thought it would be a better idea to buy them from Jack instead.

The floor of his van was littered with the usual cabbage leaves and onion skins, and Jack was kneeling in them, trying to mop up a large puddle of water with his handkerchief.

'I only want some apples,' I explained when he gave me a flustered look.

'Just a minute, Cassie. I've got to clear this lot up before it runs under the matting.'

'What happened? Did you spill something?'

'I wish that were it. No, the fridge conked out. I've got a whole

174

load of meat and fish in there that'll go off if I don't do something quickly. No good taking it home; there's too much of it.'

'Oh. What are you going to do, then?'

Jack leaned past me to wring his handkerchief outside. 'I think the pub landlord might be able to store it for me. I'll just mop this up and then I'll run round there and ask.'

'I'll help,' I said. There was a rag in the carrier on Margie's bike, so I took that and knelt beside Jack.

'You're a good girl, Cassie. But mind you don't get your nice frock all dirty.'

I smiled at him, hoping he might give me a Mars bar or something. When the job was done and no treat seemed forthcoming, I pestered to go with him to the pub, on the grounds that because the landlord seemed to like me he would probably agree more readily to Jack's request.

'Oh, I don't know, Cassie. Won't Mrs Thoroughgood wonder where you are?'

'No. She thinks I'm over the rec. with Sylvia Tanner. Please, Jack? I can help you carry the stuff in.'

Finally, he agreed. I was to follow on the bike and meet him in the pub car-park, and if I was a good girl I just might get a Vimto and a bar of chocolate. I pedalled after him like someone in a race.

The pub provided lunches and evening meals, so the landlord, Mr Reede, had a large chest freezer in the kitchen which, luckily for Jack, was only half full that day. We hurried in and out with packets and cartons of frozen food until our fingers felt as though they were frost-bitten. Then, because Mr Reede refused to accept any payment for the storage, Jack felt obliged to offer his custom in the saloon.

'But you must let Mrs Thoroughgood know where you are,' he told me. 'Tell her you've been helping me and I'm treating you, if that's all right with her. There's a phone in the passageway. Here.' He gave me a fourpence. 'Then we'll sit in the garden.'

I had never used a public telephone before. It had two push buttons marked A and B but no instructions on their use; and I remembered Gran saying that public telephones, like public lavatory seats, harboured germs. Besides, I was twelve years old, Mrs Thoroughgood wasn't my mother, and I honestly didn't see why I should have to account for my whereabouts like a little kid. I picked up the receiver half-heartedly; the mouthpiece was wet with the condensation of somebody's breath. No, I thought, that fourpence could be better spent on something else, and I dropped the coins into my pocket. Then I went outside to wait for Jack.

He came out with a tray, and on it a bottle of Vimto, a pint of beer, a small glass of something stronger, crisps and chocolate.

'Did you get through all right?' he asked, unloading the tray on to a table.

'Yes.'

'So she knows where you are?'

'Yes.'

'That's right. You must always tell people where you're going and who with, Cassie.'

'I know. Dad's always getting on to me about it.'

'Quite right as well. You can't be too careful these days. And how is your dad? Coming home again soon? I'd have thought he'd be rushing home to see his poor mother.' Like most people, Jack's powers of conversation seemed to increase with a drink in front of him.

After a while, he asked how I liked staying with Mrs Thoroughgood. 'It's all right,' I said.

'Don't you find her a bit – well, a bit peculiar?'

'No. Why should I?'

'I heard she makes you wear Margie's clothes. Isn't that one of her frocks you have on now?'

'No, it's mine. My mother sent it for my birthday.'

'She does make you wear Margie's clothes sometimes, though?'

'She doesn't *make* me do anything. I don't have to wear them if I don't want to. But why shouldn't I? She'd only give them away or burn them otherwise.'

Jack nodded. He was silent again for some moments, then he said, 'I didn't like Margie very much. She wasn't a nice little girl like you, Cassie. And she used to steal from my van. She thought I didn't see her, but I did.'

'What sort of things did she steal?' I was thinking of the fruit chews and Blackjacks I'd made a habit of pocketing whenever Gran went out for her groceries.

'Oh, silly things sometimes. Once it was a handful of Brazil nuts. I saw her throw them away as she went down the road.'

'Why didn't you say anything to her, then?'

'I did. Last year, just about a week before she went missing. I had fireworks on sale, and Margie helped herself to them while I was serving someone else. When it came her turn she asked if I had any Catherine wheels left. I told her I thought she had most of them in her pocket. The little bitch turned on the waterworks, of course. She was sorry, she'd never do it again and please don't tell Mummy; all that sort of nonsense. When she saw it cut no ice and when I told her I knew it wasn't the first time, well, she started screaming and swearing. I've never heard such foul language from a young girl.' Jack paused to stub his cigarette out. 'The worst part about it was that I used to love Margie – before I found out what she was really like. I bet she had one or two people round that little finger of hers.'

I stared at his hands. He was wrenching at his fingers, like someone very nervous.

'Her mother knew all about her ways,' I said to distract him. 'She blames herself, you know.'

'Perhaps she's right. But you'll be safe with her, Cassie. You're a good girl. You wouldn't steal from me, would you?'

'Of course not.'

'And I'd never hear you swear, would I?'

'No. Can I have another Vimto?' I didn't like the way he was comparing me with Margie; it reminded me of Mrs Thoroughgood.

'Please,' Jack reminded me.

'Sorry. Please can I have another Vimto?'

While he was fetching it I began to think about the uncomfortable situation I was in. Half the village knew I was staying with Mrs Thoroughgood, that I'd been going around in Margie's clothes and riding her bike, and they were all talking about it. She was ill, I knew that now, and I didn't want to go back to her. But what else could I do? I thought of telephoning my mother again, but that would only reinforce her belief that I was lacking proper care. Not that she wanted the trouble of me herself.

When Jack returned I was tempted to tell him it was true: Mrs Thoroughgood did make me wear the clothes sometimes. And I wanted to tell him about the brandy she drank; how one minute she was silent and still, the next jumping around chattering excitedly; how Mr Thoroughgood had once accused her of using me as a Margie-substitute. But somehow I couldn't say any of this. I still felt sorry for her, and because she had been so kind to me in her way it would have been disloyal. So I played with the pub dog until it began to get dark, then Jack loaded the bike into the van and we drove to Allgoods.

'I suppose you'd like a Mars bar?' he said as we pulled up. 'Okay, hop through and get one. And don't forget to brush your teeth before you go to bed.'

I climbed over the cab seat to reach the shop, switching on the light so he could see I wasn't helping myself to more than the Mars. Jack allowed customers to advertise goods for sale on his van, and it was my habit to scan these carefully for anything that began 'Free to a Good Home', just in case I could persuade Gran that what we really needed was a puppy. Among the postcards haphazardly stuck on to shelves and trays was a photograph of an old lady; it had been there for as far back as I could remember, but I'd never paid it close attention before. It was a black and white snap, slightly spoiled in one corner by sun on the camera lens, but I could still recognise the houses in the background as those we called The Potteries.

'Jack,' I called. 'Who's this lady on the old photo?'

'What? Oh, that's my grandmother. I used to live with her when I was a little boy, just like you live with your gran.'

'But those houses are The Potteries.'

'That's right. That's where we used to live. Hurry up, Cassie. You'd better go in or Mrs Thoroughgood will be worrying.'

It was quite dark when I stepped off the van and Mrs Thoroughgood had a light on in the sitting-room. I could see her shadow on the curtain, restlessly pacing up and down, and I was afraid to go in. Perhaps the sound of Jack's van starting up reached her ears, because while I was nervously standing at the gate and wondering what excuse I could invent, she drew back the curtain a little way and saw me. So many times I'd done something wrong, knowing it to be wrong at the time but telling myself it didn't really matter – and regretting it very soon afterwards. But I'd never regretted anything so much as not making that phone call.

Mrs Thoroughgood marched out of the house and screamed at me: I was a wicked, thoughtless child, I deserved a hiding, I wasn't to be trusted and I had let her down. And then she dragged me indoors, panting with the exertion of her screams.

We faced one another in the sitting-room, she in a fireside chair – I noticed an empty brandy glass on the table beside it – me standing resentfully before her.

'Well, Cassie? Where have you been?'

'To the rec. like I told you, with Sylvia Tanner.'

'Don't you *dare* lie to me, Cassie! I telephoned Mrs Tanner nearly an hour ago. Sylvia was already home, and she said you hadn't been to the rec. all evening. Well? What have you got to say now?'

I sniffed, started to cry; but Mrs Thoroughgood was unmoved.

'Well?'

'Down the pub with Jack Knowles.'

She repeated my words as if they were too incredible to be true, so I gabbled out the whole story; how Jack's fridge had broken down and how I helped him mop up and transfer the food to the pub landlord's freezer. 'Then he bought me a Vimto and we got talking, and I – well, I sort of forgot the time.'

'And it never occurred to you to telephone and let me know where you were?'

'Yes. Jack told me to. He even gave me fourpence for the call.'

'And?'

'I didn't know how to work the phone. I didn't understand the buttons and there were no instructions.'

'You could have asked, Cassie.'

She sounded calmer now, and I was so relieved I began to cry again.

'All right, Cassie. All right. You just didn't think, did you? But don't you realise how I felt when you didn't come home? It was like Margie all over again. As for Jack Knowles, he ought to have known better. That horrid little man! Just wait until I see him!'

'But it wasn't Jack's fault! I kept on at him to let me help.'

'He still should have known better. A grown man going off with a little girl after what's happened . . .'

'But Mrs Thoroughgood, Jack wouldn't hurt anyone. I'm sure he wouldn't. My gran's known him for ages. He used to live at The Potteries when he was a boy, so she must have known him years.'

Mrs Thoroughgood knocked her brandy glass to the floor. 'The Potteries? Jack Knowles lived there?'

It was some minutes before I realised what I had done. They said Colonel Cartwright had the well covered over so long ago that only a few people knew of its existence. If Jack had lived there as a child he would certainly have known.

18

Sergeant Jordan and a young WPC came to see me in the morning. They asked me the same questions over and over. Why had I gone with Jack? Was he in the habit of giving me free sweets? What had we talked about? At last, just as I began to think I must plead with them to leave me alone, they saw I'd had enough and let Mrs Thoroughgood take me from the room.

Later she told me Jack had been held at Wickstead police station all night. He'd agreed with everything I said about that evening, including the conversation we'd had about Margie, but he denied having anything to do with Margie's death.

Sylvia Tanner, calling by the next afternoon to find out why I hadn't been to school, supplied me with more information gleaned from her parents' conversation. At the time Margie was last seen alive, by her mother's daily help at approximately twenty minutes to nine that Monday morning, Jack should have been somewhere between his home in Wickstead and Defford, his first call on that day. But now it appeared that he hadn't followed his usual schedule. He had left home slightly earlier than was his practice in order to pick up some sacks of vegetables, but he'd forgotten his glasses and had to return for them. Therefore, although he arrived at Defford at a quarter past nine as confirmed by his customers as part of general questioning a year ago, he was twenty minutes late. Which left both Jack and Conny Jennings, who had helped load the vegetables, with shaky alibis.

This was bad enough, but now, according to Sylvia's father, Cyril Jennings had suddenly remembered seeing Jack's van in Upper Grisham that Monday last October.

'But I think that's just stupid,' said Sylvia. 'I think old man

Jennings is just saying that to draw people's attention from that dimwit son of his.'

'You don't think Conny had anything to do with Margie's death, Sylve? You *can't*. Conny wouldn't hurt anyone.'

'I don't know. He had a – a crush on Margie, didn't he? Anyway, I know one thing; the police are all over the village today. They've been to the school again, my little brother told me. They're checking attendance records because they think Margie played hooky and faked the sick notes from her parents.'

Now that was something I wouldn't have put past Margie.

Mrs Thoroughgood changed dramatically after that. She spent hours sitting in her armchair, sometimes sipping at a glass of brandy, sometimes listening to her opera records over and over – always staring ahead, as if she were watching, or waiting for someone who never came. She wouldn't let me go to school because I had 'let her down and couldn't be trusted', and I was glad of this in one way; I would have been afraid to leave her for long because she was drinking so heavily. She wandered unsteadily around the house, leaving burning cigarettes on table edges and the arms of chairs; and she went up and down the stairs without holding the banister, both hands being full with glass and bottle. The house she had once taken such a pride in became neglected. She had fired the daily help a few weeks ago and at first made some efforts at housework herself. But now she couldn't even be bothered to hoover or dust, so I did it as well as I could, although I was far too frightened of her beautiful, delicate china to do more than flick round it with a soft cloth.

I tried to prepare our meals from the tinned food she had in the larder, but she seldom ate much. And one day, when I found it necessary to do some shopping if Muffin and I were to eat at all, she wouldn't let me leave the house. I had to steal some money from her purse and wait until Conny Jennings went by on his way home, when I asked him to buy cat food, eggs and a loaf of bread. Even then it was a fearful game, and I kept turning around to make sure she hadn't followed me out of the back door.

'Loaf of bread, eggs, and cat food,' Conny repeated.

'Can you remember that?' I asked doubtfully.

''Course I can.'

'All right. Get as many tins of cat food as you can for the money. And Conny, find out what's happened to Jack, will you?'

'Jack? A-all right, Cassie. I-if you're sure.' He stared at the half-crowns I had given him, trembling and sniffing the way he did when he was nervous. I thought it was because he guessed I had taken the money without asking, and knowing his love of animals I appealed for Muffin's sake.

'He'll starve if you don't buy the food for him, Conny. Mrs Thoroughgood isn't well, you see, and I can't leave her. You wouldn't want Muffin to starve, would you?'

'N-no, Cassie. But . . . Jack . . . Cassie, I . . .'

'You *what*, Conny?' I was losing patience with him.

'Nuthin'. Cassie, I – I like you as much as I liked Margie. I like you more 'n I liked Margie.'

'All right, all right! So get the stuff, okay?'

He slouched off, looking over his shoulder with every half-dozen steps, and I felt guiltily aware that I had just treated him as badly as Margie used to do. I would make it up to him, I told myself. I would take another shilling from Mrs Thoroughgood's purse and give it to him for chocolate.

She was asleep on the sofa when I went back inside, her head resting on a cushion, her hand on her temple as if she had a headache. I sat on the floor beside her. She had always looked younger than her true age, and never more so than as I saw her that day. There were shadows under her eyes, she had lost weight rapidly, and her skin was greasy with neglect. But there was something so delicate in her face, which reminded me of her best china, so that I wanted to touch her but was afraid to. Her clothes were crumpled and creased with three days' wear, and her perfume had a peculiar smell under the more familiar one, as though she had sprayed it on to disguise the fact that she hadn't washed.

Once again I felt myself torn between seeeking outside help and hanging on until Dad came home or Mr Thoroughgood returned. If I took the first course I would be betraying Mrs Thoroughgood; the whole village would know she was ill and I might be sent to the children's home. If I let things go on as they were she would simply get worse until I was unable to cope with her.

And Jack – where was he? I had told the police how he wanted me to telephone Mrs Thoroughgood that evening and I had disobeyed, and I told them what a good friend he had been when Gran was taken ill. I thought they must have released him from questioning by now, yet he had missed his last two rounds. Jack would have understood and forgiven me, and he would have known what to do now. Where was he?

Mrs Thoroughgood stirred slightly, so I got up and went to sit by the window, and I asked myself, What would Gran tell me to do? Like Alice, who found it impossible to play croquet against herself without cheating, I found it impossible to play the part of Gran in my head without getting the most unwelcome answer. She would tell me to ask for help, and – as usual – she would be right.

I tiptoed into the hallway and looked up Dr Savage's telephone number. Yes, it was the right thing, I said aloud, feeling Muffin weaving in and out between my ankles. Even so, when I had dialled the number I put the receiver down with a bang. Muffin made a plaintive little miaow, his sapphire eyes looking up at me trustingly, expectantly. He was hungry. There wasn't a tin of cat food, or any other meat, in the house; and Conny, good-natured and biddable though he was, might easily come back with bird seed by mistake or forget the errand altogether.

I redialled the number, and this time I managed to close my mind to all doubts until I heard the doctor's voice and it was too late for a second thought.

He didn't know who I was at first.

'Casse Wade,' I repeated. 'You came to see my gran at the top of Joshua Road a little while back, and you sent her to hospital. Lilian Wade, you know. She has pernicious anaemia. I'm her granddaughter, Cassie.'

There was a snorting sound at the other end of the line, and I wondered if he thought I was some silly kid just messing about on the phone for a laugh.

'You must remember me,' I said. 'You keep calling me Elaine.'

'Aa-ahh.'

'Well, I'm with Mrs Thoroughgood, and I think she's ill. Will you come and see her, Doctor?'

'And is Mrs Thoroughgood one of my patients, young lady?'

'I – I don't know.' I hadn't thought of that. 'But I'm one of your patients.'

'Ah, but you're not the one who's ill, are you? I assume you mean Mrs Rochelle Thoroughgood, the mother of young . . .'

'Margie, yes. And I don't know what's wrong with her, but – '

'Look, Elaine, I suggest you telephone Mrs Thoroughgood's own doctor.'

'But I don't know who he is, and I don't think she's likely to tell me. Dr Savage, I'm all alone with her. Her husband's away somewhere, my gran is in hospital, my dad's still abroad, and I don't even know where my mother is . . .' The receiver was becoming wet with perspiration from my hand and I felt my knees trembling. I wasn't used to the telephone. And besides, having gone through measles, chicken-pox, and all the other childhood ailments, I knew how well my doctor lived up to his surname.

'All right, all right.' He made another snorting noise. 'This is a tidy kettle of fish, I must say. But I'll see what I can do. You'd better tell me what seems to be the matter with your guardian.'

'We-ell, she's just not herself. She roams around the house all night. She won't let me go to school, and she doesn't change her clothes any more or wash. And she hardly eats. She just drinks brandy and smokes. There's next to no food in the house and I'm afraid to leave her, even to go to the shop.'

'Yes, yes, I see. All right, Elaine, I'll find out who her GP is and have him call round as soon as possible. Do you think you can manage until then?'

'Y-yes.' I thought if I said no he might contact the Welfare people, so I repeated the assurance stoutly – 'Yes, sir. Thank you,' – and prayed that Dad would be here before the doctor.

Mrs Thoroughgood was still asleep, so I crept outside to wait for Conny.

He was dawdling along the road, a paper carrier in his arms, and looking more than reluctant to meet me. He's got it wrong, I thought; he's forgotten what I wanted and asked for the first thing that came into his head. It was a dull morning, misty in the distance and with very fine rain in the air. Conny, dressed in a slate grey jacket and charcoal trousers, seemed to blend into the day. He wouldn't look at me, but thrust the carrier into my arms and turned to go.

'Wait a minute, Conny.' I looked into the bag and found the loaf, a dozen brown eggs, and eight tins of Kit-E-Kat. 'That's just right, Conny. Thank you. Would you like a shilling for chocolate?'

'No, ta, Cassie.'

'Sixpence, then? It's all right; Mrs Thoroughgood would like you to take something.'

Conny stood looking at his shoes. I asked him if he were angry with me for speaking so sharply to him before, but he only shook his head and gave a wet, bubbly sniff.

'Did you find out about Jack?'

'Yeah. I knew anyway. Father Steven told me.'

'Told you what? How is he, Conny? When will he be back on his rounds?'

'Ain't comin' back. 'E died.'

'*Died*?' I was shaking my head, but at the same time I had an awful feeling that my mouth was fixed in a smile of disbelief. 'But he can't be dead, Conny. He *can't* be.'

''E is, I tell yer, Cassie. There's gonna be a funeral. Next week. 'E got ill at the police station an' they took 'im to 'ospital, but 'e pegged out on the way. Comin' to the funeral, Cassie? Me dad went to Colonel Cartwright's funeral an' there was cake afterwards.'

I ran back into the house, dropping two of the eggs on the way, and screamed for Mrs Thoroughgood to wake up. She looked dazed, then frightened.

'Mrs Thoroughgood – Jack's dead! Jack Knowles is dead!'

'Dead?' Her eyes were focused on my face, but there was little recognition in them. She might have been watching a dull television documentary for all the response she showed.

'Yes, *dead*! He was taken ill at the police station while they were questioning him. Mrs Thoroughgood, they thought he killed Margie – but he couldn't. Not Jack. Jack wouldn't have hurt anyone, I'm sure of it. What are we going to do?'

'Do about what?'

'Don't you see? If it hadn't been for us – me – they wouldn't have taken him for questioning, and then perhaps ... Mrs Thoroughgood, when's your husband coming home? Please, hadn't we better phone him?'

Her eyes wandered from my face, as if the effort of looking at me was too much. 'He's not coming home.'

'Not ever?' I took her arm and tried to pull her to her feet. 'Let's phone him now, Mrs Thoroughgood. Let's find his parents' number and call him. Please? Get up, Mrs Thoroughgood.'

'I can't.'

'Yes, you can. It's only because you haven't been eating properly.'

'Leave me alone, Cassie. You'll never take Margie's place. Go away. Go to school, go over the rec.; I don't care. Just leave me alone.'

I kept trying to get her to her feet, and it did seem as if she really couldn't move, though not through any lack of physical strength. Nor was the brandy to blame; she had drunk the last of that some time ago. But some force that I couldn't put a name to had drained from her so that she found it an effort to move or speak. Until now, I had been worried, uneasy and nervous with her; but not even when I saw her dropping her lighted cigarettes everywhere or tottering downstairs with her brandy had I felt half afraid as I did now. I suppose I had clung to the hope that, because she was an adult, strong, wise and infallible, she would recover herself. Now I knew that was impossible and I was frightened.

'Mrs Thoroughgood!' I screamed at her. 'You must get up!' Still she wouldn't look at me or make an effort to move.

But at least I could now be confident that she wouldn't fall and hurt herself or set fire to the house if I left her to find help, and I was just making up my mind to run to the vicarage for Father Steven when the front door bell rang. The doctor, I thought, and I started to cry with sheer relief.

But the young man wasn't a doctor. He had a suitcase with him instead of a doctor's bag, and he knew my name.

'Cassie!'

I stared hard at the short fair hair, the moustache of a slightly darker colour, the smart suit; but it wasn't until he spoke again that I recognised him. There was no mistaking his lilting Welsh accent.

'Cassie, whatever's the matter?'

'Jeff! Jeff, where's my dad? Is he coming home?'

'Soon, very soon. He's in Colchester at the moment, making some arrangements about a new job. Perhaps he'll be here by teatime. Cassie . . .' He followed me into the house, wrinkling his nose as if the place smelled. Probably it did, due to neglect, and I hadn't noticed because I was there all the time.

When Jeff saw Mrs Thoroughgood he telephoned for an ambulance straight away and sent me from the room. So I fed Muffin and went to wait in the back garden, feeling the same hot prickles on the nape of my neck that I'd experienced when Gran first became ill and I thought she was going to die. Muffin ate his fill, then came to join me, rubbing his head gratefully against my legs. Poor Muffin. I would have to persuade Gran to let us adopt him.

In a while, Jeff came out and told me Mrs Thoroughgood had been taken to hospital; we could go home.

'We must take Muffin. We can't leave him to starve. He was Margie's cat. Please, Jeff?'

'All right, Cassie. You go and find your street door key and I'll get Muffin. You're right; we can't leave him.'

We must have made quite a spectacle walking along Joshua Road, Jeff with a struggling Siamese under one arm, me clinging to the other. And I couldn't help looking at this new Jeff with his short hair and neat suit. He still had that slow way of speaking and moving, and he still used his hands in an oddly expressive way whenever he spoke, but without the shoulder-length locks and loud shirts, not even the most imaginative inhabitant of our village could have called him effeminate. At last, I had to remark on the change in him and ask why. Jeff smiled, but more to himself than to me.

'Well, Cassie, I suppose you could say I don't have anything to rebel against any more.'

This was an unsatisfactory explanation, but I was glad no one would be able to call him names now or imply horrible things about my dad, and I decided to let the matter rest until later.

Once we were home, he took some clean sheets from the airing cupboard, changed my bed and made me lie down for a nap. 'And in the mean time, I'll find somewhere for Muffin to sleep. You know, he might not stay, Cassie. Cats are well known for finding their way back to their old home.'

'I read once that a good trick is to put butter on their paws. We could try that, Jeff.'

'Hmm. I suspect we'd end up with more butter on ourselves and your gran's furniture than on Muffin's paws. We'll see. Close your eyes now, Cassie, and try to have a little sleep.'

I tried, but with my eyes tightly shut all I could think of was

Jack. I could see him standing there with his head on one side, his front upper teeth fastened over his lower lip, just the way he used to look when Gran and I went to collect our weekly order and he drove me mad with the same remarks time after time.

When I awoke I was surprised to find myself at home in my own bed and not in the cramped spare room at Allgoods. Dad was there, more sun-tanned than usual, but anxious as well. After I had hugged and kissed him I saw that my mother was there too, and I almost laughed at how quickly her concern became irritation once she was sure no real harm had come to me.

'What is it about this child that attracts trouble? It's just one thing after another with you, Cassie.'

'The most important thing is that she's all right,' Dad said. 'How do you feel, Cass? A bit better?'

'Yes, but Daddy – poor Mrs Thoroughgood! What will happen to her?'

'She'll be well looked after, don't you worry. It sounds to me as if she's had a nervous breakdown, which is hardly surprising, poor woman. But she'll recover in time, and maybe she and Mr Thoroughgood will be reconciled.'

I thought he meant reconciled to Margie's death. Then my mother gave him an angry look, which I didn't understand.

'At the moment, though, it's you we're concerned about,' Dad went on. 'Why on earth didn't you tell someone what was happening?'

'I didn't like to. I thought the Welfare people would put me in a home.'

At this, my mother became quite triumphant. 'You see? None of this would have happened if you hadn't been gallivanting across Europe, Arthur.'

'Perhaps not. But I don't intend to spend the rest of the day weighing the blame. If Cassie's feeling well enough later I'm taking her to see her gran.'

'So everything's all right, is it? She could have ended up like the Thoroughgood kid – dead at the bottom of some well. The trouble is, your mother lets her have her own way too much, and you're never here to keep an eye on things.'

I wondered why Dad was receiving her accusations so impassively. His usual response, if I remembered correctly, was to give as good as he got, and often better. Then he said, 'Well, all that's going to change now. I'm going back to the Army – but a desk job in Colchester. You see, Isabel, I intend remarrying in the spring.' And turning to me, 'I'm sorry, Cassie. I hadn't planned to break the news quite like this. I wanted you to meet Olwyn first.'

'Olwyn? Jeff's sister?'

'That's right. You're going to like her, Cass.'

If my mother had had sails sprouting from her back I would no doubt have seen the wind dropping from them. Deflated was the only word I could think of to describe her just then.

'Congratulations, Arthur,' she said after a moment of confusion. 'I hope you'll both be happy.'

'I'm sure we shall. Now, is there anything you'd like to discuss with me? Anything with regard to Cassie, perhaps?'

'No. If Cassie's happy with your new plans I suppose I am too. She can always come to me for a visit, can't you, Cassie?'

Having Dad home for good made me magnanimous. 'Of course I can, Mummy. I'd like that.' And I kissed her without being prompted, for once.

For a moment I was really happy. Then I remembered Jack and I told them both what had happened that evening and how, in trying to reassure Mrs Thoroughgood, I had aroused her terrible suspicions.

'Now Jack's dead, and I can't help thinking it's because of me, Daddy.'

'Oh, Cass! You don't really believe that, do you? Jack had a heart attack. It could have happened at any time.'

'That's right,' said my mother, agreeing with Dad for almost the first time in memory. 'And he should have known better than to take a youngster off like that – even if it was only a stone's throw away – and bring her back after dark. What were the police to make of it? Don't forget, they still haven't caught whoever killed Margie.'

'Perhaps they never will,' I said. It was certainly beginning to look that way.

Dad thought otherwise. 'There's a lot of police activity in the village at the moment, and as they haven't issued a statement about Jack it seems as though he's been ruled out. But even if he was innocent, I wonder if it's possible that he gave them a new lead? Someone in his job is bound to see and hear more than the rest of us.' He stood up, suddenly brisk. 'Well, that's your adventure over at least, Cass. Come on, let's get ready to visit your gran.'

'Yes, please!'

But it wasn't over for me yet.

19

Gran was allowed to leave her ward and go downstairs to the day room, the only part of the hospital where children were allowed to visit, and she had some wonderful news.

'I'm coming home tomorrow,' she said.

'Already? But Gran, I'd planned to get everything ready for you first. I meant to polish everything, make it look all nice and bright.'

She laughed. 'Never mind, Cassie. It'll be just perfect the way it is, dust and all.'

Dad told her of his future plans jobwise, which pleased her enormously, but he didn't mention Olwyn. That, like my escapades, must wait until she was home.

Then Gran launched into praise of the treatment she was being given. It must be one of those new 'wonder drugs', she insisted, and would have no truck with our explanation of a dull old vitamin. 'It cured me overnight,' she proclaimed.

We thought that was a bit of an exaggeration, although she certainly looked well.

'Not cured,' the consultant told us. 'There's no actual "cure" for pernicious anaemia, but after an injection of B12 many patients do find their symptoms disappear literally overnight. These injections will have to be continued at monthly intervals indefinitely, however. But cheer up, young lady; your gran is quite a character, and she'll be able to take needles in her stride. And you'll find she's able to live a perfectly normal life. A few years back she wouldn't have been so lucky, you know.'

It was almost dark when we left the hospital arm in arm, and gazing up at Dad I felt all the old pride return. He was so good-looking that even if I was the tiniest bit jealous of the new woman in his life (which I wouldn't have admitted anyway) I certainly couldn't fault her taste. But was it my imagination, or did I really have a much shorter distance to look up to his face?

'You're growing, Cassie,' he said, reading my thoughts. 'You'll soon be the tallest twelve-year-old in town.'

'Like Katy in *What Katy Did*,' I said, not displeased to have something in common with an old favourite of mine.

'And how's the French coming along? Shall I book that weekend in Paris yet?'

'I don't think so, Dad. All I can say that makes any sense is, *Nous avons passé deux jours à Paris avec un ami.* And I'm not even sure that I said that right.'

We laughed, and I felt another moment of real happiness. Gran would be home tomorrow and Dad wasn't going abroad any more. Perhaps I could even have the puppy I'd always wanted. Then I remembered Jack, and I told myself I had no right to be happy.

Life soon fell into the old familiar pattern when Gran came home. She supervised my homework as before, moaned if I didn't eat a proper breakfast, and regularly told me what too much television or reading could do to your eyes. Luckily she took to Muffin – as he did to her – and so I had a pet for the first time since Tigger died. Jeff stayed with us for a few days before having to fly back to Cyprus, and Gran and I enjoyed speculating on the change in his appearance.

Yet the atmosphere in the village had changed. People were tense, watchful of the renewed police activity, watchful of their children just as they were last October when Margie first vanished. I think we all felt some breakthrough had been made in the investigation, and it was exciting to go to school and have all the other girls, especially the older ones, envious because Upper Grisham was the centre of renewed drama.

I had been thinking about my school project, 'Our Village', that the first years were meant to be working on in lieu of 'real' homework for this term. My efforts so far had been half-hearted and the results made for dull reading, so I thought a photograph of Upper Grisham taken from the top of Sandy Path might liven it up. I had two exposures left on the film in my new Brownie and was wondering how best to use the remaining one when Gran came in.

'And where do you think you're going?'

'It's for my school project. I thought I'd take a picture of the church. It's one of the oldest in this part of Suffolk, Father Steven said, so I mean to devote at least two pages to it.' I knew she would never allow me up Sandy Path on my own, it was too out-of-the-way. And the church would actually make a very good picture, so I had only told a half-lie.

'All right. But don't you wander off.'

'No, Gran.'

She was still upset about Jack because she had known him for so long and, like me, was convinced Cyril had lied about seeing the van in Grisham that Monday. I was still upset too, but I was trying not to think about it, to block it from my mind as only a child can do when her own conscience is involved.

I decided to take the Sandy Path picture first. It would make a stunning contribution to my project and was therefore the most important; and if I jogged the camera at the crucial moment, well, there would still be one exposure left. To get there, you had to go past Colonel Cartwright's old house and right to the end of the narrow road called Potter's Lane. Then you came to this steep path on the left, its entrance almost hidden by two barren hazel trees and as dark as any man-made tunnel. The ground gave the path its name; a coarse, dirty sand, seldom dry except at the height of summer. Trees met overhead, and on one side you could look down on to the gardens belonging to The Potteries; I remembered how Petey Scammel had once shied stones down at Cyril Jennings' cucumber frames and had actually managed to hit one. As you progressed the higher and steeper the path became, and when you reached the open once more Grisham was far below. Here the way widened into a rough track, thick on either side with buttercups, ragwort and moon daisies in summer, but now almost bare, what was left of that year's growth trampled in the mud. I followed it round almost to the water tower, where there was a gate I could use to steady my hands when I took the picture.

Conny was there. He was sitting on the top bar of the gate, shivering in his inadequate jacket and trying to smoke a hand rolled cigarette.

''lo, Cassie,' he said, spluttering.

'Have you been pinching your dad's tobacco again?'

''e won't miss it. What 'ya doing?'

'I'm going to take a photograph for my school project.'

Conny jumped down, grinding his cigarette into the mud with his boot. 'Whass a project?'

'It's – oh, it's something you have to write on a particular thing. I've got to write about this village, so I thought I'd take a picture to go with it.'

'You ain't arf clever, Cassie.'

I ignored this piece of flattery. Conny thought everyone who could read and write was 'clever'. He watched my careful preparations intently, and I started to ham it up a bit, stepping backwards, then forwards, looking through the view-finder and muttering about the light. Eventually, Conny wondered aloud if it wouldn't be easier to draw the picture, and after giving him what I hoped was a scornful look I took the snap.

'Good, ain't it?' said Conny, meaning the view. 'I can see the church.'

'I can see my house.'

We stood looking for a while, pointing out various landmarks, watching the smoke from garden bonfires curling upwards and forming a light cape of haze over the village. Then Conny said, 'Jack Knowles died.'

'I know. You told me. Don't you remember?'

'Will someone else come with the van now?'

'I don't know. I don't think so.'

'I used to call him Uncle Jack.'

'Oh, yes, because Jack and your father are cousins or something. And you used to help on the van sometimes, didn't you?' I wanted to ask about the morning Margie went missing, but that would make it look as if I thought he had something to do with it – and I didn't. It would have been no use trying to explain my feelings to an adult; they would have said, 'You're a child, and you can't understand.' Or in the case of pompous Mrs Woodruff, 'Kindly allow your elders and betters to be the judge.' It was just that I felt *safe* with Conny – if I hadn't, I wouldn't have been standing there alone with him at the top of Sandy Path, but would have turned back the moment I saw him. I felt that he would never hurt me, or allow anyone else to hurt me. Conny was a high-spirited but very biddable child in the body of a man.

'I used to 'elp sometimes,' he agreed after a long pause, as if he'd had to think about it. 'Uncle Jack 'ad a bad arm. So I always lifted 'eavy stuff for 'im.' He looked at me sideways, and I was struck, as so often before, by his beautiful eyes and long, girlish lashes. 'Is it my fault 'e's dead?'

'Of course not, Conny! Whatever gave you that idea? He had a heart attack. You know that.'

'I should've bin 'elping 'im a coupla days before. Only I didn't. I slep' late.'

'It's not your fault, Conny.' In trying to reassure him, I had to face that which I was trying to block out. 'If it's anyone's fault, it's mine.'

'Yours, Cassie? Why?'

When I explained to Dad why I felt responsible it had been comparatively easy; but everything, every sentence had to be simplified for Conny, as if you were dealing with a five-year-old. He tried so hard to understand, sometimes frowning, sometimes nodding his head sympathetically, but I was gabbling and not making it at all clear. At last, when I got to the part about disobeying Jack and not telephoning from the pub, I started to cry.

Poor Conny didn't know what to do. 'Aw, Cassie . . .' he began, reaching out his great, soft hands, then thinking better of it and withdrawing them. 'Aw, Cassie. Don't cry.'

'You see? It was all my fault. If only I'd let Mrs Thoroughgood know where I was, then she wouldn't have made all that fuss. And then perhaps . . . You know what, Conny? My dad once said that some people's lives are full of If Onlys.'

He patted my head, a slow, deliberate action that would have been funny in different circumstances. He smelled of oily, unwashed clothes and mice, but somehow it was comforting, and I was going to suggest we walk back down Sandy Path together when the strange thing happened.

Cyril Jennings came across the field behind the water tower, his red shopping bag – probably containing something poached – in one hand and a nutting stick in the other. When he saw us he dropped the bag on the ground and ran at Conny, grabbing him by the collar.

'You never bloody learn, do you! How many times have I told you to stay away from these girls?' He began hitting Conny around the head, and Conny, though flinching under each clout, made no attempt to defend himself, physically or verbally. He took the assault – there was no other word for it – as a matter of course.

'Mr Jennings!' I shouted, afraid Conny was really going to be hurt. 'Mr Jennings! Don't hit him! He wasn't – '

'You shut your trap and speak when you're spoken to.' He stopped hitting his son and began to shake him. 'Do you want to be put away? Because that's what'll happen if you get into any more trouble. I'd have thought you would've learned your lesson with the Thoroughgood kid.'

Conny was as tall as his father, yet he seemed to be looking up at him. 'Margie didn't mean it, Dad! She always said things, but she didn't mean it!'

'Get home! Go on, get home this minute.' Jennings turned to me, suddenly calmer but still panting from his exertions, and he smiled. I'd often seen him smile before and I didn't like it. 'I have to be strict with him, Cassie,' he said. 'He doesn't mean any harm, but there's things he just can't understand. I have to protect him, don't you see? Look, let you and me have a little talk, eh? You wait there a tick.' He went back to retrieve his bag, the contents of which had fallen out.

He didn't need to be strict with Conny, I thought, just firm. Conny only needed a little telling now and again and he was fine. It certainly wasn't necessary to hit him around the head, in my opinion. And hadn't Jennings once come close to hitting Gran? I wasn't going to wait around for 'a little talk' with someone like him, so I started to walk away. Then, for some reason I could never quite understand afterwards, I slipped through the fence on one side of the track and ran down the sloping field to Potter's Lane. I don't know if Jennings tried to follow, although I heard him swearing at me, and I didn't dare stop to see. But he was in his late fifties and a heavy smoker, whereas I was a tall twelve-year-old made fit with all the netball and hockey at school; if he had followed, he'd have been hard pressed to catch me.

There was a gap in the hedge where the Joshua Road boys had stolen branches for their bonfire on Guy Fawkes night, and I squeezed through it – getting a scratched leg and a shoeful of mud in the process – coming out on the lane just opposite Colonel Cartwright's old house. There I paused, wondering what to do next.

I should have gone straight home, of course, and told Gran what had happened. But I felt somehow that I was in the wrong by being with Conny in the first place, and a child who has done wrong doesn't generally go straight home. So I wandered down into the heart of the village, one-and-six left-over allowance money jingling in my pocket and thoughts of sherbert dabs in my head.

A mist had come up from the river, which ruled out taking a picture of the church as I had planned, and when I got to the shop I found it closed. The rec. was deserted; no one wanted to sit on a damp wooden seat and clasp the cold, sweating swing chains in their hands when they could be cosy at home waiting for Lucille Ball in *The Comedy Hour*. I thought about going home myself. There would be Gran's muffins for tea, or home-made scones still warm from the oven, perhaps. We would sit around the fire in the Best Room and I would time Dad at his crossword puzzle.

I had almost made up my mind to go when I started thinking about Conny.

Margie didn't mean it, Dad! She always said things, but she didn't mean it!

Instead of turning back the way I came, I started off along Alexandra Road, drawn irresistibly to the Thoroughgood house, the inaptly named Allgoods.

It no longer struck me as the most desirable house in Grisham, the sort of place Elvis Presley or some other big American star might have, as I once used to think. Allgoods looked desolate, so probably Patrick Thoroughgood still hadn't returned. I stood by the gate for some minutes, fingering the laurel leaves and looking at the spiders' webs dripping and sparkling in the mist; diamond necklaces, we used to call them. Margie would have destroyed them with one sweep of her hand.

Poor Mrs Thoroughgood. No one could tell me which hospital it was they had taken her to, and I hoped it was a cheerful, cosy place with pictures on the walls and a record player so that she could listen to her favourite operas when she began to recover. And I would have liked to write to her, just to let her know Muffin was being looked after.

198

I turned away at last, wondering if Donkey Hoty and all the other soft toys were still where we had left them and if the silver Moulton was rusting away in the garage after all.

The village was so quiet, unnaturally quiet, and the mist had turned into a thick fog. Gateways, hedgerows and road-signs were dripping, and when I stood still I could actually hear the drips, an almost metallic sound, yet distant and muffled.

'Earth stood hard as iron,' I said aloud, watching my breath spiral. 'Water like a stone.' This would be the first night of true winter.

As I walked toward my house I became aware of a car's headlights, hazy and shivering yellow, approaching from the top of Joshua Road. Then I heard the police bell, and my instincts told me who they were looking for. The black Humber drew level with me, and the two CID men, Inspector Washkansky and Sergeant Jordan, pulled me inside.

The Sergeant almost shouted at me. 'Cassandra Wade, where the devil have you been?'

'Cassie,' I reminded him. 'My name's Cassie.'

20

It was some time before I was able to understand what all the fuss was about. The disgrace of being brought home in a police car with the neighbours watching, the way they practically pounced on me with their questions the minute I walked in, and most of all Gran's low but audible demands for 'an examination', were confusing. It turned out that neither Dad nor Gran had the slightest idea what had been happening, only that Conny had run to Mrs Woodruff in tears and babbled my name over and over. Mrs Woodruff had naturally telephoned the police, and when it appeared that I was missing the general panic set in.

'I went to photograph the church,' I told them. 'Only it was too misty. So then I went over the rec. That's all. Daddy, I've been thinking. Couldn't we find out where Mrs Thoroughgood is and write to her, just to let her know Muffin's all right. It would ease her mind, you know.'

'We'll see, Cass. But I think the Inspector would like to ask you some questions first.'

I told them what had happened, what had been said as far as I could remember it, including Conny's odd statement that Margie was always saying things she didn't mean; and when they were satisfied I was unharmed, they gave me a good scolding for worrying the daylights out of Gran and left me to face her.

'You told me a lie, Cassie,' she said. 'You told me you were going to photograph the church for your project, but you went up Sandy Path instead.'

'But I got this better idea, Gran. I thought a picture taken from – '

'You lied to me, Cassie.' She placed my tea in front of me: a boiled egg that had gone cold and scones minus the jam.

It was a miserable evening we spent together. Dad filled in his crossword silently, Gran did some sewing, and I watched Lucille Ball without being able to raise so much as a chuckle. And I had left my Brownie, a birthday present from Dad, outside Allgoods.

But the day wasn't yet over, and just before nine, my bedtime, Mrs Woodruff knocked on our front door. Cyril Jennings had been arrested, charged with killing Margie – and he had admitted it.

When the whole story came to light almost a week later, Dad and Gran explained it all to me as simply – and honestly – as possible. I'll always remember that honesty, because it was the first time I felt like an almost-adult.

Cyril had always been ashamed of Conny. Before his marriage he had cultivated the bit-of-a-lad image: a great success with women, virile, the kind of man one would expect to produce strong, healthy children (preferably sons). Conny had given that image a severe blow. Later, when he was classed educationally sub-normal, Cyril felt more ashamed of him than ever. If the boy's backwardness wasn't enough, he had to get himself in trouble at the Flower Show, relieving himself behind the hedge because he was too shy to use the proper lavatory behind the pavilion. Then he began making a nuisance of himself with the teenage girls in the village, chasing them and trying to kiss them. He meant no harm, of course; he watched too much television. But Cyril thought of his own mother's uncle, imprisoned for indecent assault, and he trembled to think of the shame his son might bring on him if he were not watchful. So he began to threaten Conny with talk of 'a home', and the 'cat o' nine tails', and in the mean time Conny was still watching television, studying the behaviour of other people with whom he was trying to identify. Cyril was therefore horrified when he came in one day and announced that he was 'in love' with Margie Thoroughgood.

Cyril knew enough about Margie to see that here was a double threat. He had watched her leading her special pals about the village, heard her rudeness in the shop, even suffered from her nasty remarks about his dirty appearance. And the coalman had told him how Margie once tried to blackmail his own son after she'd seen him shoplifting in Wickstead. Cyril warned her to stay away from Conny. He wasn't to know that telling Margie not to do a thing was a sure way of getting her to do it. He even tried bribing her. She laughed at him. Then he discovered that when Margie dodged school she was persuading Conny to let her into the house while he, Cyril, was out on his odd-jobbing round.

The next part of the story had come from Conny himself as told first to Mrs Woodruff, and later, with more tears, to Inspector Washkansky. Although it was related third-hand by my dad, I could visualise it more clearly than the rest: Margie, having made sure Cyril had left, knocking on the door and telling a doubtful Conny, 'It's all right. I only want somewhere to stop until half-past three. You do like me, don't you, Conny? Let me in, then.'

Once inside, she would settle in front of the television, perhaps eating all Cyril's chocolate biscuits (which Conny would take the blame for), or persuading Conny to roll her a cigarette. When she tired of television she would roam around the house, trying on what little jewellery Mrs Jennings had owned, even putting on one or two of the dresses Cyril still kept for her memory, until poor Conny was almost jumping up and down in fear of his father coming home and catching them. He loved having Margie there, loved making her mugs of coffee, beans on toast, and generally waiting on her, but it could be nerve-wracking if Margie was in one of her difficult moods.

I saw this all so clearly and as Dad went on, sometimes inserting the third-hand dialogue which may or may not have been accurate, I felt that this was almost a fictional story and if Dad could only change the ending Margie might not be dead.

When Cyril found Margie's pencil case in the house he challenged Conny, who admitted to having let her in. Cyril gave his son the hiding of his life. In future, he would make sure the boy was out over the fields or wherever he roamed off to before leaving for work himself, and he would lock the door.

But Conny didn't worry about being locked out. If he became hungry during the day he would simply climb in through the kitchen window. So that Monday morning, after Margie had had the row with her mother and decided to skip school, he was alone in the house once again. Margie knocked on the door, ready with the charm she could switch on at will, her most winning smile, and, as an extra bribe, a pack of cigarettes she had stolen from her father's desk.

'I can't let you in, Margie,' he told her sadly. 'Me dad says I've not to. 'E'd kill me if I didn't do as 'e says.'

Margie's smile had slipped a little. 'He's not here, is he? What the eye doesn't see, and all that. You're not afraid of him, are you?'

Conny admitted that he was, and she laughed.

'I'm not. Let me in, Conny. I've brought you some ciggies.'

'No. I durs'n't.'

Margie became angry. She wasn't used to hearing 'no', especially from one who had previously treated her almost royally. She would make him sorry, she said. She knew all about his trouble a couple of years back, frightening Mary Thorby and trying to kiss Pamela Grundy. She would get him into real trouble; she'd tell someone he'd touched her and tried to do bad things to her.

She didn't mean it; Margie was always saying things.

Only this time Cyril Jennings overheard her. He had returned for his secateurs, which he'd left behind accidentally. When he heard Margie's angry shouts and then the threats she was making, Cyril must have been sick with panic. He saw himself in court, listening as the judge passed sentence on his son. He imagined reports in the papers, the whole village talking about him, his friends – such as he had – shunning him. It mustn't be allowed to happen. Somehow he must find a way of shutting that little bitch up. Reasoning with her, bribery, returning her threats; he didn't care how, just so long as he buttoned her lip for her.

Cyril stepped into view and Margie, probably realising she had gone too far this time and horribly frightened, began to run. That was the last Conny saw of her (which was why that day remained so clearly in his mind), running down the lane, her white-blonde hair flying, satchel bobbing up and down on her back, Cyril in pursuit.

Conny retreated to the kitchen, miserably preparing himself for the hiding he was bound to get. Margie hadn't meant those things, he knew that. You could always get round Margie by being nice to her – which in Conny's case meant grovelling to her and giving her things like the chocolate biscuits or the odd half-crown from Cyril's savings tin. No, she hadn't meant it.

Cyril returned some twenty minutes later, his face set with the expression he wore when anyone made hints about his poaching.

He took up his secateurs, as well as a crow bar, then told Conny to go and find his Uncle Jack, who would be somewhere near Defford, and make himself useful on the van for the rest of the day.

'Where's Margie?' Conny asked.

'Gone home. Now you can bugger off too. I've got to go back to the churchyard and get all those brambles cleared. Can't have the place looking like a jungle with Remembrance Sunday coming up.'

Conny, wondering at the strange way his father had avoided looking at him, went off in search of Jack. His spirits were high as he left Grisham and headed for Defford. He'd escaped the beating and he had no doubt it was due to Margie, who must have charmed his father with her smiles.

Of course, Margie could do anything.

Jack was late that morning. He'd forgotten his glasses and had to go all the way back to Wickstead for them. It would be getting on half-past ten by the time they reached Grisham, he said. But Conny didn't mind; Uncle Jack was good to him.

That evening, Conny learned Margie was missing. 'You'll have to say you were with Jack all morning,' Cyril told him, putting Germolene on the scratches he'd got from the brambles in the churchyard. 'Because if anything's happened to Margie people might think you had something to do with it. You don't want to have to go into that home, do you?'

'The home' became Conny's overriding fear, the place they would send him if he didn't behave himself, and eventually he began to wonder if that was what had happened to Margie. Especially in the following months when his father began to use her as another useful check.

'You know what happened to Margie, don't you? She opened her trap once too often, and now she's gone. You want to watch you don't go the same way.'

Poor Conny. I wondered what would happen to him now. He wasn't capable of looking after himself, and I supposed he'd have to go into the dreaded home after all.

'He'll be all right,' Dad said. 'I heard he's being sent to a special centre near London. They'll look after him there, don't worry, Cassie.'

'But did Cyril mean to kill Margie?, I asked.

'I believe so, Cassie. You must remember he was a very fright-ened man. But even then it's possible Margie could have escaped. If only she hadn't run into the dell and panicked.' Of course. She didn't like the dell; she had a claustrophobic fear of the trees, the branches that met overhead. 'She must have fought like hell. But if she left marks on him, he had a good excuse – '

'The brambles in the churchyard,' I said. 'Will he hang, Dad?'

'I don't know, Cassie. Come along, now. That's quite enough on the subject for one day. I have a letter to write to Olwyn, and it's time for your bath.'

Cyril Jennings didn't hang. He was given a life sentence, but only after an appeal for clemency, and died in prison some years later. Conny settled well at the centre, where he was permitted to work in the garden, eventually becoming wholly responsible for its upkeep, which made him proud and happy.

Mrs Thoroughgood spent over two years in hospital. Later, still estranged from her husband, she went abroad. I never saw her again.

I didn't like Olwyn when we first met; she was too young, in my opinion, and too pretty. But she had no intention of trying to buy my affections – as I feared she might. Instead, she would chatter gaily on, just as if there wasn't a twelve-year-old scowling at her from across the tea table. This made me feel left out, so I began to ask questions, just to get her attention. And she always answered matter-of-factly, using her hands expressively as she spoke, as her brother did. It was Olwyn who explained the change in Jeff's appearance; those awful clothes and girlish hair-style had been a form of rebellion against his father. I couldn't fully understand this at the time, but Jeff was a good friend and whatever his problems had been, I knew Gran and I were just happy they were resolved.

Olwyn was patient, and so I grew to like and then love her. I remember actually feeling jealous on one occasion because Dad was getting all her attention.

Six months after Dad and Olwyn were married, I was a brides-maid again, this time for my mother and Ray. I believed at the time – and I believe now – that my mother only remarried so as not to be 'outdone', as Gran put it. But, surprisingly, the marriage was a happy one.

We moved to Colchester, Gran as well, and I started a new school. I told them I came from Wickstead, not Upper Grisham, but it didn't really matter because the Thoroughgood case, once national news, was already fading from the minds of those outside the area.

My family did everything possible to help me forget; yet there was a time when I thought of Margie almost constantly. Margie, The Girl Who Had Everything. I wondered what became of her bike, the soft toys, and all her beautiful clothes – especially the red dress. Margie wouldn't have liked anyone else to have them, and I certainly didn't want them any more. We had taken Muffin to live with us, and I used to talk to him a lot, especially at night when he lay curled up on my bed.

'I don't think Margie would mind, do you?' I would whisper. 'I think she'd be pleased to know you were being looked after.' Because whatever Margie's faults, I knew she had genuinely loved that cat. And was it all Margie's fault she turned out as she did? Gran didn't think so.

'Nobody's born bad,' she said, 'just as nobody becomes wholly bad. Probably Margie was insecure and unhappy. Rochelle was neurotic about her upbringing. I think Margie began to rebel at an early age and then simply went too far. It's past now, Cassie. Let it rest.'

It was time to discard an old ritual – after four hundred and nine days – and I threw the diary out, though I still shut cupboard doors twice and look under the lavatory seat for earwigs.

But it was the memory of Jack Knowles that endured in my mind. It must have seemed an amazing piece of luck to Cyril Jennings when I brought suspicion on Jack, and he probably lied about seeing the van that morning in order to settle the matter. If only I had telephoned Mrs Thoroughgood from the pub.

'You can't go through life saying, If only, Cassie,' Gran said. 'Jack had a bad heart to start with. That was the real reason he sometimes got Conny to help him lift things, not a bad arm. He just didn't like to admit his heart trouble. So you see, it could have happened at any time. You've got to learn to stop blaming yourself.'

It took me a long time to realise she was right, but I managed to accept it in the end.

Gran was always right.

If you have enjoyed this book and would like to receive details of other Walker mystery titles, please write to:

Mystery Editor
Walker and Company
720 Fifth Avenue
New York, NY 10019

F
SUM

Summerfield, Lin

Count the days

$18.95

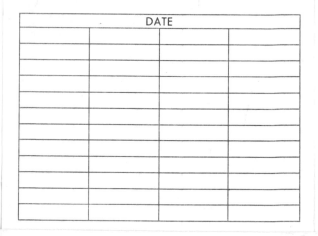

DATE			

© THE BAKER & TAYLOR CO.